Guardian

Sky Road Trilogy: Book Two

by Sandra Hurst

Praise for
The Sky Road Trilogy

Reader's Favorite – 5 Star Review

"… Hurst breathes authenticity into an ancient world. Each character has been crafted to become a friend or family member. To read Y'keta is to become one of the People."

5 Star Review - In'Dtale Magazine

"… Y'Keta offers an intriguing story with a solid setting. A coming-of-age story that while different also feels familiar, yet in a good way."

Amazon Reviews

"… breathtakingly beautiful."

"… well-crafted, poetic, and deeply moving."

"…takes the reader through that last rush from childhood into young adulthood."

Dedication

This book is for Rebecca, Tajia, and Laurie.
For coffee, love, and encouragement without end.

And for Titch, who knows who he is.

For Mike and Cameron, Always.

A Note on Pronunciation

For people who, like me, want to know 'how to say it properly', I have included a pronunciation guide at the end of this work.

WINTER

One

<<<Y'keta>>>

The smoke of burning corpses rose into the cold night sky, spreading an ugly smear across the ever-watching stars. Shards, these things stank when you burned them. I stepped back, coughing from the acrid smoke that billowed out as Pey't added the last of the scaly bodies to the pyre.

The Utlaak were attacking with almost every new moon. It had started when the high pass from the Ice-Lands opened. As soon as the Eye of the Watcher was hidden, they would slink out of their barrows and pour into the valleys, terrifying the nearby villages and pushing further and further south.

It's not that the hordes of leathery grey slugs were that hard to fight. They died rather easily, driven as they were by fear of the vicious whips of their leaders who were always behind them. There were just so many. It felt like their numbers never dropped.

Walking away from the putrid smoke, I tried not to look at the flaming pile of lizard-like bodies, hoping my stomach would calm down. By now I should be used to the sights and smells of battle. "D'vhan is right," I muttered under my breath, "whether we kill ten or a hundred this moon, just as many will be back next."

"I'm tired," D'vhan complained, tugging at his wild red hair and grimacing when his hand came away covered with soot. "Clean up and let's get away from this corpse pit."

The warriors were milling around, just waiting for the command to return to the scouting camp and debating who would make the long run to the village to report that another foray had been stopped.

"Look," I said, peering through the greasy smoke that hung like a curtain in the still night air, "even the sky refuses to carry them. The Road doesn't want their spirits." Gesturing towards the sliver of a moon hidden behind the clouds in the late-night sky. "Even the Watcher doesn't want to see what's left when the Utlaak die."

My stomach clenched when I saw D'vhan bent over against the trunk of a tree, coughing harshly.

Glancing from the sky to the patches of ash-covered snow, he said, "The wind is the wind," and straightened up slowly, his grim voice sounding thinner and even more gravelly than normal. "The Utlaak have their own Road, it's just unfortunate that it cuts across ours." Saving his breath, he motioned silently to his warriors to gather anything we may have had left behind. "We need to get back to the scouting camp by morning," he wheezed, shuffling over to lean back against the stone outcropping where they had finally cornered the Utlaak. "Leave nothing that could give away our presence in this area." I tried to keep my face from showing my concern, as I watched D'vhan's breathing start to calm. The Reds were ,as efficient and silent as the smoke that hung in the air, hardly disturbing the night as they combed the forest for any sign that we may have left behind. Coen, a lanky, pale-haired boy who had come to Esquialt last cycle walked up to D'vhan, carrying a piece of bark.

"What do you have there?" D'vhan asked, reaching for the crude parchment.

"I'm not sure, Kalixt," Coen replied. "I found it near the fire we built to burn the corpses. It looks like they were trying to write or draw something."

I peered over D'vhan's shoulder, squinting at the piece of bark. Nothing was obviously legible in the smoky light of the funeral pyre, but just as D'vhan's forearm tensed to fling the flattened piece of white-bark into the fire, something seemed to stop him.

"The Utlaak don't have a written language," he muttered. "There's no record of their own language at all, so what are these markings? They seem deliberate, but crude. Maybe scratches made by a charcoaled stick or a soot-covered rock." Tucking the bark into the breast of his jerkin, D'vhan nodded at Coen. "Good eye, young one," he said. "I'm not sure what this is, but something tells me it's more than just white-bark. We'll have to get Laban to look at it. Forget the scouting camp tonight, we'll head straight back to the village." Raising his voice, D'vhan assembled the small band of warriors and gave orders to start them on the dark trek back to Esquialt.

"Esquialt? D'vhan, that's too far to walk in one night, and after a battle!" I said. I could do the walk, although my feet would hate me for it, but I knew that with his damaged lungs that D'vhan could not.

"Move!" D'vhan ordered.

Stubborn, stupid old crow. Even now, five cycles after the lung infection that almost cost the People his life, he still wouldn't admit that he had limits, wouldn't let his warriors care for him.

§

The weary group of warriors walked into the village as dawn on the second day approached, turning the dark shadows of trees to a dull shapeless grey. Waving the others into Red Lodge to sleep, D'vhan and I crossed to the main cookfire and thumped wearily to the ground.

"I'm too old for this," D'vhan complained, shoving his gnarled hand through the short braids, making his hair look like someone had disturbed a nest of ruby snakes.

Grimacing at the ache in my feet, I humphed at him. "You aren't that decrepit yet, old crow. Besides, we tried to make you stay behind at the scouting camp. You threatened to follow us on your hands and knees because you're so sure we couldn't do things properly without you."

"Hush, hatchling." D'vhan's eyes twinkled mischievously, trying to look angry at the familiar teasing. "It's amazing how little respect you have for your elders. I should send you to work with the green feathers for a few moons. That would improve your attitude."

I felt the blood drain from my face at the thought, every muscle in my stomach clenched with tension. "Now, D'vhan. You know that Iamaat, the green leader, has issues with me…"

D'vhan's deep laugh echoed across the sleeping camp at the sight of my discomfort. "I know. I know, cub," he said. "Right now, I wouldn't wish Iamaat on anyone. Something has stung her and she's more difficult to deal with than ever. Now, get busy. Do something to help your poor elder. Get a fire going. It's cold just sitting here with my leathers getting soaked from the dew."

Peering around surreptitiously, to be certain that the camp still slept, I whispered *"Tlegu."* Calling, in my own language, for the Lightning to restart the remains of last night's campfire. The embers spat and sputtered, burning off the moisture from overnight and then, as I fed twigs into the pit, sent flames dancing along the kindling. D'vhan reached past me, adding a few larger branches, and starting to shape the fire so that it would be ready for Hahnee when he and the cooks got up to start the morning meal. Squinting at the brightening sky, D'vhan pulled the white-bark parchment from his tunic and spread it on the rapidly drying ground.

"What do you make of this?" he asked. "I've never seen these symbols before."

I didn't know. My finger traced lightly over the four symbols on the bark. Three of them were irregular squares, longer than they were wide, but with high-domed tops. The fourth was strange, it seemed to be a diamond shape, but rough, with jagged edges and facets. "I can't understand what this would mean. I didn't think that the Utlaak wrote at all."

"I don't think they do." A soft voice from behind me made us both straighten up quickly. The sudden movement wrinkled D'vhan's leathery face with pain. I could tell his back muscles complained at the unexpected movement. Laban squatted down between us, chuckling at our surprise. "Surely you didn't think that all the noise you two made out here would go unnoticed? You were chattering like magpies."

"Ren woke up early?" D'vhan's not-so-innocent smile made the bland statement challenging. As anyone who had ever lived in Red Lodge knew, Ren never slept beyond the first birdsong of the morning.

"She's not feeling well." Laban shrugged helplessly, his grey eyes troubled. "She's not eating, not sleeping, something has to be wrong."

D'vhan looked up. I think he was hoping the morning sky would give him guidance. Then with a whuffed-out breath, he dove in. "Have you asked her what is wrong? She probably could tell you."

"This is the third day in a row that she's felt ill in the morning. I'm thinking of asking one of the shamans to look at her. But I'm almost..." Laban's expressive hands waved about dramatically as he scrambled for a word adequate to cover Ren's likely reaction. "She doesn't like to be fussed over."

"Ask," D'vhan insisted. "It's likely that she knows what's happening. In fact, I'll bet my favourite knife that she knows." D'vhan passed the white-bark to Laban. "But before you let her yell at you, you were saying that you knew what this means."

Laban closed his eyes wearily, dropping his chin to his chest. "It's hard to explain," he said. "You can't look at this as a warrior and see what you need to see. Think about the way a child would draw on a parchment. Remember that with the Utlaak grubs we are dealing with juveniles at best. From what happened five cycles ago"—Laban gestured towards where Y'keta squatted scowling at the painful memories the shaman's words were evoking—"we know that the adults never leave their tunnels. If you had never seen a lodge building, but wanted to explain one, I think this is what they would look like."

We jumped to our feet, swivelling around to scan the waking camp. All seemed normal and quiet. Hahnee had come out of his lodge and was stoking the cookfire and starting the boiled grain for firstmeal. Titch, the three-legged mongrel who led the camp dogs, was wandering in between the smaller lodges looking for scraps. And the hulking, not-quite-square shapes of the large lodges were casting black shadows in the grey morning. D'vhan and I stared at each other, each wanting the other to say it, not wanting to be the one to bring the words out into the open where the fear that we could see in each other's eyes lived.

"They are looking for villages," D'vhan finally said, his gravelly voice dropping tiredly. "Just like the bark shows, every village has three major lodges: Green, Red, Grey. It's the same with the People everywhere."

"So," Laban said, slipping unconsciously into his Shaman voice, echoes of power drifting through his words, "that means the fourth symbol is the important one. What is that a picture of? Remember, the Utlaak are trying to make pictures of things that they have never seen."

I stared hard at the rough diamond shape on the small piece of bark, cursing violently. "Son of a raven, it's Siann's crystal. They've been moving further and further south with each raid. Never going back to a village. They are looking for us."

"Yes," Laban said, the power in his voice drawing answering sparks from the Lightning Staff he carried. "They seek the Lifebinder Crystal. Soon they will find it, and her."

Two

The elders stood in council around the small fire inside Grey Lodge. Its flickering light cast shadows up and into the depths of the Grey Lodge, flashes of light catching the crystal eagle that hung from the rafters and then glinting away into the dark.

"We need to decide how to deal with this latest threat," Laban said, his footsteps loud on the packed earth of the lodge. His cape of mixed green, grey, and red feathers cast its own shadow as he paced. "The Utlaak may not find us, but we can't rely on that, we have to be ready if they do." A quiet babble rose from the Elders, each one offering suggestions for dealing with the Utlaak and being praised or contradicted by the others.

Iamaat spoke, her imposing presence quieting the chattering Elders. "This is what happens," she said, almost hissing the words, "when our traditions and teachings become corrupt."

Pushing D'vhan aside, she elbowed her way to the centre of the lodge and stood, hands on hips, in front of the council fire, the green gems in her hair cast a living halo of emerald sparks around her. But it was more than her substantial physical body that demanded their attention—her eyes flashed, and she was wrapped in a cloud of crackling anger.

"We have become too lenient, impure, losing too much of ourselves to the paths of strangers." No one missed the glance she shot at where Y'keta lounged with Pey't just outside the open entrance. "We have accepted strangers in our midst and they have brought this upon us."

With a sharp motion of his hand, D'vhan cut her off in mid tirade. "We have heard your hateful words before, old woman, and we will not hear them again. This is a council meeting about threats to the People, not about whatever twisted version of purity you believe we should live up to."

Iamaat's rheumy eyes blazed at the older warrior. "Twisted? It is not for you to call anyone twisted, you…"

"Peace, Iamaat," Laban interrupted, stepping in front of the Eldest Mother, hands raised in supplication. "Your concerns are known, and we are not dismissing you, but right now we need to decide on actions, not place blame."

Blustering under her breath, Iamaat roughly shouldered her way between the standing Elders and ducked out of the entrance, stalking angrily towards Green Lodge.

"Now," Laban sighed, "does anyone have any…less absurd, more rational options to suggest?"

"Wait," Ren answered. "We have already decided to send messengers to the other villages suggesting that their shamans and warriors come to the spring festival with their Kit'na. It can be discussed when all are here."

Laban looked at his mate where she leaned against the side of the Grey Lodge, her pale face ashen in the firelight.

"Do nothing," she continued. "We cannot destroy every Utlaak in all the burrows by ourselves. Send out the messages to the other villages, ensure that the young ones arrive safely, call for support, and wait."

Laban chuckled, his gentle voice breaking the tension around the fire. "Trust my mate to cut through all the opinions and find an action that we can take now." The smile he sent towards Ren was warm, the love that was always there obvious.

Turning back towards the other Elders to arrange messengers, Laban didn't see Ren clutch her stomach and slide bonelessly down the side of the lodge. It was only Hahnee's sudden gasp that spun him around to see Ren, stretched out like a broken doll, limbs sprawled awkwardly on the hard-packed ground.

"Ren!" he cried, dropping to her side, ignoring the mud stains and the audience as though both were of equal import. "Little hawk! Wake up. Ren!"

Pale-green eyes opened slowly, the normally fierce gaze met Laban's muzzily. "What happened, Laban? Why do you look so frightened?"

"You fainted, my heart." Laban lifted his mate from the mud, cradling her lean body against his chest. His hands held her so carefully as if she were made of spun moonbeams rather than being the strong warrior that the village held in such high regard. "Please, love, please let the healers look at you now."

"If I must," Ren sighed. "I'm sure nothing is wrong, I'm just overtired." The pale green of her eyes seemed to be faded, as though the ferocious light that always burned there was flickering.

Laban's grey eyes flashed towards Y'keta. "Get my mother." He didn't wait to see if the young warrior was listening, just stood up, carrying his precious burden and went into the family area of Grey Lodge.

"Don't fuss," Ren scolded, looking up from the pile of furs where Laban had deposited her. "You're making faces at me, and laughing upsets my stomach."

Laban's uncharacteristic scowl didn't move an inch as he gently stripped the cold leathers from his mate's body and wrapped her in a warm, dry tunic. "When you stop looking like a breath could shatter you, then I'll stop fussing."

"You didn't need to call for your mother. Of all people, Laban!" Ren's lips tightened, her pointed chin and sharp cheekbones throwing her gaunt features into worrying relief. "Couldn't you just get Siann or even Sawiea to look at me? Your mother is too old and frail to be bothered with such minor troubles."

"Will you stop, little hawk." Laban's usually gentle eyes hardened as he looked down at his mate. "You are not a minor inconvenience. You will never be minor to me, or to this village." His warm hand cradled her cheek, frowning again at the contrast between his warm, tanned palm and her pale, clammy skin."

Ren had never felt so treasured, or so undeserving. All pretense of strength that she had held on to, any illusion of distance that she tried to maintain disappeared as she turned her face into his hand and sobbed. "You need me to be strong, and I'm failing you. I'm too weak."

"Little hawk, listen to me." Laban lifted her into his arms as though she was weightless, holding her tight against his chest and speaking urgently, face buried in her long blonde hair. "I need you for more than your strength or your spirit in battle. I need you for the joy you bring to my heart when your eyes meet mine, for the way your ideas challenge me and make me a better leader for the People, for the way your hair feels as it flows through my hands. I cannot lose you."

Laban's intense whispers were interrupted as Y'keta entered the room with Inkiss. Laban's mother was old, ancient for one of the People, but she still smiled contentedly as she made her faltering way across the lodge and knelt down beside the pile of bedfurs.

"So, my daughter," she said as she smiled at Ren, her faint voice breathy and weak, "what brings you to your knees in the dirt?"

Ren glared at Y'keta, who didn't have the grace to blush.

"Yes," Inkiss said, laughing, "the young warrior told me. How can I help you if he doesn't let me know what you need?" Shooting an unhappy glance at her son, she continued, "Since you and my stubborn son refuse to tell me."

"Maskim, I—"

"Enough, Laban. Let me see to your mate, then we will discuss what you should or should not be telling your mother." Inkiss humphed under her breath. "I may be old, and getting frail, but I am neither stupid nor in need of protecting from difficult situations."

All irritation erased from Inkiss' wrinkled face as she turned back to the pale woman smiling up at her from the bedfurs. There was nothing Ren liked more than seeing her mate try to weasel his way out of trouble.

"What has been happening, daughter? Tell me all of it, for I will surely find out if you don't. My son"—a pointed glance flew across the lodge—"will not be trying to protect me again."

"About a moon ago I started feeling tired all the time," Ren admitted. "Then in the last few days I've been just wrong. I can't eat, even grains and berries in the morning make me violently ill. And, Maskim, I can't think, I cry, I rage. I'm just not me."

Inkiss smiled delightedly, in the five cycles since they had mated this was the first time that Ren had called her mother.

Inkiss stood up slowly, stretching her aching back and rubbing the stiffness out of her knees. "You are perfectly you, just you and a little bit more. My dearest heart, you are expecting a child. Probably within 6 or 7 moons. The little one is still learning their place within your body, be kind and let them develop a little."

"A baby?" Laban's voice was loud enough that his mother shushed him automatically and Ren giggled, which made Y'keta stare. He had never heard Ren make such a sound.

"Yes, my son, a babe for you and your mate to cherish and raise in the sight of the Elder Stars. We are blessed."

Three

Siann looked like she had swallowed a thunderstorm as she marched towards the Grey Lodge, the dark hair flying around her face crackling with its own electricity, eyes flashing dangerously. Y'keta stepped back instinctively—those were danger signs with the young shaman, and who knew, it might be aimed at him.

"Hatchling?" His nasal voice rose, making the ever-present insult into a cautious question.

"Where is Laban? I need to talk to him, now!" Siann's normally pleasant voice sounded like it had been dredged in ice. Whatever has her feathers ruffled, Y'keta thought, I want no part of it.

"He's in the lodge with Ren," he answered, stepping between Siann and the door flap as she stalked forward, anger sharpening her soft features. "Ren isn't well, Siann. She fainted." Y'keta pushed her shoulder with his square-fingered hand, barring her way into the lodge. "Can you leave them be for a few moments. We don't know what's wrong yet. Inkiss is with them."

Siann looked like a sudden, cold wind had blown past her. "Ren is ill? What's wrong? Why did no one call for me?" Siann's hand went instinctively to the pouch around her neck, where the Lifebinder Crystal slept. "Let me go in, perhaps I can help."

Y'keta squeezed Siann's shoulder gently, surprising himself at how strong she felt under his hand. Then, he snatched his hand back awkwardly, suddenly aware that he'd allowed his touch to linger. "There isn't anything you need to do for Ren. Inkiss says she'll be fine, it's all quite normal." His smile was a bit confused. After all, children were rare among his People and he wasn't quite sure how to explain to Siann that Ren wasn't really ill.

Siann's face grew calculating and her expressive lips pursed as she mulled over the poorly arranged information. "So," she said, "Ren is sick, and fell down, but Inkiss says it's normal?"

Y'keta nodded, not sure what to add.

"She's pregnant!" she shrieked.

Shaman, healer, whatever, Y'keta thought, Siann can still act like a green feather when she wants to, and this news has her as excited as a child on her name day.

"That's so wonderful!" she said, bursting into an infectious giggle. "I can see it all—Laban will hover like a raven with only one egg and Ren will be annoyed because she won't be able to fight and hunt."

Y'keta snorted. The reactions would be so typical for both Ren and Laban. Running a hand through his shaggy blond hair, he tried to picture someone telling Ren that she couldn't join the hunt or track down the Utlaak; he was glad it wouldn't be him.

"So," Y'keta said as Siann's excited bouncing slowly settled down, "you came out here with thunderheads crashing around you. Laban is busy, but would it help to tell me what had you so ruffled?"

The joy faded from Siann's eyes almost immediately and they became once again the cloudy brown that he had seen a few minutes earlier.

"I'm sorry," he said. "I shouldn't have asked."

"No," Siann replied. "If Laban isn't available, I should tell you, D'vhan, someone. I'm afraid that things are really out of control in the Green Lodge."

The back of Y'keta's neck started to itch at this—it felt like his crest feathers were rising, even though he didn't have them anymore. "Wait," he said. "I'll get D'vhan, this sounds like we need an Elder."

"Please, just D'vhan, no one else," Siann asked, her voice uncharacteristically polite.

Whatever this is, Y'keta thought worriedly, it's important enough for her to call a ceasefire in our never-ending war of words.

Y'keta chased across the main village clearing, ducking and weaving between the children playing in the dirt, headed in the general direction of Red Lodge.

"Y'keta!" D'vhan's voice called from his left, near the small lodges where the mated warriors and shamans lived. Skidding abruptly, Y'keta tripped over Titch, the three-legged mongrel that had been darting in and out among the children, and landed face first in the ash beside the campfire.

"Shards!" he cursed, glaring at the brindled dog before reaching over to scratch between Titch's ears and caress his greying muzzle. "Careful, old one," he said, rubbing the ash from his face and trying not to look around. He really didn't want to know who had seen him, especially didn't want to know if Siann had. But of course, she had, her merry laughter echoed from one side of the fire and D'vhan's gravelly rumble matched it from the other.

Trust it, Y'keta thought, any time I mess up, do something stupid, make myself look like a total shellhead, she's there. Standing up with as much pride and self-possession as he could muster, Y'keta brushed the ash from his hands, straightened his leathers and turned towards D'vhan.

"What was so aching urgent that you had to kick the dog to get to me?" D'vhan asked, the twinkle in his dark eyes betraying his amusement. "Or did Titch trip you just to be funny?"

Y'keta snorted. "You know, I'm not so certain that he didn't do that." Bending down to give the old dog a final pat he turned to face a grinning D'vhan. "The hatchling wants to see you." Y'keta's head twitched in the direction of Grey Lodge, a slight motion but enough to make D'vhan look over to where Siann stood, arms wrapped tightly around her chest. "She said it was urgent and Laban hasn't come back to earth yet." Y'keta scowled. "Something has blown a cold wind under her wings. She's normally snappy at me, but that's just me. This is the first time I've seen her really angry."

"Well, let's go and see what she's upset about. You're right, it's not like Siann to jump at shadows, unless they are your shadow." D'vhan smiled, the superior knowing smile that Y'keta had learned to hate over the last five cycles.

"What now, old crow? You've got that look again."

"Look?" D'vhan's voice was the very essence of innocence. "What look would that be?" The beads flashed in his red hair as he turned towards Siann, leaving Y'keta to trail behind him, his face covered in dog hair, ash, and suspicion. "So, what's happening, young shaman?" D'vhan wheezed as he got close enough to speak to Siann, the simple act of crossing the campsite stressing his breathing in the early-morning chill.

"If you would just let me…" Siann offered for the—shards, hundredth? thousandth?—time.

"No."

That was it, no relenting, no room for negotiation. D'vhan would not let Siann use the Lifebinder to heal him. Again, for the thousandth time, Siann decided that she had to speak to Laban about it. The village needed him, and he was just being stubborn. She didn't have to go nearly as far to heal him as she had when she healed that shellhead, Y'keta. She glanced over to where the young warrior stood, catching an unguarded expression of concern on the stolid face. Shards, Siann thought. He really does care about D'vhan. He's worried sick. I would never have guessed with the way he talks to D'vhan, always arguing and tormenting.

As though he felt the intensity of her focus, Y'keta's strange orange eyes drifted from where he had been watching the older warrior and focused on her. The black circles around his pupils made her feel like a bird of prey was staring at her with its piercing gaze. Instantly pulling a mask of disdain over her face and shovelling any respect for Y'keta or his feelings under it, Siann nodded distantly. "Hatchling?" she inquired. "Did you want something? You seem to be staring."

Clenching his lips in an angry line, Y'keta pulled the bottom of his tunic straight and stalked off towards the Red Lodge, leaving D'vhan and Siann staring at his back, each keeping their own thoughts.

D'vhan's thoughts, at least, must have been good ones. His lips twitched with restrained laughter as he glanced from the figure of the warrior in full retreat to the frowning face of the young shaman.

"Enough play," D'vhan said breathily. "What was so aching urgent that you had to send Y'keta to chase me down?"

"I think Iamaat is going down a broken road," Siann said in a rush, words tumbling over each other as she tried to say the unthinkable. Iamaat had been a part of the village since she was a child, had been the green leader when Siann was a green feather. I have to be wrong, she thought, I have to be. Her normally ruddy face paling with stress, stomach aching at the memories, Siann looked at her boot, watching idly as it made paths in the dusty floor around the campfire. "It started this morning," she said.

Four

<<<Siann>>>

The morning had started quietly enough, which should have made me suspicious. Quiet, gentle mornings had disappeared along with so many other things in the five cycles since Mother died. The green feathers were rampaging through camp, playing some kind of chase game and screaming like kuniak on the hunt. I was cleaning up the lodge after breakfast and getting ready for my day when Napaay's head burst through the hide flap, looking as solemn as that round berry-smeared face knew how to look.

"Siann," he said as his stocky form followed the head through the lodge entrance. "You keep the Lifebinder stone? Right?" I could feel the tingle of the stone against my chest—it seemed aware, listening, as my little brother piped on. "You used it to save Y'keta when the village was attacked."

"That is true, Napaay," I answered. "Although not normally something to be spoken of."

I had tried very hard over the past few cycles to make people forget the events of that night. The blood and feathers that had floated in the air, the smell of death and lamp oil.

"So?" I prodded. Napaay stared at the rushes on the lodge floor and kicked them around self-consciously. I could see the dirt-covered ankles peeking out from the bottom of his kaal-hide breeches. They didn't fit anymore. He was growing again. Sometimes it seemed that all the little Gooshoo did was eat and grow. Staring at the floor, shoving the reeds around with the toe of his foot, Napaay gave all the normal signs of a youngster in trouble. "Did you get in trouble in the Green Lodge again? I've told you not to be nasty to the little ones. You used to be little and stupid too."

"I didn't do anything!" he insisted. "It's just weird over there. I don't like it anymore."

My heart jumped. So even a little troublemaker like Napaay was starting to feel it. There had been a wrongness in the Green Lodge since Matra died. Something that just itched at my feathers whenever I had to go there. Squatting down, I put my hand under his chin and lifted his eyes to mine. "What's wrong, little bird?" I asked in what I hoped was something like my mother's voice. "What is making you feel uncomfortable? You can tell me."

Napaay looked around our lodge like someone would come sneaking out of the walls, then leaning close he whispered, "There is something wrong with Ihkopi. Can you use the Lifebinder to fix him?"

Frowning, I collapsed to sit cross-legged on the floor in front of him. "Wrong in what way?" I asked, trying to remember if I had heard of any problems with Napaay's quiet friend. "I don't know that anything is wrong with Ihkopi."

Napaay looked up at me with eyes far too serious for my little brother. "Iamaat says he's bad and broken." Napaay brushed the dirty mop of brown hair away from his face. His eyes shimmered. "He's my friend," he said, all dignity lost as he threw himself against me, blubbering uncontrollably. "Fix him, Siann, fix him!"

My spine jerked as Napaay's weight crashed into me and my arms wrapped around his pudgy shoulders automatically. *Iamaat again,* I thought. For the last few cycles any trouble in the village had started with her, our Green Mother, teacher of the young ones. Taking a soft cloth to Napaay's runny nose and tipping his face up to meet mine, I tried to explain to his innocent soul.

"Do you have red hair, Gooshoo?" I asked, making him laugh with the old nickname.

"No," he snuffled.

"But D'vhan has red hair. Does that make him wrong? Or just different?"

"Hair is just hair." The eternal pragmatism of a ten-year-old child pushed away the emotion. His sister was being stupid again.

"What about Titch, then?" I continued, bringing his favourite dog, a brindled mongrel from the pack that roamed around the camp, into the conversation. "He only has three legs. All the other dogs have four. Does that make him wrong?"

"Stop being shellheaded, Siann." Napaay snorted, wiping his nose on the sleeve of his kaal-hide tunic. *More cleaning for me*, I thought, *wonderful*. "Titch is just a clumsy dog. He's supposed to have four legs, but one got hurt."

"You're right." I nodded. "Hair is just hair, and legs are just legs. We all have differences. Ihkopi is different, Napaay," I explained quietly. As a child it had always annoyed me when a serious question didn't get answered. If my brother could ask real questions, he deserved a real response. "His heart is built a different way than yours. That is not wrong, or strange, just different."

"Iamaat talks about him all the time, uses him as an example of what happens to bad kids." Napaay's voice rose, colour rising in his thin cheeks. "I like him and it's wrong that she's being so mean!"

The Lifebinder, tucked inside my tunic, warmed and pulsed against my leg. Something Napaay was saying struck a warning note from its power. Trying to ignore the pulsing against my breast, I picked

Napaay up and brushed the twigs and dirt from his well-worn leggings.

"What is the best thing to do when a friend is sick, or sad?" I asked, trying to distract him while my mind raced madly, trying to figure out the crystal's warning.

"Well," Napaay answered, "a sick person needs a healer, and a sad person needs a friend."

Ruffling his already messy hair, I straightened him up and turned him towards the entrance of the lodge. "So, since we know Ihkopi isn't sick, maybe he just needs someone to be his friend until people learn that different doesn't mean wrong."

"Iamaat will scold me." His arms wrapped around his chest defensively.

Like any youngster, Napaay had gotten in his share of trouble with the other green feathers, but this could bring him directly up against the temper tantrums that Iamaat had become famous for over the last few cycles.

"But different isn't wrong, and Ihkopi is just different." Napaay nodded to himself resolutely. The decision to stand up for his friend shining in his tear-bright eyes.

"There you go, young shaman," I said, laughing as Napaay wrinkled his nose at the thought.

"I'm never going to be a shaman," he insisted. "They have too much to learn, and they never get to have adventures. I want to be a warrior like Y'keta, he's the bravest!"

My stomach lurched, tightened and tried to crawl up my throat. "Oh, you think he's brave, do you, little warrior?" I asked, trying not to let it show that Napaay's idolization of that shellheaded hatchling made my temper bristle. "What about D'vhan? Or Pey't? They have been warriors much longer."

Napaay thought for a minute, his eyes scanning the painted sides of the lodge for answers. "No," he concluded with the bluntness only a child could wield. "Pey't is too old and too round, and no one will ever be like D'vhan. Y'keta is just a warrior. I'll be like him!"

"Then go and help your friend," I said. Giving Napaay a final hug and straightening his wrinkled tunic, I shooed him out of the door. I hope he didn't know how much I wanted him to go. I needed to think, to try and figure out what was happening. Why the Lifebinder was warning me so insistently.

Five

Finishing her recitation, Siann shuffled her weight from one foot to the other, waiting for D'vhan to say something. Tell her she was wrong, that she'd misunderstood what Iamaat was doing to Ihkopi. Tell her that it was not her job to make those judgements. Tell her something. But he was silent. He just stood there watching a few late-winter snowflakes drift by on the morning breeze, seeming almost mesmerized.

"D'vhan?" Siann said, coughing nervously to get his attention. But when his night-black eyes finally focused on her, she really didn't like it, they were fever-bright and filled with a lifetime of anger.

"Sorry, Siann," he said, the glare in his eyes fading as he saw the concern on the young shaman's face. "If what you tell me is as serious as your brother claims, then we have a problem with the Green Lodge that I'm not sure that I can address."

"Can't you talk to her? You've been on council with her for ten cycles, surely she would listen if you told her to stop."

"Iamaat? Listen to me?" D'vhan's laugher was like nothing she'd ever heard from the warrior leader before. The sarcasm in it was almost at the edge of pain, and the laugh had nothing to do with humour. "Iamaat and I have had differences ever since I came to the village, little one. At times, only Matra's presence kept council meetings from becoming outright war. Now with her gone..." His weather-beaten face was impassive, but the gentle touch of his hand on her shoulder offered comfort from his words. "With her gone."

He didn't need to finish. Even though she wasn't invited to the council meetings, Siann had heard the raised voices and several times she had seen Iamaat stalk away from Laban and D'vhan, raging across the campsite like a green-robed thunderstorm. Siann knew that many of those arguments had been about the decision to allow Y'keta to remain in the village.

Iamaat was convinced that the Utlaak had only appeared because the village took in someone from outside. She knew that Y'keta was not one of the People, though over the past cycles he had done all he could to fit in. But he was a warrior, and under D'vhan's protection, there was little that Iamaat could do except be nasty to the shellhead whenever possible and blame every bad hunt or broken bone on his presence.

"But what she's doing to Ihkopi is wrong, D'vhan." Siann's voice sharpened from its normally soft tone. "It's wrong, not just for what it does to him, but for what it's teaching the young ones." Straightening her soft grey tunic, the young shaman met D'vhan's eyes unflinchingly. "Someone has to talk to her. You, Laban, someone has to before things go too far."

D'vhan nodded, hearing the power rolling in Siann's young voice. *She doesn't know yet,* he thought sadly. *She still can't hear the echoes of thunder in her voice, the times when she's so much more than just Siann.*

"I'll talk to Laban," he promised. "We'll find a way to pull that viper's fangs."

Siann glanced around the campground, hoping that no one else had heard how very casually D'vhan insulted Iamaat.

Her forehead wrinkled into a frown noticing that the green feathers were playing around their lodge, but that Ihkopi, twelve cycles old and scrawny as a birch bough, was scraping hides alone at the lodge entrance.

Scraping, Siann remembered, had always been one of the punishments Iamaat handed out to the green feathers when they seriously displeased her.

Twitching her expressive lips, she directed D'vhan's gaze towards Green Lodge. "Whatever you are doing, D'vhan," she said warningly, "do it soon. Something in this feels wrong to me, and the Lifebinder burns whenever I think of Iamaat."

D'vhan's eyebrow shot up into his rusty hairline. The Lifebinder was Siann's burden, the great crystal that had healed Y'keta and had given her warning when the village was in danger. It reacted to Iamaat not just as an annoyance or a stubborn old fool, but as a threat?

"Laban will know," he said. "I promise, he will know."

Siann rubbed the back of her neck with one long-fingered hand, wondering why she still felt so uneasy. D'vhan had listened to her, taken her seriously. The weight of responsibility was off her shoulders. The Elders would deal with it. So why did she feel like someone was peering over her shoulders? Why did the day itself feel somehow ominous and filled with danger?

§

In the heart of the Ice-Lands, in a cavern so massive the roof stretched away into invisibility, the Utlaak matriarch sat.

She was ancient for one of her kind, her skin brittle and stretched over a frame that had once been powerful. Her physical power had left her cycles ago, the ancient one thought, but she didn't need it now. Her gnarled hands moved ceaselessly, caressing the pulsing red crystal she held.

The crystal glowed with a sickly light, barely brighter than the lichen that grew everywhere along the cavern walls, its irregular facets worn smooth by eons of constant handling. One matriarch after another had used its power to maintain their position, sowing fear among the other adults, fear that the red death would come for any who opposed them.

Until now, the ancient one thought, one bony claw sliding over a flaw on the side of the crystal. *Until it shattered.* Its power, her power, was failing. Soon every ruthless kill she had made to claw herself onto this throne would come back to haunt her as the adults realized that she no longer steal their life by drawing it into the crystal.

Holding the stone over a rough map of the bright lands beyond the wall she watched as it pulsed slowly. The further south she moved over the map the faster the baleful light flashed.

The crystal pulsed. Just for a second the image of a young woman appeared in the darkened cavern. "We're close now," the matriarch cackled in a language as harsh as the ice itself. "The horde is getting closer. Even if I must destroy every village in the lowlands, I will have the shard, and the upstart who dares wield it."

Six

"Iamaat, this has to stop!" Laban's shouting disturbed the peaceful afternoon. Heads popped out of each of the smaller lodges, anxious faces swivelling towards the Grey Lodge where the disturbance seemed centred. Glances flashed from lodge to lodge, but no one ventured out. Iamaat's formidable temper was well known in the village and the sight of her, standing outside Grey Lodge, wrapped in a thunderstorm of self-righteous anger, was enough to keep the foolish in their lodges discussing matters they didn't understand, and the wise in their lodges keeping silent.

"I am not going to accept this, Laban of Atiskaat." They didn't have to strain to hear Iamaat's voice, shards, she was loud enough this time that the mountains should have heard it. "My word has become nothing in this place. You ignore and blaspheme our most sacred traditions, you act on the words of a stranger, someone not even of the People, over mine. And worse." She threw a poisonous glance from D'vhan to where Y'keta stood near the Red Lodge, a bewildered scowl on his plain face. Then, deliberately lifting her foot, she scraped the mud from her boot heel off onto a rock near the campfire. "This tolerance for deviants and your habit of taking in strays will bring disaster on the village. I have said so, and it is true." Flecks of spittle flew from Iamaat's lips as she raged. "I am Green Mother for Esquialt. I will govern the children as seems best to me, and no one, especially not these offal, will interfere." With a swish of her green cloak and a last glare at D'vhan, Iamaat charged across the campground in the direction of Green Lodge. Children could be seen scuttling out of the way, headed back to hide in their parents' lodges or wherever they could find shelter, until the storm that was Iamaat subsided.

"I told you, Laban." D'vhan's shoulders slumped in defeat. "She will not listen to me, or to anyone. An evil flower has blossomed in her brain and she is gone from the woman we knew." He turned and gestured helplessly at the worried faces peering from lodges around the campsite. "Look at what she is doing to your People. This can't continue."

Laban's normally gentle eyes were hard and hooded, and his short grey hair looked like a windstorm had run through it, not just his fingers. "I know, D'vhan," he admitted. "I just hoped that she could be reasoned with. What she is doing is wrong, and in some part of her mind Iamaat must know it."

"I have to believe that at one point she did," D'vhan said. "But now she can't admit it, not even to herself, let alone to you. Especially with me in the room. I am the symbol for all she despises."

Laban nodded sadly and clapped the older warrior on the shoulder. "She is wrong, you know. You are the heart of this village and know more than either she or I ever will about loving and protecting the People. But enough of that," Laban said, shaking his head to clear the pounding caused by Iamaat's thunder. "The Kit'na ceremony is coming up with the next new moon and with each young one travelling with a warrior or a shaman for protection, we have extra work to do to prepare for it."

D'vhan frowned, trying to pull his thoughts away from the last few minutes and focus on the day-to-day work of the council. "Do we expect many newcomers this year?" he asked.

"I don't know," Laban said. "With attacks on so many of the villages lately, the other councils may try to keep their young hawks at home. No one likes to lose a warrior in times like this."

"True," D'vhan conceded. "May I make a suggestion for this year's ceremony? Something a bit unusual that I'm sure Iamaat will not like."

Laban chuckled. "What do you want to do? After this morning, just the fact that Iamaat will not like it makes it almost certain that I'll approve!"

D'vhan humphed merrily. Restoring the twinkle in Laban's grey eyes was reward enough for his impudence. "I'd like to get Y'keta to stand in for me at the Kit'na ceremony this year. He knows enough about the rites to do it properly, and honestly I just don't feel like I could do it honour the way I should."

Laban's grey eyes clouded over, and his brows lowered as he quickly looked the older warrior over. D'vhan was the way he always was, whipcord thin, topped with a living flame of unruly red hair. "I know that you are not well. But is it worse? Do I need to speak to Siann?"

"No. I'm fine, Laban." D'vhan shrugged. "I don't know why I feel this way. Something in the back of my head says this is Y'keta's time and that I need to let him step up, or make him step up, which is probably what will happen." D'vhan cricked his neck, left and then right, and then left again. "It's time for the young bear to take his place among the People. We'll need that soon. I just don't know why."

"Young bear?" Laban asked quizzically. "Not hatchling any longer?"

"Winter is ending." D'vhan's deep voice was abstracted, as though he struggled to put the feelings that crawled through his heart into words. "The bears have slept the peaceful times away while the hawks soared in the forests. Now spring comes, the Utlaak are prowling and the bears will be needed to protect the village. Y'keta is the first of the young bears. Warriors sent to us to prepare for this battle. There will be more, and they will be his warriors, not mine. He must do this."

D'vhan's thin lips twitched toward Red Lodge where Y'keta was patiently teaching Coen how to sharpen the bone daggers he had made. "See there, he already takes the position without even realizing it."

"He's only been with us five cycles," Laban argued. "Will the village and, more importantly, the shamans from the other villages, accept him as your substitute?"

D'vhan chuckled, the sound rumbling through his chest and making a noise like rocks themselves were trying to laugh. "You already agree with me. You'd only try such a limp-winged excuse for an argument if you'd already given in."

A quick blush covered Laban's face, painfully obvious against his pale eyes and even paler hair. "You know Y'keta won't want to do this. So, how do you bait the young bear?" he said, quickly changing the topic. "What do we do to wake him up and get him roaring?"

"I'm working on it," D'vhan said. "I'll let you know, or more likely he'll come to you to try and get you to talk me out of it." D'vhan's smirk was pure mischief, his eyes danced, and there was a light in his face that had been missing for several cycles. "I'll trap my young bear into doing what I want. You'll see."

Seven

"I won't do it, D'vhan," Y'keta snapped. Bushes bent and swayed as the young warrior barged his way into the forest, paying no attention to the trail or to the game he was scaring away. "I don't care what kind of reason you and Laban have dreamed up, I will not take your place at the Spring Ceremony." His voice was beyond angry, snapping and snarling like a trapped animal. "You are the Kalixt, the village needs you to do this. They do not want or need me!"

D'vhan dropped onto a rotted stump beside the trail and looked up at the wildly gesturing young warrior. "Sit down, hatchling," he jested, ignoring the young thunderstorm that circled around him. "It's hurting my neck to look up so far."

The bare branches of the forest arched above them, and the pale winter sky above that. D'vhan felt like he could look straight up forever, past the trees, the clouds, the sky itself, to where the Elder Gods reigned and the sun, the great Eye of Riad, shone undiminished. Waiting patiently, he stared at the wispy clouds drifting back and forth across the sky, blown by the last of the winter winds.

Finally, Y'keta sat. His shoulders shook with a heavy sigh. "I thought we were out here to track the latest Utlaak raiding party, or is this another one of your 'get the hatchling on his own' manoeuvres?"

Shamefaced, D'vhan grinned. "Both, really," he said. "I needed to talk to you about this and we do need to find out where the last raiding party came from. And more importantly, why they turned back before we caught up to them. Now listen, hatchling."

"No, Kalixt. You listen." Y'keta's hands waved animatedly, thunderheads starting to flash in his strange orange eyes. When those eyes focus on me like this, D'vhan thought, I can still see the hawk behind his human form. "I didn't choose to come to Esquialt five cycles ago, you know that. But I am the one who made the decision to stay." Y'keta's face became solemn as he remembered the painful confrontation with his father because of his decision to stay with the People. "And that means that this village is my home, my People, even though I'm not really one of them."

D'vhan snorted impolitely. "You're as much one of our own as any other war—"

"I will never be one of the People," Y'keta interrupted, "not all the way, not like someone born in our villages. Because of this, if nothing else, they will never accept me as Kalixt."

"Who said you would be Kalixt?" Back snapping straight, eyes blazing, D'vhan pounced. "Are you so eager to replace me?"

"But you said you wanted me to conduct the Kit'na ceremony—I assumed."

"You assume too much." D'vhan's eyes crackled fiercely. "Just because I ask you to take on a task for me doesn't mean that I'm quite ready for the hania to pick my bones."

"Never, D'vhan," Y'keta protested. "I never meant to say that I wanted to replace you! I would do anything you ask of me, Kalixt!"

Y'keta didn't hear the trap under his feet until it snapped closed. The older warrior had word-danced him into a corner he couldn't back out of. A quiet smirk replaced the feigned anger on D'vhan's face. "Then you will act in the Kit'na ceremony for me. Good." Jumping up from the soggy stump and brushing the debris from his leathers, he strode into the bush without bothering to glance at the bewildered face behind him. "Now, we have Utlaak to find," he said. Get moving, cub." A vague muttering, liberally sprinkled with what D'vhan assumed were curse words in Y'keta's language, followed his back as he parted the undergrowth and disappeared into the bush, smiling.

A few hours, and many curse words, later D'vhan and Y'keta came out of the brush and into a small clearing about half a day's march from the village. The ground had been beaten flat and in the middle of the clearing the remains of an old campfire pit hastily covered with dirt showed that someone had been there not too long ago. Grabbing a stick, Y'keta stirred the embers, releasing puffs of gritty ash but not a flicker of fire. "At least three days," he said disgustedly. "They are well back into the mountains now."

An errant gust of wind blew ash into D'vhan's face, causing the older warrior to choke and cough for a few moments.

"Look around," he ordered when his breath came back. "See if you can find anything, another bark picture, something that will tell us why they were here." D'vhan squatted in the weak sunlight of the clearing, chest heaving, struggling to breathe.

"D'vhan," Y'keta said carefully.

He had tried so many times to get D'vhan to see the healers, but the prickly old crow wouldn't hear of it. "You can't heal old," he would say and brush off Y'keta's concern with a shrug.

"Don't," D'vhan shut his concern out before Y'keta could even give voice to it. "Finish checking out the campsite and let's get back to Esquialt. I don't like the clouds over the mountains. Something is blowing in from the north and I don't want to be caught in it."

Shrugging helplessly, Y'keta searched the bushes around the dead fire for any sign of the Utlaak's plans. Scraps of food and the odd bit of scaly hide stuck to the forest floor, but nothing that said why they were there, or more importantly why they had left.

"Y'keta..." D'vhan's voice was weak and husky from coughing, but Y'keta was listening for it. He swung around, looking towards where the older warrior was kneeling, moving aside the matted underbrush. "They left a cache of food buried here."

D'vhan pointed at a hollowed-out area that had been quickly covered by trampled grass. The small lined pit was filled with the grey jerky-like substance that the Utlaak had force-fed to Y'keta when he had been their captive. He shuddered at the memory, even now, five cycles later.

"If they left supplies, then they mean to come back," D'vhan continued. "We should make a camp near here and watch this site."

"A good idea, but not for right now," Y'keta said. "We have only one moon until the Kit'na ceremony and the new warriors and the other shamans are expected to arrive in just a hand of days. We can't be away from the village right now."

D'vhan's expressive lips twitched mischievously. "Oh," he said. "Now you are concerned about the ceremony? Just a few hours ago you were looking for a way to avoid it." Laughter shook D'vhan's thin shoulders, and the rueful light in Y'keta's face made it all the more potent. "Come on, cub," he said. "Let's get you back to Esquialt so you don't have to worry."

SPRING

Eight

Laban paced back and forth in front of Siann, his square-fingered hands twisting together anxiously. "Are you sure, Siann?" he questioned, peering at the young shaman as she sat on the lodge floor looking, to his mind, far too at ease considering what she was proposing.

"I know how much we need D'vhan." Siann sounded far older than her twenty cycles, her eyes were calm and clear.

Stars, Laban thought, *she reminds me so much of her mother*. Nothing had shaken Matra, not the back and forth of politics between villages, not the struggle of raising two children alone after her mate passed away. She had always been strong, at least outwardly.

"D'vhan is important, yes," Laban agreed. "But so are you. Siann, this village needs you just as much. You are not to risk yourself."

Siann blushed. "I'm not trying to be self-sacrificing, Laban," she said. "I've been bothering D'vhan about this for the last five cycles. He just won't let me heal him. I'm not sure if it's because he's scared of hurting me, or if somehow..." Her words trailed off and she stared intently at the gloves she wore to hide her scarred hands. "I think he doesn't want to get well," she said, her voice so quiet Laban scarcely heard the breathy admission. "He's tired, feeling the winters, and Iskine has been gone for almost ten cycles. I think he is giving up." Siann's eyes were clouded, their normal sparkle dulled and sad. "Bone tired, soul tired," she continued. "It's like he's doing things by rote, because they are needed, not because the spirit is in him anymore."

Laban looked at the worried young shaman, weighing his options. Yes, the village needed D'vhan, but even the best warriors could be replaced. Siann was something different. Her power, whether from the stone she carried or the Lightning that had scorched her soul at the Thunderstones, had put in her a unique position, given her a gift that no one else understood or could carry. "What does the Lifebinder say to you, shaman?" he asked formally. "What will be the cost of restoring our warrior?"

Siann pulled the pink crystal from its pouch around her neck. Noticing, not for the first time, how its long diamond shape looked like a dagger. *Pointed both ways*, she thought, unconsciously caressing the strangely warm stone. *To give life, I must take it, from myself, or perhaps*—the thought seemed to come from somewhere beyond herself—*perhaps from another*. Siann's whole body jerked unconsciously. The very thought of draining someone else to pour life into D'vhan made her shiver in the darkness of the lodge. There was an evil in the thought that curled up in her soul like a snake just waiting for its chance. All it would take was a moment of weakness, anger, revenge and the crystal would strike. The Lifebinder could kill. There was no way to forget it, that knowledge was a part of her now, it would twine around every choice she made, every day for the rest of her life.

"I think I can do it without damaging myself too much," Siann said thoughtfully. Listening to the echoes of Lightning the Tiamat had burned into her hand and the whispering snakes of the Lifebinder. "I can't make him a young man, but I should be able to heal him enough to bring him back to where he was before the lung fever."

Laban looked solemn. "Are you sure, young one? I cannot lose either of you—I will not lose both!"

Siann nodded, her eyes flickering with the twin powers that she held.

When her eyes flash like that, Laban thought, *it is hard to remember that she is not much more than just a young, very young shaman.* "Agreed," he spoke decisively. "I will speak to D'vhan as his Salixt. Order him if I must. He cannot be allowed to fade." Laban took up the Staff of Lightning and Thunder and draped himself in his ceremonial cloak before turning towards the doorway out of the lodge. "Do what you must to prepare, Siann," he said. "I'll bring him back here."

§

D'vhan looked up inquisitively as Laban pushed his way into the Red Lodge. It wasn't like him to come into the warriors' territory uninvited. "Salixt?" he questioned, watching as the assembled warriors gave way to the squat Shaman. He was in full council garb, D'vhan noted. His staff crackled with power, his cloak flashing with the crystal shards woven into it. "Is there a problem?"

Laban didn't speak to him, didn't acknowledge him at all. He simply looked around the lodge at the other warriors relaxing around the smudge fire and said, "Out!"

There was a flurry of movement as Coen, Y'keta and Pey't rushed for the exit. Apparently, Laban was not happy, and the glances they flashed each other as they scrambled out of the lodge made it clear that they didn't want to attract the normally gentle Shaman's attention.

"Laban, what is wrong with you?" D'vhan asked, the formality dropped now that the others had gone. "You come charging in here with the thunder flashing on your staff as though you are headed into battle."

"I am in a battle, D'vhan," Laban said solemnly. "I am fighting for the very soul of the village."

D'vhan quickly stood up from where he had been lounging on his bedfurs and looked around for his weapons. "What danger comes?" he said sharply. Every thought of disruption, every question forgotten, the village was in danger—he stood ready.

"Someone is trying to take one of our most valuable assets, a person with a power the village cannot lose, and I'm struggling to know how to stop them."

D'vhan's face tightened, shoulders squared, ready to meet the challenge. "Who comes for Siann? Have the Utlaak found us already?" he asked. "Should I put out more guards? Or do you want her moved into the main lodge for safety?"

"I'm not speaking of Siann," Laban corrected. "I speak of one older than the shaman, one with influence over the young of this village, a voice in council that could not be replaced."

"Ahh," D'vhan visibly relaxed, dropping his daggers back on top of the weapons piled against the lodge wall. "You mean Iamaat. I cannot help you with her. You know that she and I have old differences that are not likely to heal. She needs dealing with, yes, but I'm not the one to do it."

Laban stalked around the inside of Red Lodge, so different to the Grey Lodge that was now his home. In Grey Lodge, every item was significant, nothing was out of place or random. Tradition and history guided everything from the placement of the scrolls to the type of wall hangings and parchments. Red Lodge was...chaotic was the only word Laban could think of, weapons piled loosely by the doors, clothing and food scattered around the sleeping areas. It was much more a home than merely a place of ceremony for the warriors. Only the Salixt ever lived in Grey Lodge, and then only in the private area. The main area was for teaching, for ceremony, not for bits of leather and unwashed tunics.

"No, D'vhan," he added again. "I mean you."

D'vhan's head tilted and he blinked at the squat Shaman uncomprehendingly. "Me? No one is taking me from the village, and I hold no such place and power."

"You are our Eldest on council, you are the head of our warriors, you have fought for the life of this village more times than any other warrior. You are the heart of our village, D'vhan, and you are in danger."

D'vhan snorted. "I'm in no danger, even if I agree with you on the other parts, which I don't. There are many who can stand in my place, I'm merely an old warrior."

The pale face under his characteristically wild red hair was far too bland to be honest, Laban thought. *D'vhan was never that calm, that emotionless. He hadn't even argued and D'vhan always argued.*

D'vhan hacked loudly, obviously trying to emphasize his weakness and lack of importance. Unfortunately, the attempt worked too well, and he grabbed onto one of the large poles in the centre of the lodge to support himself as a real coughing spasm doubled him over.

"I'm not debating with you, D'vhan," Laban insisted. "I'm telling you this is so. You will allow Siann to help you, to bring you back to as close to healthy and whole as she safely can."

"But," D'vhan argued, his hands waving protests in Laban's direction.

"No arguments," Laban interrupted, "not this time. I promise you that I won't let Siann go so far that she harms herself, but the risk is worth it if we can get you back even close to your earlier health."

"You can't change old," D'vhan said, his shoulders slumping at the admission. "I'm old, Laban, and I'm tired, bone tired, soul tired. Leave me be."

"Not this time, old crow," Y'keta's voice came from behind them, making both elders jump. His strong, stumpy hands seized D'vhan's shoulder in a white-knuckled grip. "You have hidden behind this illness for the last five cycles, slowly passing off things to other warriors, pushing away those who care about you. No more." The orange pupils of Y'keta's eyes flared and faded to black as he concentrated on the older warrior. "You will fight this, just as you have fought for this village ever since you arrived so many cycles ago. You will fight for us again, and if this time it means fighting your own demons, then that's what it means!"

Muttering under his breath, D'vhan allowed the two younger men to forcibly manoeuvre him out of the Red Lodge and across the camp towards the Grey, not caring that every eye in the camp was on them. His eyes were locked on the entrance to the Grey Lodge. Young Siann would be waiting inside and he was dreading the ordeal that they, that he, was about to put her through.

"You promise me," he insisted, glaring over his shoulder at Laban, "you will not let her harm herself in trying this. She is our hope."

Ignoring the bluster, Laban roughly shoved D'vhan towards the entrance to Grey Lodge. "Y'keta,"—he turned to the squat young warrior—"stay at the door. No one, not council, not Elders, not the Stars themselves, enters here until we are done."

Y'keta nodded solemnly, trying hard not to let his disappointment and relief show. He wanted to see what happened, but at the same time, knowing how great the powers were that Siann could call on, and how often her hot temper was directed at him, he didn't want to be anywhere near her when the Lifebinder Crystal was active.

Nine

Siann paced back and forth over the hard-packed earth of the lodge, her hands never still, turning the pink Lifebinder Crystal over and over obsessively. As though examining it one more time would reveal its secret, make it less dangerous, less two-sided.

"I can do this," she muttered to herself, "I can control it, make D'vhan whole." Her normally tanned face was pale, the angles of her cheekbones sticking out in sharp relief against her solemn brown eyes. A rustle at the entrance spun her around, bringing her face-to-face with a very resentful D'vhan.

"D'vhan, I..."

The older warrior turned away from her, the stiff cant of his head and the spear-straight back their own silent manifestations of defiance.

"You told me once," she tried again, a different approach this time, "what the most important words one of the People could say to another were. Do you remember?"

D'vhan humphed, still not facing her, but at least, she hoped, listening.

"I was little, my skin was burned from the sun and I had been sick with the heat-fever for three days. When you asked how I got so scorched, I told you that I had been out catching pricklefish for a full day. All the other children had been working in pairs and groups to fill their buckets, but I was determined to catch the most, take the biggest prize back to Green Lodge, and I was so sure that I could do it alone. Do you remember that?"

D'vhan humphed again, but this time she heard the humour in his tone and his shoulders softened, no longer looking so much like a warrior, but more like the D'vhan who had taken time for a serious young child with big dreams.

"You scolded me about trying to do things alone, putting myself in danger for nothing more than my stubbornness," Siann continued. "And I *was* stubborn, and young, and full of my own self-importance."

"That you were." D'vhan's deep voice finally broke the tense air in the room. "Convinced, at six cycles, that you were going to be the greatest shaman the village had ever known."

"Do you remember what you told me the day they finally let me out of the healers' lodge?" Siann asked. "When I insisted on going back to the pond to catch more fish? You said that the most important thing that one of the People could say was, '*Let me help.*' Were you wrong?" she asked of D'vhan's silent back and tense shoulders. "I have the ability, I have the gift, I can help. So..." Siann raised the crystal, letting the afternoon sun that peeped through the entrance catch in its facets and send spinning pink ribbons across the hide walls of the lodge. "Let me help."

Laban placed a firm hand on D'vhan's shoulder, spinning him around to face the earnest young shaman. The solemn concern on her face, the affection and worry in her eyes, the knowledge of power echoing in her voice, all pulled at D'vhan's heart.

"Young one," D'vhan said, his voice gravelly and lower than drums in the dark, "you were always my favourite of the green feathers, more like own my hatchling than just another child in the village. If you are harmed, my heart could not survive it, Siann." D'vhan's black eyes, usually full of mischief and purpose, shimmered softly.

He couldn't be crying, Siann thought. *D'vhan doesn't cry.* "Then let me be whom you taught me to be, old crow." Siann insisted, "I swear to you, by the Sun of Riad, I can control the Lifebinder. It cannot harm me if I stop at just healing your lungs."

D'vhan's shoulders slumped as he gave in before the power building in her eyes. "Do what you must," he said. "But remember, I will not lose you. My spirit will Walk away from the Road and wander this world unformed before I see you damage yourself on my behalf."

"Sit down, D'vhan." Laban's hands on his shoulders pushed him onto the ceremonial white hide in the centre of the lodge. "And don't be so concerned. Siann has learned to hold her power well. This will not drain her too far."

Daring a glimpse at the crystal Siann clenched in her scarred left hand, D'vhan gasped to see drops of blood red oozing out between her fingers and running down her forearm.

"There must be blood," her voice, no—it wasn't really her voice—the voice of her power spoke. "Blood for the life of the People."

Laban shivered, this was the voice he remembered from the Thunderstones, the voice of the Elder Stars, only now it had been amplified by the Lifebinder Crystal and was booming through the small body of a frightened young woman.

Gnarled fingers tightened on a broken crystal.

"The Forest," she said. The shaman hides in the forest.

Siann shook with the strength of the power gathering within her. Her eyes glowed, flashing from an eerie white to blood red and back again as the powers within her fought for dominance.

"We see you, Dovhan of Atiskaat, D'vhan, Kalixt of Esquialt."

D'vhan's face went as white as salt and he gasped, trying to make sense of the unthinkable. The Elder Stars knew him, they knew where he was born, they knew his name.

"You have walked a Road alone, stood apart your whole life." The power speaking through Siann continued in a voice neither male nor female, but cold and distant as the winter stars. "You fear your own heart. Do not."

An incredible heat burned through D'vhan as Siann's small hand touched his upper arm. *Her empty hand*, he thought thankfully, knowing instinctively that if the crystal had touched him, powered as it was by the echoes from the Thunderstones, he would have been unmade.

Heat surrounded him. Roughly, intrusively, it burned into every fibre of his body. D'vhan's mouth twisted into an inaudible scream as the light poured into him in what felt like an unending assault. When, finally, he knew that one more second of exposure to such raw power would turn him to ash, it changed, going from an unending fire, to a warm caress, filling him with a sense of ease and comfort that he hadn't felt in cycles.

"Live, D'vhan, Elder of Esquialt! Lead your People once again," the strange un-voice chanted. "This is not your time to Walk the Road. We give you to your future, to the future of the People, and to the one who comes for you."

The glow around him faded and D'vhan blinked, trying to focus in the shadowy dusk of Grey Lodge. *I'm glad Laban made me sit down*, he thought. *I don't think my legs would hold me if I begged them to.* Feeling Laban move from his position behind him, D'vhan glanced over to where Siann knelt on the rush-covered earth. Her eyes blazed, wells of burning copper in her pale face.

"I'm all right, old crow." Her weak voice was not very effective in reassuring him. "Laban, stop fussing," she insisted, clambering up to her feet and knocking the dust from the knees of her leggings. "I'm not Ren. I'm not pregnant, and I'm certainly not going to fall apart. All I do is provide the conduit for the powers. It's not so bad." Siann's brown eyes flashed from Laban to D'vhan and back again, unwilling to admit in front of the seated warrior just how much the healing had taken from her.

"Tell that to your eyes," D'vhan heckled, catching the quickly averted glance and feeling the old urge to tease the solemn young shaman. Slowly getting up, D'vhan stretched out the stiffness in his knees, waiting for the cough, the pain in his joints, all the signs that his physical body was slowly collapsing. Rusty eyebrows climbed into his hairline as the pain didn't come. D'vhan frowned and tried a tentative squat but heard not a whimper of pain from his knees, which would have been screaming if he had tried to bend them that way just moments ago.

One final test. D'vhan breathed in deeply, listening for the wet rattle that had settled into his lungs five cycles ago. Silence.

Laban and Siann prowled around him like hungry kuniak, watching every movement, looking for the first sign of weakness.

"It worked," D'vhan said turning to Siann. Taking her lightning-scored hand in his, D'vhan turned her hand palm-upwards and, careful not to touch the lightning scar, brought it to his forehead. A gesture of allegiance, devotion, and honour that Siann had read of in the scrolls but never seen for herself.

"D'vhan," she protested. "Don't do that. It's—"

"Appropriate," Laban grabbed her other hand, the one that still gripped the bloody crystal, and repeated the gesture. "Thank you, Siann Lifebinder, you have returned D'vhan to the village, and more importantly, I think, to himself."

Pulling back the heavy flap that covered the entrance to Grey Lodge, Laban stepped into the sunshine, breath making frosty puffs in the cold fresh air. He turned to the stern-faced young warrior standing guard at the entrance.

"You can come in now, Y'keta. It's done." The words hadn't come out of his mouth when the squat young warrior bowled him over, pushing him into the walls of the lodge in his rush to reach D'vhan. Laughing merrily, glad to feel the release of tension after the events inside, Laban looked around his village. It was going to be all right. D'vhan would be well, Siann would be guarded, and Ren was carrying their child. Surely the stars were smiling.

Ten

Ren and Laban came out of the lodge a few mornings later looking so much like themselves that Y'keta's lips twitched with amusement. Ren's lanky figure strode to the campfire without ever glancing sideways, her path as straight as an arrow. Sliding her ever-present blades into their sheaths, she nodded politely to Hahnee, grabbed a bowl of the spicy stew he had been working on all day, and settled near the fire. Laban stretched leisurely as he shambled along behind her. Stopping to greet the people and settle the plans for the night's Kit'na ceremony, a short, squat canoe paddling his steady course behind a deadly green-eyed shark.

Y'keta smiled as Laban approached him, bowl in hand. "So, Shaman, how does it feel to start your fifth full year as Salixt? Were you as nervous at your first Kit'na ceremony as I am about the one that happens tonight?" Y'keta's hand thrust through his coarse hair, making the spikes stick up even more than normal. He couldn't believe that he'd let the old crow push him into doing this.

Yesterday, shamans from all the other villages had arrived, accompanied by their warriors, and with them were all the youngsters who came seeking to Walk with the People of Esquialt. That was another change in the ceremony that had caused a furious outburst from Iamaat who felt that all the People's traditions were being ignored.

In peaceful times, the young ones had walked into their new villages alone. But last cycle two hatchlings walking from Atiskaat to one of the northern villages had been slaughtered when they ran across an Utlaak raiding party. The Utlaak hadn't cared that they were children. At the harvest festival that autumn, a combined meeting of the shamans and warrior leaders had decided that, at least for now, it would be wiser that a shaman and a warrior would escort each group of hatchlings. Because this group was coming to Esquialt, it was understood that the head Shaman of each of the other villages would be accompanying their Kit'na.

D'vhan sat at the edge of the firelight, tugging idly on the red rat-tail braids in his hair. There was something unsettling about the night, or maybe he was the one who was unsettled. He'd never been good at staying in the background and it was sharding hard to sit back and watch Y'keta act for Red Lodge in the Kit'na ceremony.

The cub didn't claim to be Kalixt, didn't want to be leader, would never push D'vhan out of his position, but D'vhan knew it was time someone else stepped forward. The decision was obvious, he'd known it five winters ago, when the lung fever had left him weak and shaking. Siann had healed his lungs, and he was thankful, but it was still a lesson that he had needed to learn. No one lasts forever, no one can be allowed to be irreplaceable. He had to train someone to take his place, and that someone was Y'keta.

Y'keta watched as the newcomers milled around aimlessly among the villagers. There were only five Walkers this time. Word of the Utlaak attacks against the northern villages was spreading. Last cycle, nine young ones had come. Of course, some those had been nothing but eager hatchlings looking to get their names in the scrolls, certain that they were meant for the glory of battle. That kind went home quickly.

It still feels strange though, he thought, *only five cycles ago I was one of them, frightened, but determined to make a place with the People. Now, here I am, leading Red Lodge in the same ceremony where I came so close to failing.*

Not that leading the Reds in the ceremony meant much. There were only a few of them now. D'vhan was still leader, despite his reluctance to take on the ceremonial duties. Siann had brought him back from the edge of the Road, the lung fever from five cycles ago had been close to stealing him from them. Siann had stopped that, but even now there was a shadow that walked beside D'vhan. Sometimes Y'keta saw it hiding behind his eyes. Sawiea had been away for a few moons, visiting her oldest child up-coast. It was just him, Pey't, and the young hawk, Coen, who had come to the village in last cycle's ceremony.

Drums called people from their lodges to gather around the central campfire where Laban, his ceremonial cloak flashing in the shifting light, waited in silence. This wasn't the gentle, jovial Shaman that the village had come to know. Tonight would be a time of power, and the echoes of that power could be seen swirling in his grey eyes.

"The Elder Stars are watching," he said, glancing up at where the constellation that the People called the Watcher's Eye wheeled above them. "Five young ones have come, seeking to join their Roads with ours. Will we welcome them, my People?"

"I will not."

Of course, it was Iamaat, Y'keta thought as a harsh voice interrupted the ceremony. Of all the Elders on council, she was the only one who would speak out deliberately to embarrass Laban in front of the other villages.

"No shame to these young ones," she said, gesturing at the stunned group of young people who stood, feet shuffling, beside the campfire. "They have not Walked. This new decision about the ceremony was made without regard to our ancient—"

With a sharp gesture, Laban cut her off in mid-tirade and several people shook with supressed laughter as Iamaat almost visibly deflated. "Iamaat, what should we have done," he said tiredly. "You are the Mother of our children, would you wish them put in danger just to preserve a tradition? There is no difference between two Kit'na Walking together and one Walking with a shaman or a warrior. Let it go."

"You bring dishonour to this village and your Lodge, Laban of Atiskaat. I will be no part of this. None will join the Green Lodge who comes in such a manner."

Laban's eyes snapped, and his voice became as cold and smooth as the whisper that a dagger makes when you draw it from the scabbard. "I am Laban of Esquialt, Iamaat. You would do well to remember that the traditions you revere so highly placed me as Salixt of this village. If you cannot be civil, *be silent.*"

Ignoring the green leader's disruptive personality, Laban turned to apologize to the watching visitors, only to be waved off by Kalita, the tow-headed powerhouse of a warrior from Maskwatin, where Pey't had grown up.

"Iamaat has reasons for her rages," she said, shrugging. "I knew her daughter, Taynia. She was Red Lodge in Maskwatin." Her blue eyes softened a little as she reminisced. "When Taynia was killed, Iamaat blamed it on some untraditional training methods designed by our Kalixt. But I was there, Taynia died in a battle with the Utlaak, we were overwhelmed, no amount of training would have helped. In her grief, Iamaat couldn't see that, she's convinced that if things had been done 'properly,' according to tradition, her daughter would have survived."

Laban's eyebrows bunched up, emotions flying rapidly across his expressive face. Kalita's story explained why Iamaat hated anything new or even slightly untraditional and he could see how that would lead her towards a twisted sense of belief and then fanaticism.

"Thank you, Kalita," he said. "I didn't know that, and it explains much. I'll try to keep it in mind and deal with her a bit more gently." Fortunately, there were none seeking Green Lodge membership this cycle so he didn't have to challenge Iamaat's refusal to accept newcomers. With Iamaat's reputation, it was hardly a surprise that no one wanted to join Green Lodge in Esquialt. There was an old saying among the People that when the mother went mad, madness ruled the entire household.

Three of the five newcomers were hoping to join the Grey Lodge, students and mystics come to train under his guidance. The remaining two had asked to be accepted into the Red Lodge. After the ceremony, Pey't had agreed to take them under his wing, claiming that he was too old and lazy to be much good at anything but acting as den mother

Laban watched, smiling slightly as Y'keta, acting for the Red Lodge, stepped out to perform the traditional invitation.

Y'keta approached the central fire, feeling the nervousness of the five Kit'na standing in front of him and hoping no one noticed that he was shivering. He wasn't sure if it was the drums or the ancient songs and dances, but every year as he watched the lodges take their traditional places, his mind went back to the angry young man he had been when he had come to Esquialt five cycles ago. How much he had resented his exile to the village and how completely convinced he had been of the superiority of his People over the mudwalkers his father had forced him to live among.

Y'keta watched as Laban welcomed the new Kit'na, invoking the Elder Stars and seeking their blessing on the night. The grey smoke from the herb bundles that the Shaman had thrown into the fires made his nose twitch and their smell made him uncomfortable, reminding him too much of the cloying minty scent inside the healers' lodge. The drums rolled loudly before dropping back to their steady heartbeat rhythm.

Y'keta breathed in and out for a few beats then stepped forward firmly, his odd orange eyes giving nothing away. Taking a sharp indrawn breath, he started to chant.

> *We are the guardians, strength of the sky;*
>
> *We walk the dark places, fight fear in the night.*
>
> *Will you walk beside us to serve and to die;*
>
> *To hold safe the People, keep honour alight*
>
> *As we take up our spears on the Sky Road.*

An uncontrollable shiver ran through him as he spoke the ancient words. He had heard them repeated every cycle since he came to Esquialt, but tonight was different. Tonight, he was the guardian. Not D'vhan, whom everyone knew would guard the village with his life. Not Pey't, who had been in the village for almost fifty cycles. But tonight, the Elder Stars called him, Y'keta, son of Surta, and Red Warrior of Esquialt. Another shudder ran through him as the voices within him built one on top of another to a deafening crescendo. He was Waki'tani. He was a warrior of Esquialt.

And tonight, before the Stars themselves, he was called to be the guardian. Even if just for this moment, the safety of the People was his responsibility. It terrified him. *What if D'vhan refused to step back into his position as red leader?* Y'keta thought. *What if I'm forced to keep the mantle of authority he tricked me into wearing tonight?* No, he promised himself. *I will not let myself become anything more than a warrior. If I wanted the responsibility of being an Elder or a Guardian I would never have left the Roost.*

Eleven

<<<D'vhan>>>

I watched as Laban bent to release the tension in his back, stepping into the firelight, the grey beads woven in his cape throwing shards of multicoloured light around the gathered faces.

"The Elder Stars have heard us, my children," he said. "We give thanks for the new souls that will Walk beside us on the Road and for those warriors and shamans who came to guard their path to our fire."

We may as well address the situation head on, I thought, knowing he felt the same way. Iamaat would not let anyone forget that the Kit'na did not Walk alone.

"In times of peace we would end our ceremony with a dance of thanksgiving." Laban walked around the circle of light created by the campfire. He looked at the faces sitting in the shadows, some tired, some injured, all more used to war and hardship than any of us had ever wanted them to be. "And tonight, despite what our fear tells us, we will give thanks," he said. "The People are living still, and although our lives change, they are still bright under the Watcher's sky. Dahi of Konahi Village has asked to give thanks this night. He dances for the People."

A spear-straight warrior stepped out of his place in the shadows, gave a half-bow to his shaman, and entered the circle of light. "I thank you, Laban," he said, and moving in perfect rhythm with the drums, began to dance.

The dark-haired man moved effortlessly in the empty space between the fires, muscled body shining copper in the firelight. Tattoos of red and black twined around his upper arms and across his chest, like vines clinging to the branches of a sacred oak. Feet stamping with every beat of the drums, spear raised over his head in mock challenge, he embodied the spirit of the warrior and the strength of the spear.

"I'm too old for this," I rumbled under my breath. But I couldn't stop watching, fascinated, as the dancer leaped over the fire and made a feint at the green feathers sitting beside Iamaat. The children squealed, half excited, half afraid of the ferocious figure in his ceremonial robes.

The insistent drumbeat slowed and stopped, leaving the dancer standing motionless under the Elder Stars. An unmoving point of strength at the fulcrum of the worlds.

"You honour us, Dahi," Laban said, stepping out from where the shamans of the four villages were gathered.

"I thank you for the opportunity," Dahi said in a light tenor. "I dance for the Elder Stars." His words were not disrespectful, but unexpected enough that I glanced up sharply. My eyes met his and my heart jumped. Like the sky just before moonrise, Dahi's eyes shone back at me, I fell into their endless violet depths.

I couldn't hold his gaze. I stared nervously at my campfire boots, inspecting all the places where the beading had fallen off. *Shards, I need to get myself in order*, I cursed silently. *This is not the time to start fantasizing about a warrior who will be leaving with the sunrise. Deep breaths. In. Out. Focus on your breathing, don't think about long hair or copper skin. In. Out. Shards!*

Looking up, I saw Dahi talking quietly to Xliat, a shaman from his village, and Laban. I slid over just close enough to pick up on the conversation.

"Laban, if you will permit, and if Xliat will allow, I would spend a cycle here in Esquialt with your Red Lodge." Dahi's voice was soft and respectful as he spoke to Laban. But his eyes held a world of challenge as they locked on to mine. "If your red leader will accept me, that is," he said.

Don't say yes, I willed Laban to hear me, *don't let this one into Red Lodge. I'm not strong enough.*

Xliat nodded, gesturing to Dahi and then around him to the darkened village. "Dahi is one of our best warriors. But I break no confidences when I tell you that he lost most of his family two winters ago and has been restless ever since. I do not know what he is searching for, but maybe in Esquialt, he can find it."

Laban examined the warrior standing confidently, arms held loosely behind his back. "What do you seek here, Dahi? We welcome you, but I fear that you seek in our village the healing that must come from your own heart." Laban shrugged and gestured towards me. "D'vhan is our red leader, speak to him and arrange lodging among the warriors."

I pulled my "red leader" face on and stood up, brushing the pine needles from my leggings.

Dahi looked at me and nodded slightly. "Respects, Elder D'vhan," he said. "I seek to Walk with this village, to find a reason to serve and perhaps the missing piece of my heart that will allow me to once again serve well."

"I am D'vhan, Kalixt of Esquialt," I said, trying to sound casual and in control. "Be welcome among us, Dahi."

Twelve

The next morning, D'vhan wandered through camp in the pre-dawn light, long before the mourning doves started their songs. His eyes were red-rimmed and glassy, and a distinct smell of stale wine tainted the breeze when he passed downwind.

"Shards, you look awful," Y'keta said, coming up behind him and grabbing a bowl of boiled grains from Hahnee's cauldron. "Did someone poke your eyes with a stick?"

"Disrespectful cub," D'vhan complained, swatting playfully at Y'keta's head. "I worry about the future when I see how mean-spirited you youngsters are."

Y'keta grinned merrily as the older warrior rubbed at his bloodshot eyes. "I'll respect you when your head isn't the size of a wintering bear and your eyes don't look like all the dust of the high plain has blown into them. Just how much of the ice wine did you have last night?"

"Not enough to put up with you this morning," D'vhan said sourly, and marched off to sit and eat his meal near the entrance to Red Lodge.

"Is he always this touchy?" Dahi asked, coming out of the small lodge where he had chosen to stay. The new warrior watched the red leader stomp across the campfire with dismay. "It doesn't seem to fit with what I've heard of him. Stories have him as a gentle, courteous man."

Y'keta laughed, his orange eyes sparkling. "That he is, Dahi. A gentle, courteous, pain in my tail feathers."

"Red Lodge, now!" D'vhan yelled, his deep voice rumbling through the quiet camp. From wherever they had been in the camp, the warriors ran back to the lodge, alarmed at his call.

"What's your sharding problem, D'vhan?" Sawiea snapped, running up with her bowl and spoon in hand and the signs of her firstmeal still smeared on her face. "Scorch you, old crow," she growled. "It's so early that the birds aren't even awake, and you run around yelling like your hair is on fire. This better be a crisis."

"I've been thinking," D'vhan said, pacing backwards and forwards in front of the entrance to Red Lodge.

Sawiea muttered, *"That could be a crisis,"* causing a quick laugh to flash through the tense group.

"Listen, warriors." D'vhan's hand waved her to silence. Ignoring the grumbling from the cooks, he grabbed a charred stick from the edge of the cooking pit and started tracing patterns in the frozen earth at his feet. "See this," he explained, drawing four circles in the dirt. "Four villages, four attacks, each the same.

They come on a new moon night and disappear as soon as the sun rises."

"We know that," Pey't said, brushing the crumbs of his breakfast from his grey beard. "This was worth spoiling my breakfast?"

"No." D'vhan said, "You aren't looking deeply enough, stop looking at where the enemy strikes." Taking the charcoal end of the stick, he drew lines headed north from each of the attack sites. "Look at where they come from." The lines all converged in one spot, north of the mountains, the Ice-Lands. "Until we found the parchment drawing, we thought these attacks were the work of random bands of raiders. We were wrong. These attacks are precise and intentional, they are looking for Esquialt."

"You mean to send us to the Ice-Lands?" Pey't asked curiously. "My village is the furthest north that any of the people have settled, and even we don't travel that far into the mountains."

"But we are going to," D'vhan insisted. "If something back there is driving the Utlaak grubs towards us, we need to know."

"When do we leave?" Dahi, the new warrior from Konahi, asked. "And why would they be looking for this specific village?"

"*We* don't leave," D'vhan answered pointedly, not looking at the tall warrior. "I want you, Coen, and the two youngest hawks to stay here."

Dahi's face darkened, amethyst eyes turning to stormy grey. "Kalixt, I..."

"No, Dahi. I need to have someone here to guard the village. You and the young hawks will remain."

Dahi bowed slightly in D'vhan's direction, fists clenched. "I obey," he said in a voice that held all the cold rage of a winter storm, "but I do not understand."

"Explanations will come later," D'vhan said. "Trust me that there is an explanation, this is not an arbitrary decision. I just cannot take the time right now. Y'keta, Pey't, Sawiea, get ready. We move before the mid-day meal."

§

A few hours later the small band gathered to leave the camp. The younger warriors stood nervously at the door of Red Lodge, their faces anxious and a bit lost.

"Laban," D'vhan called out to the Shaman as he walked past. "We will be gone for two moons, I leave Red Lodge in your care until my return."

Dahi grunted at that—a Shaman in control of the warriors.

"I am neither blind, nor deaf," D'vhan corrected him sharply. "Laban was Red Lodge before he became a Shaman, and he knows this village as you, right now, do not."

"Salixt," Dahi bowed towards Laban, ignoring D'vhan's mutterings, "I am sorry if I seem disrespectful, but I did not come here to be left behind."

Laban stared at D'vhan, then, when he was sure he had his attention, twitched his lips towards Dahi and the young warriors.

"Just Dahi," D'vhan mouthed silently, waiting until Laban nodded his understanding. Then, gathering up his small band, they headed north.

He had almost reached the edge of camp when a strong hand stopped him. Swinging around he came face-to-chest with a very determined warrior. "May I speak with you, Kalixt?" Dahi asked. The words may have been polite, however, the intent behind them was anything but.

"We need to get on the trail," D'vhan said, moving as though to pull away from the hand clasped loosely around his wrist.

"Just a moment. That is all I ask," Dahi insisted, manoeuvring D'vhan until the pair stood behind a low bush that bordered the trail.

"Dahi, I…" D'vhan swallowed, craning his neck to look up at the taller man. "Laban will explain." His words were rushed, his deep voice shaken.

"I will listen to Laban's explanation," Dahi said. "But you will listen to me. You walked the camp all night last night, and it had nothing to do with the Utlaak, or the attacks, or the Ice-Lands. It had to do with *this*." Dahi's strong hand tightened against his arm. "Do what you must, D'vhan. But be honest at least with yourself. You cannot avoid the Road before us."

And suddenly D'vhan was alone, Dahi had melted into the sunlit forest, leaving him looking at his arm and wondering if he'd imagined the whole impossible conversation. *Shards,* he cursed at himself impotently as he stepped back onto the trail, ignoring the curious stares of the small group that stood waiting for him. *I have no time for this!*

"Move out, Red Lodge," he said, one hand compulsively smoothing the crumpled black leather over his forearm. "The Ice-Lands won't move closer by staring at them."

Thirteen

<<<Y'keta>>>

The mountains marched away from us, purple, then grey, and finally a stark distant white. I couldn't believe that I was going up there. Even the scouts for the Roost didn't fly that far north. I had been told that the volcanoes, their snow-covered sides wreathed in steam, made the air currents unstable and that the storms could be deadly.

Surta's eyes were hooded as he settled down on the top perch of the Roost. His voice was flat, and I could tell that he had shut down. His son, his heir, was being stubborn again. That was all he heard. "The shard-brained hatchling has his tail feathers twisted," he muttered. "Why will he not just listen to me, or to any of the older, wiser voices in council, and accept things as they are?"

"But why?" The perch swayed as I landed with a bump. My claws grasped the branch, eyes flashing from black to orange. "Why do we have wings if you won't let us fly?"

"You flew up here, just to challenge me? Even after I told you that I wouldn't change my decision." Lightning crackled around Surta's wingtips. Maybe this was normal

between fathers and sons, the constant power struggle, the questioning of authority, but Surta would not allow it. I may be his son, but there seemed to be something about me that scorched along Surta's nerves like the sound of claws scraping a granite rockface.

"No 'Keta." Surta's voice was as harsh and cold as the mountains he wouldn't let me explore. "There is no reason for our scouts to fly that far north. No reason to map the ice mountains. We do not go there."

"No reason?" I could feel my crest rising, just with the memory. Knowing that, again, what I said was being dismissed without thought or explanation. "We are the guardians of this world. All of this world. How can we ignore the Ice-Lands? Is your refusal really just because of the volcanoes? Or is it just because you don't want to get your feathers cold."

"We have never flown patrols over the Ice Mounts," Surta said. "It is too dangerous and there is no reason to do it. We are not going." Surta's hooked beak closed with an audible snap. "And since when, my son, do you care about our responsibilities to this world? Your head is too far in the clouds to care about what happens to anyone but yourself. You are just looking for an adventure, and I will not indulge your foolishness." Surta's lightning-touched feathers rippled with aggravation. "We will not have this argument again, Y'keta. We fly the paths our ancestors flew, and that is all!"

I could still feel Surta's massive shadow looming over me, blotting out the stars. Even now, cycles later, my soul *shivered at the image.*

Shaking my head, I set my face resolutely towards the mountains. This was the way D'vhan said we must go. So, no matter what memories of my father were rattling around in my head, this is the way we would go!

"Well, old crow." I nodded at D'vhan, doing all I could to keep the memory of old pain out of my face. I don't know if it worked. With D'vhan, it seldom did. "Are we going? Or are we sitting talking about it? I thought we left the Elders back in the village."

"Impertinent hatchling," he mocked, his rumbling voice echoing merrily between the overhanging ledges. "We wait for Sawiea and Pey't to join us. Then we'll move. Make a fire if you're so bored that you have time to be annoying."

Scraping twigs and damp moss from around the base of the looming pines, I started a smudgy fire under an overhanging stone ledge. Feeding it just enough to keep the fire alive without too much smoke. No sense letting whatever lived in those mountains know that we were coming.

It was full dark by the time Sawiea and Pey't broke through the bushes and squatted under the ledge beside us.

"So," D'vhan said, peering at Sawiea, one rusty eyebrow jumping inquisitively. "Just what did you find dawdling in the dark with Pey't?"

Sawiea's longbow swung around quickly, poking D'vhan sharply in the chest, knocking him flat on his behind in the cold, damp underbrush. "We backtracked enough to cover up the mess you and the hatchling left as you came up here from the trail. Were you really trying to let the Utlaak know where to find you? You could have always tied beads to the trees to point the way."

D'vhan shook his head. "Blame the hatchling," he said, cocking his head towards me and giving me a look that dared me to start one of our never-ending arguments.

"If you must," I said. Something in me just wasn't willing to banter tonight. The night had gone silent. There was something malicious out there, the back of my neck knew it.

"What is it, Y'keta?" Pey't voice was soft, quiet, not disturbing the night so much as winding through it to reach us. Hand on his well-worn dagger, his eyes searched the darkness away from our small fire. "Has something put the wind under your feathers?"

In all the worlds, only these three could get away with that, I thought. They knew who I was, who I really was, and to them all that mattered is that I was now Red Lodge. I struggled to put the thunderstorm in my gut into words, there was nothing logical, no reason for my unease that didn't tie back to my father's disapproval of going into the ice mountains.

"When I was young," I said carefully—there were things that Pey't and Sawiea knew or may have guessed about me, but I wasn't sure if they knew exactly how different my *growing up* had been—"I approached my father about visiting the Ice-Lands once. He gave me story after story about how dangerous they were, how none of our people had ever gone there and that no one should ever go. Maybe that's all it is, but I feel..." I shrugged and dropped my voice. "Call me a hatchling, but I feel like the night is watching us. It's unnerving."

"Smother the fire," D'vhan ordered. "Sawiea, patrol behind us. Pey't, let's get moving." His voice was crisp and calm. I had never been so thankful that Siann, as annoying as I normally found her, had bullied D'vhan into letting her use the Lifebinder to heal his lungs. She had done as much as she could, as much as the stubborn old crow would allow, knowing how using the crystal drained her strength. And although the damage was not completely healed, at least now he could keep up with the hunters without gasping, and his voice was its normal bass rumble again.

We moved off into the moonlit forest, silent as smoke drifting between the boles of the trees. Or, I should say, the other warriors moved silently. I tried, I really did, but my sharding feet seemed to find every loose rock and snap every dry twig on the floor. D'vhan just looked at me, his eyes dancing merrily, while Sawiea rolled her eyes to the heavens every time I made noise, as though blaming the Elder Stars for giving her such a flat-footed companion.

A few hours later we broke past the treeline on top of a steep mountain ridge and I stopped, gaping. The peaks ahead of us were snow covered, glinting under a waxing moon, higher than anything I'd ever seen, with wisps of smoke trailing from their summits.

"The rocks that do not sleep," Pey't said solemnly. "My People called them that. They may look still and frozen in ice, but there is fire in their hearts and anger towards all that lives and moves on the earth."

A cold arrow shot through my heart at his words, as though something inside me hunkered down, trying to make itself small and unnoticeable. "Anger?" I asked. "Why would these mountains be angry?"

Pey't leaned backwards, stretching his spine this way and that, limbering up after the last long climb up the ridge. It made me vaguely ashamed when I thought of all the times that I had laughed at the fat, old warrior, all the jokes about hunting "just for Pey't." He had kept up to our brutal pace without a whimper or a visible sign of effort.

With an audible thud Pey't's ample backside slid down the bole of a scraggly fir tree and thumphed onto the rocky ground. "My home village, Maskwatin, is east of here," he said tiredly. "We have legends of these mountains; of things— I've always assumed that the stories were talking about Utlaak— crawling out of the lava tubes at the base of those volcanic mountains."

"That's why we came up here," D'vhan interjected, joining Pey't on the ground. "The Utlaak have been attacking from this direction, always working from these mountains southward towards Esquialt."

Picking a piece of lichen from his tangled red hair, D'vhan shrugged thoughtfully. "There has to be a major concentration of Utlaak near here somewhere. Maybe finally we can get through to their Elders, the ones who plan the attacks, and find out why."

If my eyes rolled any harder, they would have made a full circuit inside my head. "Don't be so charitable, old crow." I squatted in front of him, glaring angrily. "I've been in one of their warrens. There are no plans, no reasons." The scars on my back from the moons I spent as their prisoner pulled and stretched as I stood up, turning away from the other warriors. "All they know is pain."

"We will go carefully," D'vhan said. "But we will go. Now, everyone, get some rest. We move again at sunrise." I sat on the rocky outcropping for a long time, staring at what I could see of the mountains in the dark. All the others needed to sleep was a flat piece of ground. D'vhan was curled up against the bole of a tree, resting his head on his arm, snoring quietly. Pey't lay on his back, puffs of steam coming from his mouth every time he breathed out into the cold air. I was still too soft to sleep on command. Rocks still felt like rocks and my hip bones found every one as I stretched out along the ridge trying to relax. My eyes fluttered closed a thousand times, only to snap open again when my mind filled with images of the whips and chains, the Utlaak grubs fighting each other at the command of their Elders. Bodies clutching and grabbing in the never-ending dark, and over it all the choking smells of death and fear.

When D'vhan shook me awake in the grey of the morning it felt like every speck of dust from the gravelly ridge had made its way into my eyes. Rubbing them didn't help, it turned the normal orange into a bloody red mess.

"Come on, hatchling." D'vhan laughed, limbering up by doing a few effortless squats. Sometimes I almost wished he was still ill. At least then I could pretend to keep up with him. Scrambling to my feet I adjusted my tunic and started to roll up the useless blanket I'd spread under me the night before. It hadn't kept the cold out like Pey't promised.

Sawiea came out from the bushes below the ridge and passed around a drinking skin. "Just a mouthful," she said. "We don't know when we'll find more." I tipped the skin up and took a satisfying mouthful, then bent over coughing as the shock from the alcohol burned any lingering sleep from my system. It definitely wasn't water, although I'm not sure what it was. The skin was full of some kind of berry liquor, heavily spiced and fermented, and about as much like water as a raging flood is like a calm fishing pond. Finally, the coughing stopped, and I looked up into three grinning faces.

"Vair wine," Sawiea explained. "I get it from my home village and only use it when we've been out all night. It chases the cold away."

"Consider yourself fortunate, hatchling." This from Pey't, whose eyes were watering a little from his pull on the wine skin. "It's very rare that Sawiea lets anyone near her wineskins. I'm convinced the only reason she doesn't sleep in Red Lodge is that she wants a safe place to hide them."

Sawiea swung her bow over her head and thumped Pey't, none too gently, in the ribs with the bottom end. "The reason I don't stay in Red Lodge, old man, is that you and D'vhan sound like charging buffalo when you sleep, and no sane woman would put up with you. Besides,"—Sawiea's normally hawk-like face softened a little—"the lodge I shared with Tonki is my home, even though he's gone ahead on the Road, I still feel him there."

I looked from Sawiea to her bow and back again. Her mate was Tonki, her bow was called Tonki, and it had human hair tied at the top. My mouth flapped open and I thought about saying something then, realizing that I'd probably trip over my words, decided to keep my silence and let someone else take the risk of getting sliced by Sawiea' s sharp tongue.

D'vhan glanced over at me and nodded. Sometimes it was as though his dark eyes could see me think. He knew me better than I knew myself. *At least this time*, I thought, *he approves*.

"Move out, warriors." D'vhan grunted. "These mountains aren't coming any closer." Grabbing our travel packs and clambering down the side of the ridge, we worked our way northward.

Nights got colder, days got darker. We were all walking on blisters and eating nothing but waybread and dried berries by the time D'vhan called a stop on the fifth day. "Pey't, did the legends in your village say how far in the Utlaak camps were?"

Pey't kicked at some dried pine needles on the floor and seemed to be trying to remember the old tales from his home village. "We were not allowed to hunt further back than two days north of the first range," he said. "After that we risked running into the villages of the under-dwellers."

"Villages," D'vhan repeated. "They called them villages—that implies buildings, organization, at least some sort of government."

"You're reading into it, old crow," I protested. "We have no proof that the Utlaak are anything but mindless animals."

D'vhan stalked up to me, pulling a tattered piece of hide from inside his leathers and waving it in front of my nose. "Animals don't draw. Animals don't plan. This, if nothing else, proves that." It was a copy of the map we had found in the winter. The map that proved the Utlaak were looking for Esquialt, looking for Siann.

Fourteen

The sun was barely visible over the horizon on the sixth day when they came to a towering cliff face that stretched east and west as far as any of them could see. Stretching like an immense frozen waterfall, higher than the tallest pine tree, the cliff looked like the legendary wall around the world. The barrier that kept the creatures of the Ice-Lands from invading the forests.

Y'keta's shoulder blades twitched with the need to spread his wings and soar over the wall, to see the unending fields of ice beyond.

"You've run out of world, old crow," Sawiea said mockingly. "Even if I shot an arrow with a rope tied to it straight up, through the ice and into the rock, we couldn't scale this."

The sun inched over the scrubby pine trees at the base of the cliff, making the stone glow in its feeble light. The ice that coated the limestone cracked and flaked as we watched. Pieces as sharp as daggers fell from the cliff, large enough to impale whatever unfortunate animal wandered too close to the base.

"Well," D'vhan said, shrugging, "we know why they don't post guards. Who would need them with this on their border?"

Pey't's voice was thoughtful in the absolute silence of the forest. "I can see how anyone watching these ice daggers rain from the cliff would believe that the mountains are angry." He shrugged and took a mouthful of the water from the skin that he carried over his shoulder. "I think we've gone as far as we can. I don't see a break in this cliff anywhere."

"Honestly, neither do I," Sawiea said apologetically. "I know that you wanted to go into the Ice-Lands, but there is no way past this."

D'vhan backed away from the towering cliff, his eyes combing the rock and ice face, looking for something he had missed, any way that they could continue. The forest was silent, no rustling disturbed the underbrush and no birds chattered in the trees. Suddenly he pointed east. "See there," he said. "Hania, circling around the base of the wall."

"Probably some wandering creature was speared by the ice." Y'keta shrugged. "Nothing more than that."

"I don't think so, cub," D'vhan insisted. "That many hania usually mean more than just one corpse. Sawiea, what do you see?"

Shielding her eyes from the morning sun, Sawiea peered at the circling carrion birds. "At least two hands of hania, D'vhan," she confirmed. "Definitely more than a single kill would attract."

"We'll go as far east as that kill and if we find nothing there, I'll think of going back." D'vhan's voice made it obvious that thinking about turning back wasn't the same as going back. But at least he would think about going home.

D'vhan plodded stubbornly through the soggy underbrush, headed east towards the circling hania. He knew what that many scavengers meant. One dead animal, even a large one, wouldn't cause such a crowd. It must be a battle, but between whom? They were too far north for the village hunters or scouts and Y'keta had told him that the Waki'tani didn't fly over this mountain range. Although he didn't understand why. *If I could fly,* D'vhan thought, *there would be no limits on where I would want to go.*

"Come here, cub," he said, stopping to let Y'keta catch up. They were standing on the top of a ridgeline, looking north at the ever-rising wall of the ice cliffs. "Do you see where that mountain just to the east of the treeline touches the cliff? Where the steam is rising?"

Y'keta shaded his eyes and squinted into the early-morning sun. Of course he could see the mountain, his eyesight was better than D'vhan's at a distance, but he didn't want to show the older warrior up by making it look too easy. "What am I supposed to be looking for?"

Without warning, D'vhan's hand slapped the back of Y'keta's head. "You think that I'm being funny? I asked you, *hatchling,*" he said, the meaning D'vhan put behind that last word obvious, "because I need you to look, not just pretend to look to make an old man feel better!"

Glancing to make sure that Sawiea and Pey't were far enough down the ridge, Y'keta allowed his eyes to change completely. Dropping any pretense of being just a warrior from the village, he focused on the eastern peak and narrowed his orange eyes. Just for a moment it felt like he was changing, feathers re-growing, limbs reshaping. It was almost as though he could glide off this ridge and reach for the sky just once more. Shaking the wistful thoughts from his head, Y'keta concentrated his gaze on the mountain. The mountain was grey. *Either limestone or slate,* he thought, *with scraggly pine trees at the base—nothing unusual.* The real snowpack started at the treeline and from there, where it joined the ice cliff, the crevasses and hollows made a jagged grey and white pattern that stretched to the volcanic peak. Except, Y'keta squinted, right near the start of the snowpack there was a large black hole with a plume of steam slowly rising into the frosty air.

"D'vhan, I think there is a burrow on that mountain. About halfway up, right where it joins the ice cliff."

"Can you see any sign of Utlaak? Any movement at all?"

Y'keta scanned around the outside of the dark entrance. "The snow is packed down, lots of footprints," he reported. "I don't see anything moving, but that cave has been used for something. Someone is there or was recently."

"And that is only two fingers east of the hania," D'vhan said, using his left hand to measure the distance between the circling birds and the looming cliff. "There was a battle, we'll see the signs soon, but I'd bet Pey't a skin of Sawiea's wine that the survivors fled to that cave."

§

Cautiously they pushed their way down from the ridgetop, feeling the silence of the valley bottom weigh on their spirits like a heavy blanket. Even though they could no longer see the rising sun, they didn't need it to know which direction they were headed. No one could avoid the stench of death that filled the eastern end of the valley. It drifted through the silent afternoon—old death, pungent and vile. The undergrowth they passed was trampled and dead, saplings broken. Whatever had happened here was not recent, but the forest had not yet healed.

When they reached the skirts of the mountain, Pey't raised his hand in warning and the group came to a silent halt.

"Y'keta saw a cave near the treeline," D'vhan said. "It's pretty close to the hania, and looks big enough for trouble to hide in." His characteristic head tilt asked a question and Sawiea's nod answered it. Quietly dropping her pack and slinging Tonki over her shoulder, she set out to scout the area for danger.

Wordlessly, D'vhan and Pey't squatted back to back in the small clearing, leaving Y'keta to wander as quietly as he could between the battered saplings. "Sit down and keep quiet," D'vhan hissed. Y'keta's squat brow furrowed. He had not grown up with the wood lore that the others learned, but he thought he was doing well enough. At least most of the time.

It didn't take long for Sawiea to return. Her usually impassive face looked troubled in the half light of the forest. The sombre glance she threw at D'vhan was enough to bring the warriors to their feet, weapons in hand. "What's happening, Sawiea?" D'vhan's voice was quiet in the heavy, stinking air. "What did you find?"

"The battle was maybe a hand or so of days ago," she replied. "It looks like two groups of Utlaak fought. The bodies have just been left to rot." Sawiea swallowed thickly, her face an off shade of green. "Hania aren't picky eaters, there isn't much left."

"Anything alive?" D'vhan asked. "Any sign of where the survivors went?"

"I don't think many from the one group survived. There was only one set of tracks that I could see. They both came from, and returned to, that big cave that Y'keta saw." Sawiea clicked her head in the direction of the battle. "You all need to see this," she said. "Although you won't thank me for it."

The sights and smells of this battlefield would never fade from their minds. The grey, malformed bodies of the young Utlaak were sprawled haphazardly across the shale skirts of the mountain. Their limbs twisted in the spasms of death and their faces frozen in the final moment of fear. Wetting a rag from his waterskin and wrapping it carefully over his mouth and nose, D'vhan picked his way among the rotting corpses, shooing away the merciless hania. They didn't care which side of the battle had won or lost, to them it was just meat. So much meat.

A few disgusting minutes later, D'vhan returned to the fringe of the forest and gestured for the warriors to join him. Carefully digging a hole in the mulch under a pine tree, he buried the wet rag that had been over his face.

"No adults," he reported. "But I think that one of these groups were the ones that had the camp we found. I found similar types of food on several of the corpses. Even the hania wouldn't touch that grey stuff."

"I don't blame them," Y'keta said, gagging slightly. "Even hania have some standards."

"If I'm reading the battleground properly, our Utlaak from the campsite were the losers here. I think that's why they never came back to their food cache. Whether this was a fight between Utlaak tribes, or just because the Elders were bored, it was brutal. None escaped." D'vhan pointed up the scree slopes towards where the dark cave entrance loomed. "The winners seem to have come from there, and I think went back there as well. Now," he said, leading the small group away from the mountain's foot, "let's move away from here and find a safe place to camp. Tomorrow we'll get as close to that cave as we can and see what we find. I doubt that they are still there, but we may find more clues."

A few hours later they were safely upwind of the battleground and sheltered in the lee of a pair of large boulders. Y'keta had made a small fire and Sawiea passed around her special wine, the clear, potent liquid warming their hearts and burning the smell of the battle out of their noses.

"Y'keta." D'vhan pointed towards the top of the jagged erratic they were sitting under. "Climb up and take first watch. No wandering."

Y'keta nodded and, grabbing his well-worn blanket, started climbing the side of the large limestone rock. He knew why D'vhan had put him on the first watch. Attack was most likely in the early part of the night, before the moon rose, and his night vision was better than the others. Breathing deeply in the cold air, Y'keta allowed his eyes to change. The orange in his eyes narrowed until the dark, hawk's eyes dominated his face. He wouldn't miss anything.

Settling himself on the top of the rock, he covered up with the rough hide blanket and let himself disappear into the dark. *Why*, he thought, taking advantage of the quiet time before moonrise to try and understand everything that had happened in the last few moons, *would D'vhan insist on me handling the Kit'na ceremony? Especially now that Siann had restored the older warrior.* The back of Y'keta's neck bristled.

The wily old crow was up to something. But what? Swivelling his head back and forth to cover both the route they had taken from the battleground and the opening of the mountain cave, Y'keta tried unsuccessfully to calm the knots that were forming in his stomach. *Me?* he thought. *I stood for Red Lodge in the Kit'na ceremony?* He shook his head in amazement. Then, like the distant flash of lightning that reveals an oncoming storm, he understood.

He hadn't escaped after all. He had thought that the responsibility of being the chief's son was behind him, that when he left the Roost, he had broken free of it. But the old crow had trapped him. Even now, D'vhan was trying to push him into leadership, trying to make him matter.

A few hours later, unsettled in body and mind, Y'keta slid his stiff, cold body down the boulder and slipped into the makeshift campsite. Using the end of his spear he gently poked Sawiea. He remembered the way she had attacked him five cycles ago the first time he'd gone too close in an attempt to wake her. Her breath making frozen puffs in the cold night air, Sawiea nodded, grabbed her bow and hauled herself up the rock to take her place on watch.

Y'keta stretched his hands out to the flickering embers of the fire, murmuring to them in his own language, urging a little more heat for his frozen hands. A hiss from above grabbed his attention and he looked up in time to catch the wine skin that Sawiea had dropped basically on his head.

"One swallow," she whispered. "Then throw it back up."

Y'keta took a small sip from the skin and felt the strong drink pour through his system, warming him from the inside out and driving out the night's dark thoughts. "My thanks," he whispered as he threw the flask back up into the darkness only to see Sawiea snag it with the end of her bow, wave, and disappear back into the darkness. Throwing a few twigs onto the fire, he grabbed an old stick to shove the embers into a pile, trying to generate more heat. Then, stretching out as close as he could to the fire, all thoughts of plans and responsibilities put aside for the night, he slept.

§

Y'keta groaned pitifully when Sawiea's longbow poked him in the ribs a few hours later. Seeing D'vhan bent over the fire and Pey't rationing out their meagre supplies, he rolled to his feet, every bone aching. Scorch it! Would he ever get used to sleeping on the ground?

"You'll live, hatchling." Pey't chortled, passing Y'keta a rough cake made of dried fruit and grains smothered in honey and some of the precious buffalo jerky. "You need more padding." He laughed, patting his own overstuffed stomach proudly. "Then the rocks won't feel so hard."

"Really," Y'keta joked, pointing at D'vhan and Sawiea standing by the fire. "How do they do it then?

They don't have an ounce of extra meat on their bones."

Pey't leaned towards the young hunter, lowering his voice as though to share a deep secret, and whispered, "Pure stubbornness."

Eyes streaming with laughter, Y'keta and Pey't looked at the other two warriors, who stared back innocently, making them laugh even harder.

"Laughter is a good start to any morning," D'vhan said, "but that mountain is still up there, and we aren't getting any closer."

With that, D'vhan picked up his pack and led them noiselessly back through the shale and the fallen ice, closer and closer to the shadow of the cliff.

Fifteen

<<<Y'keta>>>

The cave mouth loomed in front of us as we moved up the slope from the trees. There were eyes everywhere. The back of my neck was prickling with warning and I just knew that somewhere in the blackness of that cave I would have to face the Utlaak again. I'd fought them many times in the last five cycles, but not in their caves, not in the darkness that a part of me had never escaped.

We slid towards the opening, our backs pushed against the cliff face, trying to be silent, but failing miserably. The bottom of the mountain was covered with loose gravel and chunks of ice that snapped and crackled with every false step. The cliff stretched before us, vanishing to the west and east as far as we could see, blank-faced limestone topped with daggers of falling ice. A signpost marking the end of the world.

Suddenly D'vhan stopped, his hand waving us all back. I pressed myself so hard against the cliff that the cold of the rock face started to seep through my tunic, leeching away whatever courage I had left. Pointing at Pey't and Sawiea, D'vhan gestured to a ledge overhanging the trail we were on. Sawiea untied herself from the rope that connected us and pulled herself effortlessly up onto the ledge. Pey't followed, with greater effort, his bulky frame moving silently but not easily onto the rocky outcropping. Gesturing us to wait, they scuttled sideways along the narrow ledge towards the gaping cave mouth. *Mouth.* Why had I thought of that? It looked like a mouth, black and gaping with icicles hanging like teeth above the opening. Right where we needed to pass.

After a few moments we saw movement above us. Sawiea's bow waved us forward, the tail of human hair that decorated the top-notch waving morbidly. D'vhan and I shuffled forward a few paces, ducking behind the last large boulder west of the opening to wait for the others.

"Ready?" D'vhan whispered. I could see in his face that the confident battle-leader from my first cycle in the village had, at least for now, returned. There was a fire in his eyes that made the normally mischievous face look nothing less than deadly. I shook my arms to loosen up the tight muscles in my shoulders, checked my daggers, and nodded. I wasn't ready, but I never would be.

"Wait a moment." Sawiea pulled her flask out and gave us each a sip of the strong vair wine. "We'll need some fire to keep our hearts strong," she said. "I don't want my hair joining Tonki's on this bow."

Pey't's eyes flashed brightly as he rubbed his balding scalp. I shook my head in amazement. Even now the old warrior found some self-effacing way to defuse the tension and steady our spirits.

D'vhan stood up, straightened his tunic, nodded and edged around the boulder. We followed. Trying to keep up with the older warrior was never easy, especially now.

Stepping out of the morning sunlight into the half-dark of the cave entrance was the most dangerous moment. I went first, blinking quickly. My eyes would adjust faster to the dark than those of the other warriors. The cave floor was buckled and littered with fallen rocks. Bodies were stacked against the cave walls like kindling, bloody and stinking. Nothing had been done to help the injured or bury the dead. They had been stripped and thrown to the sides of the cave like refuse.

Pey't swallowed thickly, pulling a cloth from his pack and quickly tying it around his mouth and nose. *A good idea*, I thought, digging through my travel pack for something to use as a mask. There was no way to know what sicknesses the foul air was carrying.

Picking our way across the uneven floor, trying to stay between the corpses, we moved deeper into the shadows of the cave. D'vhan pulled out the torches from his pack but I gestured him to stop. "Wait," I hissed. "Wait here for me a moment, but do not light the torches."

Shaking like a leaf in a windstorm, I moved forward, hoping that I looked more confident than I felt. My stomach was lurching, every step taking me further from the safety of the daylight and deeper into my nightmares. I lost sight of the others about a dozen steps away. Trying to ignore the corpses of Utlaak grubs piled under my feet, I leaned over and traced my fingertips along the cave wall. I could just make out that the wall bent abruptly about ten steps further in, turning completely away from the light. I made my way cautiously around the narrow hairpin bend in the passage and froze, desperate not to give away my position. I closed my eyes and took a few deep slow breaths. Opening my eyes, I felt my shoulders sag in almost palpable relief. The walls of the cave were lined with the phosphorescent lichen that had been in the other barrow. If we were careful, we could pass through without the lights giving away our position. One hand trailing along the cave wall, I cautiously made my way back to the others.

"The lichen on the walls will provide light for us once we pass a bend about twenty steps ahead," I said. "Torches will only draw the Utlaak as well as any other creatures that live in these caves."

I couldn't help shuddering, feeling the insects and worms that had crawled over my body as I lay bound and helpless. D'vhan's hand brushed my arm as he edged past me and around the bend into the dark. He's the only one I'd talked to about my time as a prisoner in the Utlaak barrow, the only one who knew how many nights I slept outside the lodge, just so that I could see the stars and know that I was not still lost in the dark.

Following Pey't around the bend, I whispered, "Close your eyes for a few breaths. Then open them slowly." A few moments later, I opened my eyes to see the cave outlined by the pale violet glow of the lichen.

"So, this is what you meant," D'vhan whispered, his voice echoing strangely off the limestone walls. Carefully he reached out to touch the lichen, then shook his hand furiously when it came away from the cavern wall covered in the glowing mold.

Pey't coughed softly behind his improvised mask. All that the shaking had done was splatter D'vhan's tunic and leathers with the pale spores, making him glow like some eerie creature from the under-lands.

"We'll be able to see, at least," Sawiea jested. "All we need to do is follow D'vhan."

Swatting aimlessly in Sawiea's general direction, D'vhan moved forward into the cavern.

"Why are there no bodies here," I muttered. "Once we passed the bend at the entrance there isn't a single grub."

D'vhan rubbed his hand through his hair. The gesture was so normal for him that I'm sure he didn't realize that he'd done it. The resulting sight made Sawiea trip and almost fall. D'vhan's hair was now speckled with the glowing lichen. He looked like a floating apparition, a messy-haired ghost floating in the absolute darkness of the cave.

"Get moving," D'vhan said. "We need to get as far as we can from the entrance in case another party of Utlaak come in through the cave." Trying not to chuckle as his ghostly head bobbed away from us down the tunnel, we followed.

Sixteen

For hours, the party inched its way forward, moving parallel to the wall of the cave, following the bends and turns as the passage twisted ever further into the mountain. Several side tunnels ran away from the main tunnel and the risk of the warriors getting lost was never far from their minds.

Finally, Pey't came up with a solution. Taking a handful of the disgusting lichen, he drew arrows at each junction, marking our way towards the front of the cave. The lichen was visible from several hands of steps away and pointed away from our location, marking our way back to the entrance and ensuring that anyone who followed the arrows looking for us would be going the wrong way.

When Y'keta stumbled for the third time, D'vhan finally called a halt. Sitting in an alcove that bulged inward from one of the walls, and sharing out our rations, we debated our next steps.

"How far will you push this, old crow?" Sawiea asked. "We have supplies for maybe three hungry days, or whatever passes for days in this place. But what do you think can we find down here?"

"We push on." D'vhan's voice echoed against the walls of the cave, the deep rumble at home in the depths. "At least one more full day's march." He nodded forcefully, which made Sawiea giggle. His head with its crown of lichen bobbed up and down disconnectedly in the almost-absolute darkness.

"What do you think we can find?" Pey't repeated. "We haven't seen any sign of life since the entranceway."

"That's what bothers me," D'vhan answered, the worry in his voice evident. "I can't believe that every single Utlaak at the battle just sat down and died at the entrance. Surely one of them would have tried to go through here, to get back to the barrows. It doesn't make sense." Absentmindedly, he rearranged the lichen in his hair, running his hands through the wildly tangled red mess. "One more day," he insisted. "Then we can go back."

"So, if we don't find anything in the next day, we can go home?" Sawiea chimed up from the shadows, her voice sounding animated at the idea of getting out of the caves. "This cave will still be here if we want to come back when we are prepared for a long trek."

"Shards! You hatchlings are pushy tonight! Where is the respect for your Elders?" D'vhan teased.

D'vhan took a quick look around the narrow niche they were seated in. "We'll use this alcove and rest for a few hours," he said. The entrance was narrow, and a more careful search showed no back entrances or passages leading from their alcove. "This alcove looks deep enough to hide us if anyone passes by," D'vhan continued. "If you have enough energy to argue with me, *Asawie*," he said, chuckling softly at Sawiea's old nickname, "then you can take first watch. Wake the hatchling next, then Pey't. I'll take the last."

The three younger warriors glanced at each other, the look confirming that none of them would be waking D'vhan for a watch. He was stronger since Siann healed his lungs, but he was still their charge and had already pushed himself too hard on this journey.

"Take no chances on sleeping," D'vhan continued, either not noticing, or ignoring the byplay from his nursemaids. "Being surprised in here is the same as being dead. If you start to doze, wake your replacement."

The silent hours on watch weighed heavily on Y'keta's nerves. The only sounds were the constant drip of water somewhere in the darkness and the soft breathing of his companions. His eyes shifted constantly, searching the cave for movement, looking for changes in the patterns of lichen that might mean something had brushed past and disturbed it.

Feeling his eyes growing heavy and his vision blurring, he reached over with his foot and softly kicked Pey't's boot. The brown eyes snapped open at once and, nodding, he took Y'keta's place at the narrow mouth of the alcove. "Stretch out," Pey't whispered. "I'll wake Sawiea next, then she can wake you."

Y'keta stretched and bent, loosening up stiff muscles then lying on the cold floor, hands on his daggers, closing his eyes to feign sleep. He wouldn't sleep down here, never again.

§

They came eventually. A sibilant hiss in the dark alerting Pey't, giving him just enough time to boot D'vhan into wakefulness.

"Red Lodge. Up!" D'vhan hissed, rousing Sawiea and Y'keta from their places, hands finding their weapons, eyes finding D'vhan. "Y'keta," he whispered his voice hoarse with tension. "Can you see how many we face?"

"I saw about a dozen bodies," Pey't answered D'vhan's question. "All small grubs, no adults."

D'vhan nodded, but still looked at Y'keta for confirmation.

With an apologetic glance at Pey't, Y'keta edged towards the entrance to the alcove and allowed his eyes to shift. The orange pupils gave way to the black eyes of the raven and everything changed. The pale light given off by the lichen was mostly ultraviolet and outlined everything for Y'keta in a fuzzy purple radiance. It always happened when his eyes changed this way. He quickly counted the grey forms crawling along the main passageway. "Twenty-four," he whispered. "I don't think they've seen us yet, though. They are not looking this way."

"Keep silent and stay back," D'vhan mouthed, pulling the small group to the back wall of the alcove.

Weapons were drawn silently as the wave of grey bodies moved in front of them. Each warrior stood frozen against the rock face like statues in the darkness. It almost worked.

The very last Utlaak had just moved past them and was slinking down the passage, almost out of sight when things went terribly wrong. For some reason one of the last grubs looked back, maybe to make sure that the adults and their whips weren't behind him, maybe because it didn't want to go towards the daylight, there was no way to know. But as he turned to glance back down the tunnel, the grub saw D'vhan, his lichen-covered hair glowing like a pale star in the unending darkness.

With a wild cry, the grub charged back down the passage and into the alcove, determined to get at the strange glowing figure, its crystal club swinging wildly.

The warriors met the charge with deadly knives and total silence. It wasn't enough. The sudden attack had alerted the Utlaak horde and within moments the entrance to the alcove that sheltered the four warriors was blocked by twenty or more Utlaak grubs. Their greyish hides making sandpaper noises as they brushed against each other, crystal-spiked weapons glowing in the darkness, covered with the ever-present lichen.

Grabbing Pey't, D'vhan moved quickly to the left wall of the alcove, gesturing Y'keta and Sawiea to the right, creating a bottleneck. One or two brave Utlaak advanced into the niche, only to be cut down by the vicious knives of the waiting warriors. It was a stalemate, the Utlaak could only enter the alcove by ones or twos, which would mean certain death, but the warriors couldn't leave. Even if they pushed their way out of the hollow, they would find themselves quickly surrounded and just as quickly dead.

A flickering light careened toward the back of their alcove. Some brighter-than-normal spark among the Utlaak had flung his lichen-covered mace towards the back wall in a vain hope of either hitting someone or at least getting an idea of the numbers in the cave.

"There is no reason to hide now," D'vhan said. "Pull out your torches, but don't light them yet. I have an idea that might thin these slugs out a little." Trying not to take their eyes away from the narrow opening to their sanctuary, the cornered warriors scrounged in their journey packs, pulling out the flints and torches. "Asawie, nock an arrow please," he asked, nodding as Sawiea set an arrow in her bow and looked towards D'vhan for a target.

But whatever D'vhan planned had to wait, as five scaly grubs tried to storm the narrow bottleneck at the cave's entrance. Thick hides blurring together into a rush of arms and legs, they poured between the limestone boulders at the mouth of the alcove. Pey't swung low, his knife piercing the leg of the leading Utlaak, sending him squealing to the floor of the cave, his panicked thrashing adding to the confusion of the moment.

D'vhan moved like a dancer, his bone-handled daggers dripping with the grey blood of the Utlaak. He seemed to be made of smoke, darting forward to jab at an unprotected leg or arm, then gone again before his victim could react. It was the death of a hundred daggers, each cut slowing the attacker down just a little, each stab weakening a leg or an arm, making them unable to strike back. "Drop them in the entranceway," he yelled. "Block the way."

With swift but violent obedience the five Utlaak were dispatched and their still-warm corpses piled across the entryway to the small hollow where the warriors squatted, panting.

"Now," D'vhan husked, doubling over to catch his breath. "It won't take them long to move the dead meat. Y'keta, keep watch. Everyone else get your torches out." Stripping off his tunic, D'vhan began carefully wiping every trace of the glowing lichen from his body and vigorously scrubbing his hair to get it out. "Pey't, use your shirt and scrape the walls, all the lichen you can find!"

Pey't shook his head but obeyed. Stripping his shirt over his head he started mopping the phosphorescent lichen from the walls of their little sanctuary, moving as quickly as the close quarters allowed. Soon his shirt and D'vhan's tunic were the only sources of light in the alcove.

"Sawiea, your wineskin."

Sawiea started to argue, then stopped as a skittering from beyond the bottleneck showed that the Utlaak were moving again. "Y'keta," she asked, throwing her wineskin across the small space to D'vhan, "how many?"

"Too many," he replied, his face and hair grey with the blood of the grubs he had fought. "I still count eighteen, and there may be a few more, further back in the tunnel."

Catching the wineskin, D'vhan wrapped it in his now-glowing tunic and juggled it from one hand to the other. "Pey't, do the same thing with the honey from the cooking supplies."

Pey't nodded thoughtfully and swaddled the earthen honey pot in his shirt, using the arms as a tie to keep the bundle in place.

"On my signal, light a torch. We throw these as far as we can into the middle of the Utlaak. Sawiea, use the torch to light two arrows and aim for the bundles." His explanation had Pey't and Sawiea nodding thoughtfully. Y'keta just glanced back at him confusedly. "Watch and learn, cub," D'vhan growled.

D'vhan and Pey't sidled close to the opening. "Left side," Y'keta hissed, "about ten steps down." They nodded, hefting their glowing burdens and stepping over the corpses and into the open tunnel.

At D'vhan's cry, the men threw their bundles into the mass of Utlaak bodies in the hallway. They landed together with a splat as the honey jar cracked open, spreading all over the grubs.

Jumping back into the alcove, D'vhan cried, "Don't miss!"

Sawiea laughed. "I never miss, old crow." She quickly lit two arrows from Y'keta's torch, nocked the burning arrows and sent them flying into the panicked Utlaak. The flaming arrows struck the lichen-wrapped wineskin and exploded. Heat vaporised the strong vair wine in a fireball that incinerated the closest grubs. Those unfortunate enough to be covered in honey from the shattered jar found that the burning liquid stuck to them, scorching through hide and bone. The stench made the warriors grab for the rags they had used as masks and the acrid smoke drew tears from their irritated eyes.

Y'keta coughed and husked out, "Do we run?"

"Worthless. How many?" D'vhan managed, the smoke choking him, good lungs or not. "Too far to the entrance. We have to take them all."

Y'keta let his eyes change. Smoke clouded his vision, even with the raven eyes, and the light from the fire blocked the view further down the tunnel. "I see eight—maybe ten, I'm not sure. Can we try another throw?"

Sawiea and Pey't shook their heads—there was nothing left to throw. Y'keta swallowed and tried to get words around the boulder that had grown in his throat. He had believed that D'vhan would save them. D'vhan always saved them. What would they do now?

"We fight," D'vhan answered his unspoken question. *"We are the guardians, strength of the sky..."* The words of the Warrior's Chant straightened Y'keta's spine, steadying his hands.

Sawiea's alto, and Pey't's light tenor voice picked up the refrain echoing from the sides of the alcove, *"We walk the dark places, fight fear in the night."*

Y'keta's voice joined the chorus of defiance and as one unit they stepped out of their alcove to face the charging horrors in the tunnel. *"To hold safe the People, keep honour alight/As we take up our spears on the Sky Road."*

The next few moments were a blur of flailing limbs and flashing metal. Daggers pierced the leathery hides of the Utlaak, bringing down one after another in thrashing heaps on the uneven cavern floor. But step by step they were being pushed back. First to the entrance of their alcove, then slowly, painfully, to the back wall of the alcove itself. A quick glance flew between them. This was it. There was nowhere left to back up to.

Pey't was bleeding from a deep slash to his left arm and fighting just to stay in the battle, jabbing one-handed at any arm or leg that came near his position in the middle of the defenders. D'vhan was grey with blood and exhaustion. His eyes, ancient and resigned, looked at the Utlaak with determination, but no anger. Even at the end, D'vhan would not hate these creatures. Y'keta had no such qualms, there would be no polite jabs for him; he wanted them dead. His knife aimed for throats, guts, anything that would ensure a quick death or a permanent disable.

Suddenly a collective shudder ran through the grubs and the four in front of them feinted forward and then quickly dove back into the darkness. Making room. An adult had come. It was three times the size of the younger grubs. Taller than any of the People ever grew, it towered over the smaller Utlaak. Its hide was thick, layered leather plates covered its body, and its arms ended in deadly claws. Y'keta drew in on himself, too afraid to move. He had seen these adults before. They delighted in pain and slow death, the slower the better. Pey't grabbed a torch and waved it in front of the monster—no reaction. Y'keta could have told him not to waste his time. Adults didn't live long enough to get this large if they were afraid of anything.

D'vhan didn't speak. He dove straight for the massive legs of the Utlaak, his daggers aiming for the vulnerable area behind the knees. He missed and rolled helplessly into the grubs gathered in the alcove entrance, his daggers lying useless on the cave floor. They didn't attack him, just shoved him back towards the adult waiting motionless in the torchlight, teeth filed to sharp points. *They know this game*, Y'keta thought, *you don't steal the adult's kill, and that's what this is to the adult: a game.*

"Together," D'vhan said. "He'll pull us to pieces one at a time."

The melee started. D'vhan came up from behind and jumped on the shoulders of the behemoth. He was grabbing at the limp, matted hair, trying to gouge eyes, anything a man without a weapon could do to cause damage. Ignoring the younger ones, Pey't and Y'keta danced around the giant Utlaak, daggers weaving, looking for a break in its defences and dodging the deadly shard-edged mace it swung with expert precision.

Sawiea shot. Her back pressed against the furthest corner of the alcove, she fired arrow after arrow into the armour of the creature. Grey blood ran down its legs, making the floor slippery and treacherous. Over and over Pey't dodged the huge mace, swinging his dagger with his one good arm before dancing agilely away at the furthest limit of the creature's swing.

He slipped. The great glowing club came down. Pey't screamed causing a ripple of what Y'keta assumed to be laughter to run through the grubs. Someone else was feeding the adult's need for pain today. They would be left alone. *This is it,* Y'keta thought despairingly, *Pey't is down, D'vhan unarmed, we're done.*

Seventeen

<<<Y'keta>>>

Unarmed, D'vhan dove in front of the creature, grabbing Pey't by his uninjured hand and dragging him to the side of the alcove. Pulling Pey't's dagger from his limp hand, D'vhan taunted the creature, luring it to turn away from where Pey't's unconscious form slumped against the wall.

Suddenly, words that D'vhan had chanted echoed again in my head. I don't know if I was hearing him, or just remembering. "We are the guardians," he had said. Not the warriors, not the fighters, we are the ones who guard.

The Utlaak dropped its deadly mace and swung its ham-sized fists at D'vhan over and over, relishing the painful grunts when the blows landed. D'vhan dodged, but not fast enough, not nearly fast enough. But he refused to stop, refused to allow the Utlaak's attention to turn back to Pey't. I could feel his life fading away with every blow that he took, moving a half step slower with each moment that passed.

Time slowed, it stuttered, it backed up, swirling threateningly like an ice jam on a frozen river. "Cub," he always called me, and maybe that's what I was. But if so, I was a bear cub. Not the son of the Storm Lord who had fathered me, but of this man, this laughing bear who was dying in front of me. Something in me broke free, raised up on its hind paws and roared. "No!"

Rage consumed my every thought, my every movement fuelled by the demand that this injustice end. I would not see D'vhan beaten the way I had been beaten, I would not see the whip and chain scars on his back that were forever burned into mine. I would not allow it.

Moving faster than I thought possible, I knelt and grabbed the two-handed mace the creature had used to crush Pey't's leg. With an incoherent cry I swung to my feet, the mace acting as counterweight to my pivot. At the very top of my swing I hurled the mace. The head, packed with crystal shards and moving with the full weight of my anger, crashed into the back of the Utlaak's skull, splitting it open and dropping him instantly. Blood and brains spilled to the floor. The smell was indescribable. I vomited, over and over, while Sawiea and a barely standing D'vhan waved their daggers at the grubs left in the doorway.

Something stirred between my shoulder blades. I could have said my wings wanted to unfurl, but that was impossible now. It crackled across my shoulders and down my hands like lightning, burning a path down my arms and into my fingers. I looked at the younger Utlaak and whispered, *"Tlegu."*

Silently, they exploded. Ash and smoke drifted down to settle on the tunnel floor. There was no noise, no stench, nothing to say that they had even been there. They were just gone.

As soon as the burst of power was released, my knees buckled, and I fell to the alcove floor, rolling over the corpse of the dead adult and landing against the wall where Pey't lay unconscious. My heart was racing. Every movement was sheer pain. My body had been flayed raw as though the lightning had scorched through my muscles and out the pores of my skin.

I turned to look at D'vhan, his black eyes wide with concern and fear. "D'vhan, I..."

"Not a word, cub," he said, scrabbling over the giant body to reach my side. "Are you safe? Just nod."

I nodded, unbelievingly. He didn't care that I'd just blown up a tunnel full of Utlaak, he was worried because I could have been hurt. Stupid old crow.

"Asawie," D'vhan turned to his oldest friend in the village, "I ask for your silence."

"I saw nothing," she said, looking for all the world like exploding Utlaak were something that happened every cycle or so. "Just a warrior killing the enemy in whatever way he could."

He didn't have to ask Pey't—the pudgy warrior was still oblivious. I'm not sure whether it was from the pain of his crushed leg or the blood loss, but I know he didn't see anything. The stillness of Pey't's limp form finally snapped my unnatural calm. I watched D'vhan as he shook his head over Pey't's mangled leg. Shards of crystal were embedded down to the bone. The *visible* bone. I swallowed, hoping I wasn't going to vomit again.

"Sawiea," he said, "throw my pack over here. I have the healer's pouch in there." Fishing through the supplies in his pack, D'vhan pulled out a blackened bone needle and thread made from the gut of the buffalo we had hunted last fall. "I'm glad he's still unconscious," D'vhan said, frowning at his friend's limp form. "This is going to hurt."

Tying a clean strip of leather above the injury on Pey't's arm, he twisted it tight, trying to cut off the bleeding. "Help me with this, Y'keta," he asked, passing me the needle. "You see better than I do in this light."

"D'vhan," I said, ashamed of my cowardice. "I'm not sure I can do this." My stomach was lurching left and right inside of me like a drunkard trying to walk a straight line. It didn't matter that I had just vaporised a tunnel full of enemies. The thought of sticking this needle into someone who was a friend made my gorge rise.

"Just do it, cub," D'vhan admonished, his lips twisting in derision. It seemed he couldn't believe how much of a coward I was either. "You will hurt him less than I will. Make small stitches and work from the top of the wound to the bottom."

Biting my lips, I carefully inserted the bone needle into the edge of the skin on Pey't's arm. He didn't flinch. I sighed. Passing the hooked needle through the torn flesh, I pulled it up through the healthy skin on the other side, dragging the twisted line of gut with it. One stitch.

"Don't pull too tight," D'vhan explained. "You don't want the skin to be stretched too far."

Two stitches, then three—Pey't was starting to wake up, twitching as the needle went in and out, knitting muscles and flesh together. Sweat rolled down my skin and into my eyes. I couldn't wipe it away, I was too worried about pulling on the needle or waking Pey't up. Finally, it was done.

Snipping the end of the catgut with his dagger, D'vhan tied a knot in it and padded the wound with soft cloths and a clean bandage. "Good job, cub," he said. "Remember, someone on a battlefield always needs to know how to do this."

A few moments later, Pey't woke with a whimper. *His eyes are wild and,* I thought, *not quite sane.* Thrashing madly in D'vhan's arms, he tried to strike out at the pain. Passing her torch to me, Sawiea came over and knelt next to the delirious warrior, cooing softly. "Hush, Pey't," she said, in a tone that could only be called motherly. "The evil is gone, and we are well, hush now, the pain will end soon." She looked at D'vhan questioningly and mouthed, *"Poppy?"*

He just nodded, his hands full of struggling warrior. Sawiea pulled a small pouch from the healer's bag and showed it to D'vhan. "This one?" she asked.

He nodded.

"Learn, hatchling," she said, turning to me and showing me the crimson-dyed pouch. "In a healer's pouch red is always used for poppy dust or leaves. It is very dangerous and should only be used as a last resort." I could feel the wrinkle between my eyes getting deeper, trying to remember every word she spoke. Passing me the tiny red pouch and wiping her hands on her leggings, she continued, "Take one leaf."

She looked at D'vhan, who corrected her, "Two— it's bad."

"Take two leaves, do not smell them, and do not handle them more than absolutely necessary. Bruise them between your hands and, when I open Pey't's mouth, push them under his tongue." Holding Pey't's mouth open was the hard part. I gingerly took the leaves from the pouch and wadded them up in my palms. The sickly smell made me doubt that Pey't would swallow them at all. But I put them as far back under his tongue as I could and pulled my hands out quickly as Sawiea let go and his mouth snapped shut.

Pey't coughed a few times and I could see his throat working as he swallowed the unappetising lump. His eyes cleared for a second and he glared at

D'vhan. "Fool!" he husked. "You should always let one warrior die to save the group. You know that."

"Quiet," D'vhan ordered. "You can argue with me when you stop bleeding all over us."

As I watched Pey't gather his strength to protest, I could see a cloud come over his mind. His eyes became glassy and unfocused and he slumped, not unconscious, but obviously not aware.

"Now, the hard part," D'vhan said once Pey't had calmed. "We need to pick all these shards from his leg and bind it as best we can. The bleeding will not stop until every trace of crystal is removed." I swallowed. Pey't was a warrior, and my friend. I did not want to hurt him again. D'vhan's filthy red hair rattled as he shook his head. "No needles, not this time. The wound is too jagged, there is not enough skin to knit together. Just pick out the debris and we will bind it for travel."

It took a long time. Sawiea lit torch after torch and I shifted my eyes back and forth from my human to raven vision to make sure that the crystal shards were gone. They were poisonous and would infect, I remembered. But finally, everything I could do was done. We bound Pey't's leg with the softest skins that we had and used handles from the grubs' crystal maces to make a splint, holding it straight.

"He won't walk," Sawiea said. "We'll have to carry him out."

§

She was right. It took three days for us to backtrack to the entrance of the caves. For most of it, Pey't was barely conscious, the poppy leaves keeping him awake enough to eat and drink, but not to feel what would surely be unendurable pain. We walked down endless tunnels. Sawiea and I carrying Pey't between our crossed hands. D'vhan, wielding the adult Utlaak's killing mace as a light, prowled ahead and then dropped behind, his eyes everywhere. At every rest stop he ordered us to let him carry Pey't, and at every new start, we refused.

"Forget it, old crow," Sawiea said, ignoring his bluster. "Y'keta and I are the same height. You, little hawk, are too short." They had laughed at him then, but the looks D'vhan threw at his rebellious warriors as he stalked the tunnels behind us warned that revenge was still to come.

The light blinded us as we approached the tunnel entrance, but we didn't slow down. The sight of sky and trees, and the scent of fresh air drew us like moths to a campfire. It wasn't until we stumbled down the hill and back into the sheltering forest that the three of us stopped. Looking back, we could still see the cave entrance. D'vhan's lips pursed. We were exhausted, Pey't was in pain, but it was too soon to stop.

"Further in," he said. "I won't rest in sight of that hole. Scorch it."

"Eye of Riad!" We almost dropped Pey't in surprise when he cursed. "Damn that creature to the blackest hole in the Watcher's heart. By the Stars, I don't know how you got me out of there. I can hobble on my own feet."

"Quiet, Pey't," Sawiea said, brushing her grumbling hatchling aside and firmly sliding into the role of mother. "You can annoy the healers when we get you home. Until then you can cooperate, or you can chew more poppy leaf and sleep."

D'vhan's cackle echoed through the scrubby pines and gave a much-needed air of normalcy to the day. "It feels good to hear Asawie bullying someone else. She hasn't left me alone for cycles."

"You aren't out of my care yet, old crow," she grumbled, throwing a dark glance towards D'vhan. "The first time I see you taking on too much you'll wish that you had a shattered leg. You keep acting like the Elder Stars made you alone responsible for the welfare of the world."

We walked until even Sawiea was stumbling, almost dropping Pey't more than once. Finally, D'vhan called a halt and we settled for the night. I spent the night staring at the stars, trying to be thankful that we had escaped the caverns, that Pey't was still alive. But something in the back of my mind wouldn't let go of the darkness. This wasn't over.

Eighteen

The evening meal had just finished. People were sitting around the campfires chatting and sharing skins of wine or water and catching up on the day's news. But all that stopped abruptly when the tired group trudged into the village. Y'keta came first, limping and footsore. Pey't, slung on a makeshift travois, was dragging behind him. D'vhan and Sawiea brought up the rear, looking deliberately unruffled at being a hand of days late.

"Laban," Hahnee bellowed, "they're back."

A rustling from Grey Lodge heralded Laban's arrival. His silver hair and beaming face were a better restorative than any medicine the healers could make. Clapping D'vhan on the shoulder, he knelt near Pey't and carefully pulled the hides from around his leg. The wound was ragged and in places his thigh bone was still evident.

"Get Siann," he called to no one in particular. "Someone, find her."

A few moments later, Siann came running from her home behind the Grey Lodge. Her healer's bag was slung haphazardly over her shoulder and her mouth looked suspiciously greasy, as though she had still been eating when the call came. Wiping her mouth absentmindedly on her sleeve she dropped beside Pey't, and casually pushed Laban aside.

"What happened?" she said, turning to Y'keta with a frown. "Why did you let him get hurt?"

"Now, Siann," D'vhan defended, "it was hardly Y'keta's fault."

Waving away the older warrior with a flip of her hand, Siann speared Y'keta with her eyes. "I asked you. What happened?"

"Adult Utlaak," Y'keta answered, his shoulders tight and hurting from the memories of their desperate trek through those lightless tunnels. "It cornered us in the tunnels. Pey't took a mace to the leg and an arrow in his arm."

Siann didn't look at him, just focused her eyes on Pey't, their berry-brown depths gentle and compassionate. "I have to look at it. I'm sorry," she said. "I know this will hurt."

Pey't nodded.

"We've been giving him poppy," Y'keta admitted. "It was the only way to move him."

"D'vhan." Siann turned her frown towards the older warrior. "How much and how often? You know that poppy sickness is an evil thing."

"I know," D'vhan said. "I've seen it too many times. For the first few days we gave him two leaves at a time, sun up and sun down, this last hand of days it's been one. He's had only one leaf since our last camp."

"Good," Siann said. "Now let me look." The wrappings on Pey't's leg were pulled back to reveal the crushed meat and bone that was all that remained of his upper thigh. Siann pulled a face. "It's a mess, Pey't," she said.

Pey't's face paled and his lips tightened into a thin line as she carefully moved his leg to inspect the area where the bone was broken.

"I'm sorry," she told the injured warrior, noticing how his hands trembled as she carefully straightened out the shattered bone. "It has to be straight when I heal you, and only healing you will save your leg."

D'vhan's face looked like a thundercloud, but what could he say. She had paid the price to heal him of the lung fever, drifting around the camp, pale and listless, for almost a full moon afterward. He hated the thought of her doing that again, but how could he say no. How could he tell her not to help one of his own warriors?

Pey't looked from the confident face of Siann to the anxious eyes of D'vhan and Laban. "I will heal without it, Siann. Don't risk yourself for me."

"Stars! What is wrong with the men in this village?" Siann's eyes crackled with anger. "I am neither a child, nor a simpleton. I know what is given me to do!" Her lightning-edged gaze crackled with the twin lights of her power, voice echoing with the very essence of the Thunderstones. "Now, choose! Do you want to keep your leg? Or sit around the fire for the rest of your life needing green feathers to fetch and carry for you?" Her glare was ferocious, and the ends of her hair crackled and moved in a wind that no one else could feel.

Pey't withered before her fury. "Very well, Siann," he said, one hand waving her away weakly. "Who am I to refuse such a blessing."

D'vhan touched her arm lightly, placatingly. "We do not doubt your power, young one," he said. "We just want to be wise in using it. We know the cost it bears, and we value you. Not just your power. You."

Siann stood up and, brushing the dead grass and twigs from her leggings, walked towards her small lodge. "Take him into the healers' lodge," she said. "Laban, D'vhan, I need to talk to you while I prepare. Please, come with me."

Laban and D'vhan fell into step on each side of her as she walked away from the crowd of gawking villagers and into the quiet of her own small lodge. Running a hand over her brow she spoke solemnly. "It's bad," she said. "Worse than you know. There is a sickness in the bone, probably from the crystal shards. If I cannot heal it, he will not only lose his leg. We will lose Pey't." Siann tugged at her braids in agitation. "I do understand what using the Lifebinder costs. It takes life in proportion to the life it gives, and this cost will be high."

"Siann?" Laban looked ill. How could he advise her? How could he say that her life was more valuable to the village than Pey't's was? But the awful truth couldn't be ignored. She was—infinitely—more important.

"There is another way." Y'keta stepped in from the entrance where he'd obviously been eavesdropping.

"Get out of my home," Siann ordered. "How dare you!"

"Listen, Siann," Y'keta continued, not giving a moment's space to her blustering. "My People know of this crystal. There is another way!"

"No," she said, her voice adamant, her eyes flint.

"You know!" he said, shoving an accusing finger into her chest. "You've already figured out that you can draw life from someone other than yourself. You could use my life to heal Pey't."

"It is an abomination!" she exclaimed. "Everything I believe, everything I am refuses this. I will not cause harm!"

Laban looked from one intent young face to another. Power, life, youth—whatever you called it— the fire burned bright in both of them. "Siann," he said softly, not pushing, just opening a door of compromise, "would you heal Pey't if you could?"

"Of course, in fact I mean to, no matter the cost. That is the oath I swore."

Y'keta started to speak again, only to be waved to silence by both the head Shaman and the red leader. D'vhan had caught an inkling of what Laban was trying to do and was willing to let him finish.

Laban nodded, not taking his eyes from where Siann's flashed from white, to red, and back to their normal soft brown in the dimness of the lodge. "Of course," he said softly. "No one doubts that you would give your life for any member of this village. You take your oath seriously."

Mollified, Siann started to breathe deeply, stress pouring from her in an almost visible wave. "Then you understand."

"Yes," he said. "I understand oaths, and so must you." Siann's eyebrows shot up at that. He was accusing her of not taking oaths seriously? Her?

"Y'keta has also sworn an oath. To protect, to guard, to spend his life if necessary, as the spear of the People."

Siann nodded, uncomprehending. The shellhead was a warrior. So?

"You cannot spend *your* life when *his* is offered," Laban continued, his voice firm and unrelenting. "It breaks his oath, and the oath every member of Red Lodge makes at the ceremonial fire. You cannot!"

Throwing her healer's bag across the room, Siann stormed out of the lodge, leaving them sitting amid her belongings, staring at each other bewildered. Should they stay? Should they leave?

"I don't know if she'll listen," D'vhan said. "She's always been a stubborn youngster."

"She's already given in," Y'keta said with a certainty that made the others look at him in amazement.

Laban shook his head in disagreement. "Siann never gives in."

"She does hate being wrong," Y'keta said, shrugging dismissively. "But she hates even more being wrong in front of me." He laughed ruefully. "She will wait until I leave, then come back and admit to you that she was wrong, and she will do the healing the way I suggested. Oh," he added with a smug grin. "She'll also make one of you order me to do it, rather than ask me herself." With a jaunty swagger in his step, Y'keta marched out of the lodge and went to get his meal. He would need all the strength he could find for the upcoming ordeal.

Tears rolled down D'vhan's wrinkled face as he laughed at the young hawk strutting his way across the camp. "Look at him," D'vhan crowed. "So certain that he's got the young shaman all figured out."

Laban's grey eyes sparkled. "Do you think either of them know?" His lips twitched as he saw Siann walk out of the trees near the lake, only to turn and storm away when she saw Y'keta near the main campfire.

"Not a clue." D'vhan chortled. "The next few cycles could be interesting for those two."

§

Y'keta was right. A few minutes later Siann slinked up to the lodge, looking around sheepishly. "Sorry," she muttered, "but that hatchling just twists my tail feathers every time he opens his beak. He thinks he knows so much, that he's so special."

"He's a good man, Siann," D'vhan countered, trying to defend his second-in-command.

"Man?" Siann scoffed. "I don't think so. He's hardly a hatchling, and the Stars know he's not one of us."

Laban's face grew stormy, grey brows beetling over his now steely eyes. "I'd expect that talk from Iamaat, but not from you." His voice was firm and disapproving, eyebrows lowered. Laban was not joking about this.

"I know, Laban, I know." The toe of Siann's camp boots traced guilty patterns in the sand floor of the lodge. "Y'keta's earned his place here, and I don't really believe that he's not one of the People. There is no doubt he's made that decision—look at how he stood up to his father to stay. But lightning scorch him, he annoys me."

Exchanging amused glances, D'vhan waved Siann back into her own lodge and followed her inside. They still needed to deal with the problem of the Lifebinder. "So, young one," he said, his eyes kind, understanding at least a little the burden she carried. "What will we do about Pey't?"

Siann picked up her mother's bag from where she had so callously flung it a few moments before. The memory of Matra was never far from her, especially at times like this. "Mother would have said that healing is a gift to the People from the Elder Stars. If Y'keta wants to give Pey't this gift, I can't stop him." Her voice dropped to a nearly inaudible mutter of *"Much as I would like to."*

"Would it make it easier for you to heal Pey't if the life came from me?" D'vhan offered, waving Laban's protests away. "You know that I will take his place, gladly, if it helps you to deal with this."

Siann glowered. "I just spent a full moon recovering from healing your lungs," she scolded, shaking her finger forcefully in D'vhan's face. "There is no way that I will allow the crystal to pull the lifeforce from you when I just put it there!"

"Well, I could," Laban started to offer hesitantly.

"No," Siann cut him off before the words came out. "You can't. You are our Shaman Elder, our leader, and if that isn't enough, your mate is pregnant. We need you at your best." She sighed resignedly. "I guess it has to be the young shellhead. Watcher defend us!"

"Siann." D'vhan put a gentle hand on her arm. "You need to know before you agree to this. Something happened in the caves when Pey't was hurt. Something that might affect the crystal."

Siann tugged at her braid, looking suddenly like the hatchling D'vhan had spoiled so long ago. "What?

Was Pey't affected by something poisonous? Bad air? I hear that can happen in deep caves. What?"

Laban started pacing back and forth across Siann's small lodge, a sure sign that he was trying to figure something out. "You fought an adult Utlaak, didn't you?" he said. D'vhan nodded and winced as the sore muscles in his back and legs reminded him that the battle hadn't really been that long ago.

"Was Y'keta hurt?" Siann asked. "It would be like him to hide something important like that, just to look strong."

"You are like Titch when he has a bone," D'vhan chided, tugging on his filthy red braids. *Shards*, he thought, *I need to get cleaned up—it's been days.* "Will you let go of this unnecessary conflict with Y'keta? It is not helping us right now." He turned back to Laban, mouth pursed thoughtfully. "Both of you need to know that, if it wasn't Pey't's life we were dealing with, I wouldn't reveal this, even to you, and I do not want it going outside this lodge, ever."

Laban's head snapped back in surprise. As far as he knew the older warrior had never kept a secret from him. "D'vhan," he said, stepping close enough that the two men were facing each other almost chest to chest. "If it affects the village, the council needs to know. I need to know."

D'vhan waved him to silence. "Listen and then judge," he said. "We should have died when Pey't got hurt. One man down, I'd been disarmed, and we were cornered in a cave blocked in by not only an adult

Utlaak, but with more than a dozen grubs watching from the tunnel." D'vhan wiped sweat from his brow as the memories piled up in his mind. "We would have died," he repeated, almost to himself. "If not for the cub."

This time it was D'vhan who paced the small space in Siann's lodge, the dusty path that they had made as they walked back and forth reminding Siann that she would need to lay new reeds on the floor after all this activity. Her home didn't see this many guests in a cycle, let alone a day.

"Something happened," D'vhan continued, shaking his head bewilderedly, "that I still have trouble believing, never mind talking about."

Pacing back and forth, he started explaining what had happened in the tunnels, Pey't's helplessness, his own foolish unarmed attack on the adult.

"Something happened to Y'keta, maybe fear, maybe anger, but something changed in him at that moment." Even now the disbelief was obvious in his rumbling voice. "I've never seen anyone move that fast. Before I even knew what he was planning, he had killed the adult Utlaak, its own weapon buried in its brain."

Siann gasped, but D'vhan waved her back to silence.

"That was just the start," he said. "The adult was dead, but I was hurt, Pey't was unconscious and it was too dark to fight with arrows or knives in the tunnel. Then,"—he swallowed and hesitated a moment, wondering if he should speak at all—"this must be kept secret," he reminded them, "it must be!"

Laban looked at Siann, who furrowed her brows and nodded. "The Elder Stars hold this between the three of us," he said, using the formal words of binding. "We three bind ourselves to this place and this secret. The Elder Stars witness this oath."

Siann repeated the ancient words, her eyes flashing from their normal brown to almost red as the power of the words pulsed within her.

D'vhan echoed the words, taking comfort in the ritual and solemnity, feeling the oath take effect between the three of them, a binding that only the death of the last of them would break. "Y'keta killed all the Utlaak in the hall," he said baldly. Seeing the looks of incomprehension on their faces, he tried again. "Lightning came from his hands and they exploded, all of them."

Siann blinked, thought, and blinked again. "What?" she said. "You expect us to believe that?"

"Yes, I expect you to believe it," D'vhan snapped, "because that is exactly what happened. He drew a power from somewhere within himself—it may be something the Waki'tani can all do—and the Utlaak were gone. Just gone. Twenty Utlaak turned into nothing but ash floating in the tunnel." D'vhan glowered at the young shaman. "If you doubt my word, you may ask Sawiea, although I swore her to secrecy, she will answer if I ask her to. Pey't saw nothing, he was unconscious the whole time."

Siann thumped down onto a pile of furs stacked against the wall of the lodge, her mouth opening and closing, but not finding words to say. Laban seemed to be staring at his feet, his lips pulled in a straight line and his eyes narrowed. "I believe you," he said. "We know that he was Waki'tani before he came here, and we don't know a lot about what the Storm Lords can do, other than legends." Laban shrugged. It was supposed to look nonchalant, but neither of the others were fooled. "At least," he murmured, "we know some of the legends were true."

"Siann," D'vhan said, squatting down to look the young healer in the eye, "whatever he did, however he did it, it drained him as the Lifebinder drains you. That's why I thought you had to know." He looked apologetically in Laban's direction. "That is the only reason I spoke."

They stared at each other, their glances measuring the sudden silence in the lodge, wondering who would be the first to accept this new reality.

"Stupid hatchling." It was Siann, of course it was, who broke the tension. "Trust him to find some way to make himself feel special. Son of a raven, but he's egotistical." It didn't seem to matter that Y'keta had called down lightning to save the warriors, it was all just annoying to her. "If he can survive that, I guess I won't kill him by healing Pey't." Her mischievous smile peeked out from behind the shaman's mask. "At least not on purpose."

Nineteen

<<<Y'keta>>>

It was D'vhan who told me that Siann had given in. I knew it would be. There was no way that she would admit making a mistake to me. The healing would happen in the morning, D'vhan said, to allow Pey't and I to rest me to have at least a few good meals.

I sat on my bed in Red Lodge, watching the other warriors bustle around me. D'vhan had changed into the soft leathers he wore around camp and sat playing his reed flute and staring at nothing. Young Coen was polishing and sharpening weapons near the entrance. The traditional work for the newest warrior in the lodge—I was glad it wasn't my job anymore.

D'vhan's face flipped from anxious to amused and back again, as though he couldn't decide which emotion to feel. Amusement won, it usually did with the laughing old bear. From nowhere my eyes filled with tears. I had almost lost him. I widened my eyes and clenched my fists, trying to push back against the emotion. Trying to be the guardian, the bear, that I knew the village needed. That D'vhan needed. It didn't work. I dropped down onto the bedfurs and tucked my head on my chest, feigning tiredness, hoping the dim light in the lodge would hide my eyes from the others.

I actually thought it had worked until I felt a hand touch my leg. "Hatchling," D'vhan said quietly, "come outside for a moment please."

Not bothering to grab a tunic or fur wrap, I stood outside the Red Lodge, wrapping my arms around my chest against the cold night air. I looked up to the Elder Stars, as I did every clear night, and gave thanks that I could see them. That they hadn't been swallowed by the darkness of the caves. In my mind I heard Surta's voice repeating the legends of the Elder Stars, the Eye of Riad, and the awful darkness of the Watcher's domain. *You may not believe in them, my son,*" he had said to me, *"but don't dismiss too lightly what you don't understand."* I hadn't listened, I was so sure that I understood everything that I needed to know back then. But now, after what had happened to Siann at the Lightning Stones, to me in the caves, I was prepared to admit that there were a great many things that I may never understand.

D'vhan's fingers snapped under my nose, startling me and bringing me out of my daydreaming. "Where were you, cub?" he said. "I've been standing here freezing for the last few minutes waiting for you to wake up."

I couldn't apologize, couldn't really explain what had been going through my mind. It was all a bit too new for words. "What did you need, D'vhan?" I asked. "Why couldn't we talk inside where it's warm?"

"Cub, I need to ask if you are sure about this?" Even if I couldn't see his face, D'vhan's voice was concerned. "You are Red Lodge, my responsibility. Siann, as a shaman, is Laban's. I know that you want to save Pey't, Y'keta. But I need you to tell me that this healing won't cause me to lose you both."

I shrugged. What could I say? "I don't know what will happen, old crow. No one does. But this is something that is mine to do, I know this, so do you. I have to try." I felt D'vhan's hands grasp my forearm, a greeting used only in ceremonies among warriors.

"I cannot lose you, cub," he said flatly. No emotion showed in his voice, but his hands squeezed my forearms painfully. "I won't say don't take chances—impulsiveness is a part of your nature. Just don't take foolish ones." With that statement D'vhan walked into the lodge, leaving me to follow, my heart filled with more warmth than I had ever felt towards my own father.

§

Healing D'vhan had been a private thing. I had stood guard at the lodge entrance and made sure of that. Unfortunately, saving Pey't wouldn't be. The hide walls of the healers' lodge had been rolled up to allow as much light in as possible and the whole village turned out to watch Siann heal Pey't. Muttering under my breath, I pushed my way through the crowd and knelt beside the raised platform that Pey't was lying on. His ashen face was covered with a fine sheen of perspiration that told me that a fever had taken over. One of the healers had given him poppy to stave off the pain, I could see his normally sharp eyes drifting across the watching faces, unable to focus on anyone.

Siann came out of the Grey Lodge beside Laban and whispered urgently to him when she saw the crowd that had gathered around Pey't's bed. I watched her pull her tunic straight, biting her lips nervously. Then, realizing she was being watched, she set the *I am a Shaman* mask on her face, and walked forward with a confident stride that I was nowhere near believing.

"Hatchling," Siann said, nodding to me with that distant, haughty attitude that seemed to go with my nickname. "So, you meant it." My spine snapped straight, and my stomach knotted at the implication of cowardice. Breathing hard, I made a conscious effort to unclench my fists, palms scored with the angry white half-circle marks left by my fingernails.

I breathed in, didn't look at the annoying she-wolf, didn't think about anything but Pey't. He needed—I provided. I was the guardian.

"Do what you have to do, Shaman," I said, directing my words to Laban rather than addressing his annoying shadow. "I am here to serve." I could see D'vhan nodding in approval at my words. If he only knew how much I wanted to take those words and beat the annoying smirk from Siann's face with them!

Just then, Pey't moaned. It wasn't loud, or particularly pitiful, but that small, weak sound was enough to turn Siann instantly from hatchling to healer. Turning away as though I wasn't even there, she dropped beside Pey't's bed. Shards! I just hoped it wouldn't be his bier as well.

"This isn't good, Pey't," Siann said softly. "I am afraid you have crystal shards in the wounds and that they have become infected." One small hand went to Pey't's cheek, coming away covered in clammy sweat. Siann frowned. She put her hands on either side of Pey't's face, forcing his drug-addled eyes to focus on her blearily. "Do you know what I am going to do?" she said. "I've known you since I was a child, I'll do all I can, but you need to understand that it might not be enough."

I'm not sure how much of anything Pey't could understand. His mind was so clouded by pain and the effects of the poppy leaves. Siann must have seen what she needed to see though, because she sat back on her heels and, pulling the Lifebinder Crystal from the pouch around her neck, gestured me to sit beside her.

"Are you sure about this, Y'keta of Esquialt?" she asked. Her voice wasn't really hers though, and my skin crawled at the strange mix of young woman and ancient, alien power. Every part of me wanted to say no, wanted to run, shove my fingers in my ears so tightly that I couldn't hear anything. No friend moaning in pain, no hatchling talking with triple-voiced doom in her words, nothing but my own heart beating out of my chest. But I didn't, I'm not sure why or how, I just didn't. Instead, I nodded. I don't think I could have spoken if my own life had depended on it, and maybe in some way, at that moment, it did.

Siann's eyes flashed from their normal soft brown to an eerie white, and then blood red as the powers within her started to twine. She made a gesture at Pey't's leg and I carefully pulled away the poultice that the healers had applied the day before. The smell of rotted flesh was enough to make my gorge rise. Only closing my eyes and swallowing hard, several times, stopped me from disgracing myself in front of the whole village. The wound was obviously infected. The flesh of his leg had turned from a normal wounded pink to a greying mass shot through with streaks of seeping yellow pus. I must have missed some crystal shards because blood still seeped from the festering gash.

"Blood," Siann intoned in the voice that was not her voice. "Power requires blood, requires life, the People have always known this. Who offers their blood for the life of this warrior?"

"I do," I said weakly, not quite sure who, or what, I was talking to. "I am Y'keta, guardian of Esquialt. I offer."

Siann nodded and looked up at Laban. Silently, he passed the ceremonial dagger. Those flickering eyes focused on me, the changing colours and the absolute lack of anything I could call Siann making me afraid.

Siann grabbed my arm, the strength of a mountain in her grip, and held my hand over Pey't's exposed leg. The knife flashed, striking so quickly that I didn't feel the wound. Blood flowed down my hand from where Siann had sliced my palm and dripped into the festering crushed thing that had once been Pey't's thigh. The Lifebinder Crystal flashed from white to red as Siann forced it into my bleeding hand. Closing my hand around the crystal, praying to whatever gods or Elder Stars may be watching, I fed my blood to the crystal, for Pey't.

My heart hammered in my chest as though I was heading into battle. The feeling of something, someone breaking down the walls of my mind was sheer torment, an invasion that I couldn't resist.

"What is this power touching my crystal?" the cackling voice questioned.

"There is another ...?"

Then they were there, all of them. The Thunderstones with their echoes of ancient power, holding the collected prayers and hopes of generations of the People. The Lifebinder Crystal, powerful and capricious, giving life, but only at a cost, serving no one and obeying no rules of morality or belief. And finally, Siann was there in my mind, not the shaman, but the woman behind that mask, young, unsure, and afraid, but determined to do the right thing, to serve her People. It lasted only a moment, this feeling of souls coiled around each other like twins within the womb. Then it was gone, and with it went every spark of strength that I had.

I collapsed, deflating like an emptied wine sack. I tried to catch myself as I fell across Pey't, not wanting to cause him harm, but there was nothing I could do. I landed on his bloody leg and rolled away to end up on the ground hugging my knees to my chest, feeling violated, exposed and alone—above all, *alone*. Looking around, I tried to find Siann. She was on the ground next to Pey't's bed, her small frame shaking like a tree in the winter winds, face as pale as a spirit from the Watcher's worlds. Her eyes met mine and something in my heart cried out in relief. They were her eyes, no flashing red or white power, just a bruised young woman who had done the impossible, again.

Twenty

<<<D'vhan>>>

"Because, I can't sleep!" I grouched at Inkiss, who was trying to kick me out of the healers' lodge again. I didn't tell her that I hadn't slept since we returned to the village.

I was haunting the path between the Red Lodge and the Grey, when Pey't woke three mornings after Siann and Y'keta had drawn the crystal rot from his leg. The lodge was full of the oily scent of ground herbs and I'm sure that the healers had put poppy in the smudge fire that burned near Pey't's bed. My eyes stung from the smoke and I had just stepped outside to breathe some fresh air when a shout from the lodge drew me back inside.

Pey't was thrashing on his bed, raving about flashes of lightning and swearing that his mouth was filled with the coppery taste of blood. It took three of the largest healers to hold him pinned to his bed.

"Pey't," I yelled, grabbing at his uninjured ankle, the only part of his body that I could reach under the pile of healers trying to hold him down. "You fat old turkey buzzard, stop snoring!"

His poppy-blasted eyes tried to focus on me. "D'vhan?" he muttered, straining against the healers who were strapping his wounded leg down with ropes of braided leather to make sure he didn't pull open the stitches or injure the delicate new tissue that was replacing the putrid mess left by the crystal infection.

Pey't's gnarled hand snaked through the tangle of arms and legs around him, searching blindly for something. I grabbed it and squeezed hard. "You're safe, Pey't," I tried to reassure him. "The grubs are gone, you are at home and healing."

"Home?" his weak voice answered, the frown on his face smoothing out a little. "Maskwatin?"

"No, Esquialt, Pey't, you are in Esquialt, with Red Lodge." I spoke slowly, trying to keep his attention focused on my voice and away from the work the healers were doing to rebandage his leg. "You Walked here a long time ago, remember?" I forced a laugh. "Or have you finally found where Sawiea keeps her vair wine?"

Pey't's eyes sharpened at that. "It's buried under her pillow," he said. "She knows no one will ever find it there."

Inkiss, who had slept at Pey't's bedside ever since the healing, dripped more poppy water into his mouth and smiled at the worried glances from the younger healers. "He will live," she said, shooing me out of the way, "but he will not be himself for a few more days. This is not like when Siann healed you, D'vhan. Healing from such an infected wound is a slow and painful process."

After the healing, an exhausted Siann had been carried to the Grey Lodge where she slept unmoving, watched over by Ren, who alternated between hovering over the young shaman and scolding her mate for taking such dangerous risks without consulting her.

Y'keta hadn't woken up since the ceremony. He tossed fretfully on his furs in the warriors' lodge, mumbling about snakes, and pleading with someone "not to be afraid."

Once the power surrounding them had diminished, he had searched the crowd in the healers' tent, his strange eyes completely black and unfocused, until his eyes had locked on mine. "She is afraid," he had whispered. "How can someone so strong be afraid?" Then he collapsed into a fitful sleep that the healers said was necessary.

§

The People say that only gossip can outfly a swooping hawk. And as word flew through the camp that Pey't was expected to recover, celebrations started to break out around the camp.

Stumbling awkwardly, I ducked out of Red Lodge and dropped the hide flap back over the entrance. The cool spring air made me breathe in deeply and put a steadying hand on the solid wooden support beam as the cold air made my head spin. "It's time," I muttered to no one in particular.

Iamaat watched as I walked carefully across the compound, headed from Red Lodge back into the forest where the mated warriors had their smaller, individual lodges, eyes fixed on the uneven floor, stopping and starting with every few steps. "Where are you headed, Kalixt?" she said, stepping in front of me.

"You're in my way, Iamaat," I said, shifting left to get around her bulky form. "Move."

Iamaat drew herself up to her full height. Her thick frame a large blot against the stars. She huffed mightily. "I'll ask again. Where are you going, Kalixt," she repeated as she manoeuvred herself between my path and the lodges.

"What business is it of yours, hag?" A wide step to the left took me around Iamaat but my shard-cursed balance didn't quite hold and I stumbled, catching myself on Iamaat's thick winter robe.

"Take your hands off of me, abomination!" she said. The venom in her voice could have poisoned a hundred spears. "You pretend to Walk such an honest, upright Road as a warrior, all the while you hide your perversions behind a smoke screen. First you used Iskine, a beautiful young girl bewitched by the attention of a respected warrior. Now you shamelessly take Sawiea into Red Lodge against all our traditions. She's a mother, a widow, and you allow her to wield weapons and to battle with the men! You are weak, D'vhan, and should not be allowed to lead the warriors. Iskine's son has left the village now. Her son, not yours! He carried your name, but you had no part in him. I know you!"

I could have fought back. It would have been easy to scream and yell, drag out all the secrets that I'd discovered about Iamaat. But I didn't. The cold air was sobering me up, and for tonight, just for tonight, I didn't want to be sober.

Without a word to the poisonous viper, I walked around her, moving further into the forest behind Red Lodge.

§

Weaving between the lodges and cursing at Iamaat's outrageous suggestions, I slowly worked my way back into the darkness near Dahi's lodge. I could see that he was still awake, the inside of the lodge glowed as though it was full of fireflies. Laban had asked Dahi several times if he wanted to sleep with the other warriors in Red Lodge, but he always refused.

I could almost hear his voice answering, "Thank you, Salixt, but my village's way is not the way of your village. I am with you for this season, but there are areas in my life that are still undecided. Until I know my place here, I'd rather keep some distance."

The Elder Stars looked down from a frosty sky. I supposed their twinkle could be considered laughter. Look at me, I grumped at myself, foolish old crow, what in the Void was I doing?

"Dahi, may I enter?" I asked, not really sure that I should, or even that I wanted to. The seven skins of "courage" I'd drunk were starting to wear off and I was feeling sheepish and out of my league.

"Enter, D'vhan," he said. "You never need to ask. You are always welcome by my fire."

Not quite sure how to take that, I pushed the hide flap aside and stepped into his lodge. Or I supposed it was his lodge. Dahi had lived here for three moons now and there wasn't a single thing that marked the place as his. No trinket, no bedfurs scattered across the floor. Just a simple bedroll propped up against the lodge wall and his white whalebone bow set carefully against the centre pole. There weren't even any remains from his meals. Nothing that in any way said that Dahi meant to stay.

"I've been thinking about what you said before I left." My hand itched to trace a path across his chest and down the edge of his ever-present fur vest. I could see his breathing quicken as I watched. He wasn't unresponsive to me, no matter the coolness I saw in his amethyst eyes.

"You look foolish with wine stains on your tunic," Dahi said. "Just how many skins did it take for you to get up the courage to step in here?"

I looked through the smoke of the lodge up into Dahi's amethyst-coloured eyes. My eyes took a forbidden tour of his body, hair like midnight, golden skin, legs and arms that seemed to stretch forever. "I'm too old!" I said, hoping that my words sounded certain, and didn't show any of the despair I felt in saying them.

"What are you so afraid of," he said. "Why does it frighten you that I'm ten cycles younger?" His light tenor voice carried such a weight of authority.

A part of my very soul wanted to step into the hunger in his eyes. But I knew if I moved, even a step closer, that I would be lost forever. I wasn't a youngster to play with a beautiful warrior and then walk away unburned. This fire would consume me if I...I stepped forward, stopping with the smudge fire between us.

"Are you ashamed, old crow?" Dahi asked. "Has Iamaat's poison so damaged you that you cannot be whole in your spirit? Cannot want what your body wants?" Like a kuniak stalking a stray calf, he slowly stepped around the fire, just one or two paces, close enough that I could see the strain on his face. It matched mine.

"I have lived in this village a long time, Dahi. They saw me come as a youth, afraid, insecure, much like Ihkopi is now. I married here and raised two children who have moved on to Walk another village's Road. This village saw Iskine die in my arms and they saw me suffer her loss, numb and frozen." Smoke poured into my eyes, making them red and gritty. I rubbed them resentfully.

Dahi was moving again, close enough now that I could count the beads braided through his hair and see the red and black tattoos ripple across his arms and chest each time he moved. "Does wanting me harm you?" he asked softly. "Does it offend you that I can see you? See all of who you are and guess at much of who you can be?"

"It frightens me." My heart hammered as I tried to say the words that would make this all stop. "I have given everything I am, everything I have ever wanted to this village. I have nothing left to give you."

His laughter was the last thing I expected!

"Shards," Dahi cursed. "How many nights did you spend pacing the camp and rehearsing that load of buffalo droppings? Telling yourself that there could be nothing for you other than being Kalixt." His long fingers rested for a brief moment against the red leather of my tunic, then he impudently snapped his fingers in front of my face, breaking my daze. "How stupid do you think we are? I have been here for less than three moons and I know who you are. Do you think that Pey't, whom you've known for cycles beyond count doesn't know? Do you think that Sawiea, who is as close as a sister to you, doesn't know what makes your heart and body burn?"

His hand threaded itself through the coarse hair at the back of my neck and arched my eyes up to meet him. The amethyst fire in his gaze flared like a star marking someone's passing to the Road. Then his lips were on mine and gods, all the gods, it was sweet. Fire burned through me and settled low and urgent.

His tongue swept out and over my bottom lip, stopping to pull and bite gently. His arms were like steel around me, making me—for once—not the leader. "Does this make you any less, D'vhan? Or does it finally free you to become more? You are mine," he said. "I know it, you know it. I need you— Sun of Riad, I need you. But not like this, not when you are feeling guilty and ashamed. When you come to me it will be because you are mine, not because you are afraid." His hand ghosted down the front of my leathers. "You belong to me, old crow, and I don't intend to let you back away." Then he walked out. Just like that, leaving me alone, standing in his lodge, shaking.

"D'vhan!" I heard Hahnee calling from the direction of Red Lodge. "Where are you? We need to talk before I send the hunting party out tomorrow morning." I heard him mumbling to himself as his heavy steps thumped along the pathway. "D'vhan missing, Y'keta ill, Pey't injured. Scorching Red Lodge!"

Breathe in. Breathe out, I commanded myself. *Think about the cold or rain and snow.* "Coming," I yelled.

Twenty-One

<<<Siann>>>

I dressed, made my morning meal, and got ready for my studies in Grey Lodge, following the same exact routine as every other day. Wasn't today supposed to feel different? The sun flashed in my eyes as I left my little lodge at the back of Grey Lodge. It was a simple home, but it was mine. I could have stayed in the main lodge. I didn't want to, it wasn't my home anymore, it was Laban's. My life was so different now than it had been before Mother died and the Utlaak came.

Napaay yelled *good morning* as he raced past with a gaggle of the younger children, all headed for the forest at the edge of camp in a wild flurry of arms, legs, and piping voices. I caught myself staring after him as they rampaged out of sight. Even he was gone now, living in the Green Lodge with the others of his age.

The air was filled with the comforting sounds of the camp waking around me as I walked between the aspens toward the central fire. Overhead a raucous flock of black, ill-omened birds cawed loudly, announcing their return from wintering in the southland. It was the first moon of spring, the Hania Moon. I was twenty-one today.

"Tekopi, Siann!" Hahnee called out the traditional birthday greeting from his place beside the communal cookpot. His booming voice making sure the whole camp heard him!

"Shards," I cursed under my breath. I had wanted to keep this day quiet and avoid being noticed. It would be just one more thing that brought me to the attention of the village. In the five years since people had found out about the Lifebinder, I felt like I walked around with a small and shadowed silence attached to me. I moved through the camp in a bubble. It wasn't that people ignored me—in fact, I felt respected in a way I never had been while Mother was alive. There was just a carefulness in how I was treated that grated against my sense of family. I almost wanted Hahnee to yell at me for stealing frybread, or one of the mothers to scold me because I wasn't dressed warmly enough for the spring cold.

"Is it your birthday, hatchling?" Y'keta said, coming out of the Red Lodge with D'vhan and a warrior whom I hadn't met yet. "Tekopi! You are almost a grown-up."

I growled softly. That shard-cursed, air-headed slug was never happy unless he was making me feel small or insignificant. I never had to worry about him respecting me too much.

"True," I snarked. "Almost old enough to shed my pin-feathers." He stared at me rudely and D'vhan cackled so hard that he almost doubled over. I worried that the wheezing came from the damage to his lungs returning. The new warrior just looked confused.

"Siann," Y'keta warned softly.

"Shellhead?" I replied, my face as serious as five cycles of unending rivalry could make it. "Did you want to say something?" My eyes must have given me away. Y'keta growled and ran his hand through his coarse yellow hair.

"Who, me? I never say anything." His voice was nasal and annoying. The glint in his odd-looking eyes told me that he was remembering what happened the night of the Utlaak attack. "As long as you don't."

"Now I'm really confused," the new warrior said. His voice was a pleasant tenor, slightly at odds with the grave look in his deep-set amethyst eyes. "Will someone please introduce me so that I can get in on the fun? That is, if it is all in fun?"

Y'keta looked down and coughed embarrassedly. "I'm sorry. Siann, this is Dahi, he is from Konahi Village and will be spending a cycle with us." Dahi bowed slightly. His long, tightly-woven braid flopping down his back as he straightened up. Both D'vhan and Y'keta were still wearing winter leathers, warm and lined with thick rabbit skin. But Dahi wore nothing but soft leather breeches and a vest of thin white fur. He didn't look cold though, surprisingly;

he looked comfortable even on a chilly spring morning.

It surprised me that Y'keta did the introductions and not D'vhan. The hatchling was overreaching himself again. I glanced at D'vhan, looking to see if the red leader was going to put Y'keta in his place. The look on his tanned face was odd, as if he had a mouthful of bitter gourd, but he didn't speak. He just waited until Y'keta turned to Dahi and gestured aimlessly in my direction. "This is Siann. She's a nuisance."

"Y'keta, that's enough!" D'vhan's eyes danced merrily. "Just because she has the good sense not to automatically agree with your wisdom does not make her a nuisance. More likely a wise woman who will be your Shaman one day."

I blanked out at that and missed the next few words in the conversation. That seemed to happen a lot lately. People assumed that I would take over as Shaman someday. Even Laban, who had only been our Salixt for five cycles, kept talking as though I was his heir. What would they do when I left?

Because I did mean to leave. I intended to declare myself Kit'na next cycle when the spring ceremony came around. To Walk to another village and see if the People there could accept me for who I was. Not the only child of the dead Elder Shaman, not the woman marked by the Thunderstones and burdened with the Lifebinder, just me.

"I am pleased to meet you, Dahi, and I hope that this young shellhead"—my lips twitched in Y'keta's direction and D'vhan chortled—"doesn't give you the wrong impression of the village. We are not all raving mad."

"Sun of Riad shine on your birth day, Siann." Dahi's voice was light but not at all soft, reminding me of bright sunlight over ice. "What are you doing on this warm spring morning?"

Warm? I thought. He must be living in a different village than I was. The ice was still clinging to the edges of the streams, and in the shadows where we stood my breath was still easily visible.

Dahi's laugh was light and clear. "I am from the northlands, Siann. To us, this is the middle of spring, heading into summer. At home we would be trapping marmot before their coats turned from winter-white to brown. He ran a long-fingered hand down his fur vest and D'vhan coughed noisily.

"Excuse me, Siann," D'vhan said. "I need to talk to Laban for a few minutes."

"Y'keta," I said, trying to make a good impression on the new warrior, "did you need to go with D'vhan?" Y'keta seemed to be taking on more and more of D'vhan's role in the village. It worried me.

"He doesn't need me." His strange orange eyes followed the older warrior as he walked over to Ren and Laban and squatted in front of them, talking quietly. "Now that you have healed his lungs, he is slowly getting stronger." Y'keta's voice dropped to a whisper as he spoke of D'vhan, especially when he added, "He has to get stronger."

The depth of feeling in that one brief sentence surprised me. I knew that D'vhan had been teaching Y'keta about woodcraft, history, politics, all the things a warrior of the People would need to know, but this seemed like a great deal of concern over a teacher.

I waited for Dahi to wander off to the cookpots and asked quietly, "How bad is he, Y'keta? Is he hiding things? Has the lung fever come back?" For once the annoying slug looked serious, his strange eyes meeting mine equally, no condescension in his tone.

"D'vhan is not improving as quickly as he thinks he should, Siann," he said. "Even now, he insists on keeping up with the rest of the warriors but it's wearing on him. I don't know how he made it through this past winter and if you hadn't healed him, I'm sure he couldn't have kept going much longer."

My hand flew to my chest. Inside the leather pouch, the pale Lifebinder Crystal pulsed twice, vibrations travelling from my chest, through my arm, and down to where the Tiamat had marked my left palm. The two were somehow tied together but I still didn't understand how.

My voice was hardly above a whisper. "If he is willing to try again, I think I can do more, 'Keta. I think the Lifebinder wants me to keep trying to help."

Y'keta's eyes flared with unexpected hope. "Really, Siann?" he said. "You would do this? I remember..."

His hand moved reflexively to touch the centre of his chest where a jagged circular scar marked the place where the Utlaak spear had shattered his breastbone and almost ended his life. The Lifebinder had saved him then, when even his father had given up hope. But using it had almost cost my life. "You used me when you healed Pey't—would using my strength let you do more to help D'vhan?"

§

"Stubborn old crow," Y'keta said tiredly. They had spent hours shivering in the cold spring sunlight, whispering quietly, trying to find a way to talk D'vhan into accepting further healing. "I'm willing to do anything I can to keep him going, but he will never accept it."

Siann's head snapped up as though his words had woken her from sleep. Her eyes flashed first to white and then to red. How lightning could shine out of soft brown eyes, he didn't know, but right now her eyes held a power that made the hair stand up on the back of his neck.

"I am the Lifebinder," her voice echoed. The power had risen within her, and she was no longer making any attempt at privacy. "For this, I came to your village. Use me."

"Siann?" Y'keta shook her arm carefully, not sure that the lightning in her eyes wouldn't reach out and blast him.

Siann's eyes focused and she shook her arm free. "Get your hands off me, warrior," she said, squinting angrily at him. "What do you mean shaking me like that!"

"Don't you remember?" Y'keta's nasal voice sounded frightened. Seeing Siann so far under the power of the Lifebinder had frightened him. Suddenly he wasn't sure if Siann using the stone again, or letting the stone use her, was a good idea. "You were talking in that *other* voice again. The voice I heard in your mind when you healed Pey't."

Brown eyes met orange ones and a flicker of recognition passed between them. Something had happened the day they had worked together to heal Pey't from the infected crystal wounds. For just a moment, there in the healers' lodge, a truce had been called, allowing the power of the Lifebinder in Siann to draw life from Y'keta and channel it to heal Pey't. Neither of them spoke of it, but somehow the jibes and taunts they flung at each other now seemed hollow, like an old moth-eaten cloak that they no longer needed but hadn't thrown out yet.

"I don't think D'vhan will let you try again," Y'keta spoke softly. "And I'm scared to let you try. He's doing well enough. I think what he needs now isn't healing, it's hope. And only the Elder Stars can give him that."

SUMMER

Twenty-Two

Summer came to the forest in an explosion of green. Trees burst into leaf, the undergrowth blossomed, and the air was full of the chirps and squeaks of abundant life. The only darkness in the sky over the village was the ever-present threat of the Utlaak raiders. The moment the Watcher was hidden, they would come. They had attacked Atiskaat at the dark of the last moon, tearing down the lodges even after they discovered that the people were not there.

Savohn had wisely pulled the people of Atiskaat into one of the abandoned burrows before the new moon night and kept them out of sight until the Eye of Riad Walked the sky again. The runner that he sent to warn Esquialt of the raid had not only brought word of another cycle of attacks on the villages, he had also unknowingly started another argument in council.

Iamaat proposed sending Siann away, removing the threat to the village by sacrificing the young shaman and potentially making it easier for the Utlaak to get their hands on the Lifebinder. The council had fought for days over the idea. Laban and Ren were outraged that Iamaat would even consider sending one of their own to what would be certain death if the Utlaak caught her. Iamaat was just as adamant that the life of any one person was not worth the life of the village, and besides that, Siann had brought this upon herself by picking up the crystal to begin with. The one voice not heard as the debate raged was D'vhan's. He sat through meeting after meeting, motionless on the floor of Grey Lodge, his face twisted like he had bitten an unripe vair berry. Finally, after three days of angry meetings, he exploded.

"Will you stop!" he scolded. "Listen to yourselves. You act like arguing with each other will convince the Utlaak to stay away. This is not a matter for talk, but action." Scrubbing his hands through his unusually tidy red hair, he walked back and forth across the width of Grey Lodge, scolding them all as though they were green feathers who were misbehaving in a lesson.

"Iamaat," he said sternly, "we know your position. Saying it again but louder and with more words will not convince anyone."

Then D'vhan turned to Laban, one of his closest friends in the village, and one who, if his betrayed face meant anything, had expected D'vhan's support.

"And you, Laban," he continued. "In this one thing Iamaat is right, and you know it. As Salixt for the village you must think of the whole village and not just one shaman, no matter how powerful she is."

"But, D'vhan," both Iamaat and Laban spoke at once, then glared at each other, shock evident on their faces.

"You are right," Laban said ruefully. "Iamaat's point is also right," he said, adding quickly, "although I will not agree with her reasons for making it. We cannot risk the village for the welfare of one person, no matter how much I think we will need her and the powers she controls." Laban's hands clenched in frustration and taking a few sharp panting breaths to control his temper he continued, "But I will not, I cannot, see one of our own turned into the wilderness like a kaal before a hungry pack of wolves."

Iamaat, of course, made no apology or gave any indication that she was less than perfectly correct. Straightening her robes and patting her ample stomach with a smug, self-satisfied air, she simply continued, "If she's as powerful as you say, Salixt..." She nodded regally towards Laban, and if that nod was in any way meant to show respect, she hadn't told to her face about it. "If she's that powerful," Iamaat continued, "then perhaps she is not a kaal, perhaps she is a wolf herself, and one whose teeth we may not wish to have among us."

Ren stood up, her lean form still graceful despite the obvious signs of her pregnancy. "You poisonous viper." She stalked towards where Iamaat squatted on the floor of the lodge. "You speak from the venom in your own heart. You, and your hatred, are the things I fear will poison our People." Ren glared down at the bland face below her. Iamaat didn't flinch, didn't look down. Rather, she looked pityingly from Ren's face to the small bulge where their baby was growing.

"You were not raised well," she said condescendingly. "Your parents did you a disservice. They should have taken you with them when they stepped out on the Road."

Laban gasped, his face going as pale as the snow in the northlands. Not many in the tribe knew of Ren's parentage, how her mother had become ill, and her father had chosen to leave Ren with the Green Mother of her village and step on the Road with his mate. He stood slowly, walked across to the hide flap that acted as a door when the council was meeting and, holding it aside, said, "Iamaat, you will leave our home, you will leave this council. You are not welcome in this lodge until you find a way to apologize for the damage your comment has done to my mate."

The large woman rose awkwardly from the floor using one of the side poles of the lodge for balance and walked to the doorway. As she reached the entrance, she lifted her foot ceremoniously and stepped out of the lodge, saying in a voice that was intentionally loud enough for the whole clearing to hear, "If am not welcome here, I will not be here. If am not welcome here, none of my children, none of the Greens will be here."

Glancing around the clearing, Iamaat took careful note of who looked shocked, whose lips twisted in a supressed snicker, and whose faces grew angry at her words. Some of the villagers would listen to her, she knew it, some of them had been her children, her green feathers, they would hear her. Smoothing down her green robe she carefully presented a face washed clean of any venom or anger.

"Laban of Esquialt," she said, "you have allowed your anger and your ambition to taint the traditions of our People." Her eyes flashed around the campfire, speaking to her followers rather than to the Shaman she addressed. "Your People rebuke you."

Seeing a few nods among the crowd, figuring her message had reached its audience, she gathered up the hem of her robe and majestically strode across the clearing and into Green Lodge, letting the green hide flap fall behind her with a theatrical flourish.

Twenty-Three

"D'vhan, how could you agree with her? You gave Iamaat exactly the excuse she wanted. Now the village knows that the council is fractured, and she can openly work to turn the People against me." Laban's words were hurt, his hands making emphatic motions in front of him.

"Exactly." D'vhan's answer was unhelpful at best.

"I don't understand, old crow." Ren sat on a pile of furs, her green eyes troubled. "I know you well enough to know that you don't spit without a reason. So, explain this to me, before I have to get my daggers."

"So fierce," D'vhan rumbled, his deep laughter totally out of place in the charged atmosphere. "And here I thought being a mother would calm you."

"D'vhan." Ren's temper was nothing to trifle with on good days. But now, pregnant, angry, and with her mate in pain, she was nothing less than murderous.

"Peace, Ren," D'vhan said finally, flopping down on the floor next to her. "Do you not remember the tale of the viper that we tell in Red Lodge? What is the one thing that you cannot do when fighting a venomous animal?"

Ren's eyes became thoughtful, remembering a late-night discussion in Red Lodge. She started nodding slowly. "When you fight a venomous animal, the one mistake you cannot make is to underestimate it. You must be sure that everyone knows that it is deadly."

Laban's brow wrinkled. He had been a warrior before he left for Atiskaat, but that was twenty cycles ago, far too long to remember silly lessons about snakes. Unaware of the tenderness of the gesture, Ren reached up and rubbed at the lines between Laban's eyes. "Stop frowning," she said. "It makes you look angry."

Laban smiled softly down at his usually reticent mate. "Little hawk," he said gently, "I *am* angry. No one hurts you like that. No one."

"Big bad Shaman." She laughed. "I have been tormented by people who make Iamaat seem like a child throwing sticks. She has no power to harm me. My past is my own, I will not give her the power or permission to use it against me." Winking at D'vhan, she continued, "Besides, her outburst today may have pulled the fangs from the viper. And the lines are back," she said, rubbing Laban's forehead again.

"How can you say that?" Laban's head shook, these two were giving him a headache with their Red Lodge references and all the talk about fangs and poison.

"Think of this," D'vhan said, taking pity on the confused Shaman. "How many times has Iamaat fought with you, in public, in front of the village, or in their hearing?"

"Stars," Laban said, "I don't think I can count that high."

"Exactly." D'vhan was being confusing again and Laban's brow wrinkled in frustration. "The one thing a viper cannot do is to let people know it has fangs. Iamaat has been showing her fangs for the past three cycles. Do you think that no one has heard her in here yelling the last few days? Has seen the way she treats Y'keta? Or me? Or even young Ihkopi who is one of her own Greens?"

Laban nodded, swatting playfully at Ren as she reached to brush his frown away again. "Peace, little hawk." He smiled to take the sting from his actions. "I'm trying to understand, I'm a bit slow but I'll get there. So, what you are saying, D'vhan," Laban explained slowly, "is that by showing that she is willing to go openly against the council, by attacking Siann and Y'keta so viciously, she has shown her fangs to the village. They know she is a viper now and will walk carefully around her."

"That's it," D'vhan crowed, "and she has unmasked those of the People who have been infected by her poison. We saw who nodded and went along with her. We know now which villagers we need to watch."

"Wily old crow, I am sorry I doubted you." Laban put an arm around the shoulder of the slight warrior. "But we still need to decide what to do about Atiskaat. Savohn saved his People by using the caves, but we can't count on that to stop the Utlaak next time."

"Can I suggest something without getting shoved out the door of the lodge?" D'vhan asked.

"I thought you had something brewing in that head of yours." Ren said, "You looked like someone who had taken a bite of spoiled fruit. That usually means you have a plan, but you don't like it."

D'vhan giggled. The merry sound lightened the atmosphere in the lodge and reminded Ren of all the things she missed about living with the warriors.

"Lightning scorch you, D'vhan," Laban said. "I thought you were agreeing with her!"

"I was, but not in the way she thought." D'vhan's words made Laban move from where he had been standing behind Ren and plant himself nose-to-nose with D'vhan, well chin-to-nose—D'vhan was much shorter than the irritated Shaman.

"Peace, Laban," D'vhan said. "I agree that Siann should leave the village. But," he continued quickly, seeing the Shaman start to puff up and prickle, "I think it needs to be done with a purpose, not letting her go wandering on her own. Stars know that girl finds enough trouble on her own without her wandering in the forest looking for it."

"So, what are you suggesting then, Kalixt?" Laban's use of his official title as head of Red Lodge put this discussion on a whole different level. Leader to leader, not just friends throwing around solutions to a problem.

"Well," D'vhan said thoughtfully, "first we need to talk to the hatchling. She's not a child now and the power in her is unstable and very potent. We can't just tell her what to do."

"True enough," Laban said, "and even as a child Siann was never one to just do something because an adult said so."

D'vhan smiled inwardly, remembering the Kit'na ceremony when Y'keta and Laban had come to the village. Siann had stepped out of the darkness and addressed the Elders in council, sixteen cycles old and so sure that she knew what to do. "No," he said, "Siann never was one to just keep quiet and obey. But, with her approval," he continued, "I want to suggest something a bit different. I think that the warriors, or some of them at least, should go with her."

Ren pulled her dagger from its sheath at her waist and idly flipped it end over end, catching the point between two tanned fingers. "Not enough warriors, D'vhan," she worried. "Sawiea is away, Pey't is injured, who would you send?"

D'vhan counted out on his fingers. "Myself, Y'keta, and the new warrior, Dahi. That leaves Pey't, Sawiea—who will be back in a few days, Coen, and the two new hawks to guard the village." Ren's eyes flashed cold. "Oh," D'vhan added, making it an obvious afterthought, "and I know one or two others, who might be useful. There's an out-of-practice Shaman who's mated to this woman who used to be good with daggers."

Before he could finish speaking, Ren's dagger flashed across the room and landed not a feather's width from his toes. Unfazed, D'vhan pulled the bone-handled weapon from the floor and lazily tossed it back to Ren.

"Can it wait that long? Will the Utlaak wait?" Laban questioned. "

"I'd prefer to let things settle for a moon or so, to make sure Iamaat isn't going to cause problems. It's a risk." Laban ran his hand through his short grey hair, leaving a tousled mess in its wake. "I don't want to have her raising the village against me without you there for balance, but the Utlaak have been attacking every new moon. Who knows if Esquialt will be the next target."

"Balance?" D'vhan laughed wryly. "Balance and Iamaat are not ideas that can co-exist comfortably. She has shown her fangs, whether now or in a moon or a cycle, she will strike."

Laban shrugged, the beads on his tunic making a jingling that seemed somewhat out of place with the tension of the day. "Still," he said, "We've got at until the next new moon to plan. I think we will wait at least until Sawiea gets back before I will agree to send Siann out."

Ren's expressive mouth twitched.

"And what is amusing you, little hawk?" her mate asked kindly. "Are us poor males missing something again?"

"Oh, you certainly are!" Ren's eyes danced in the dusty light of the lodge. "Which one of you brave men is going to tell Siann that the village is in danger because of her. Or once she knows, tell her that she has to stay until you think it's the right time to go?" Laban and D'vhan stared at each other. "You know her well enough, or you should by now," Ren continued. "What will Siann say when she finds out that you great and wise ones have decided to use her as bait to lead the Utlaak away from the village?"

"I think Laban's right," D'vhan said hurriedly. "If she finds out that the danger is following her, she will try to draw the Utlaak away from the village. We'll wait until Sawiea comes back, or until we know the horde is close,"

"Definitely," Laban added, swallowing thickly. There is no need to disturb Siann before it is necessary."

"Brave, brave leaders, both of you." Ren laughed, her hands cradling the small shaking bump that was her child laughing with her.

Laban's and D'vhan's rueful laughter cleared the last of the tension from the air and together they walked into the spring morning.

Twenty-Four

The sun had just gone down when an exhausted scout from Maskwatin stumbled into camp, collapsed to his knees in front of Grey Lodge, and gasped out his message. "Maskwatin. Under attack," he managed to say, sides heaving as his lungs worked for air. "Large force of Utlaak, they came out of the Ice-Lands."

The commotion brought Laban out of his lodge, frowning. "What's going on?" The Shaman asked Coen. *They must have still been eating*, Coen thought as he caught Laban surreptitiously wiping the leftover food from his face.

Coen had followed the scout in from his post on the trail and, seeing that the stranger was still trying to catch his breath, answered, "Laban, this scout came from Maskwatin, two days march to the north. He says the village there was attacked."

Laban's face went white. "Coen, go and find D'vhan," he ordered. "I want all the council members here, now!"

Ren's face peeked out of the family area as Laban re-entered the lodge, the concern in her eyes obvious to him, although no one else would ever see it. "What's going on out there?" she asked, watching her mate grab packs and start stuffing them with ritual kits and scrolls. "And what under the Stars do you think you're doing? Stop, Laban. Think!"

Laban stared at her, his eyes stunned and uncomprehending. "I need to go," he said. "I need to get ready."

Ren couldn't remember ever seeing Laban this frantic. Even in the crazy days just after Matra had died, even when the village had been abandoned and the Utlaak attacked, even when the Sky Lords themselves had walked into the village to save them. In all of this, his voice had been the calm one, steadying the People and keeping the day-to-day lives of the village on track.

"My heart." She walked up to him slowly, approaching him as though he were a wild animal in a trap. Gently putting her hands on either side of his face, Ren forced him to look at her, to find a focus in the middle of the activity. "Talk to me, Laban," she said. "Tell me what has happened to make you so frantic."

"Maskwatin has been attacked, a runner just arrived." Laban's voice held no trace of emotion, everything bled out of him with a dread that Ren just didn't understand.

She frowned, trying to comprehend. "Attacks have happened before. It is horrible, but not unexpected. There has to be more, love."

"Ren..." Laban's voice was strained, as though what he was saying was too much even for him to believe. "It's not the new moon." Rubbing the bridge of his nose to try and relieve the tension that was pounding inside his skull, he continued, "They have never attacked in the moonlight, even of a waning moon. Something has changed, and we must know what."

"So, what will you do, Salixt?" It was Iamaat. *Of course it was*, Laban thought. Who else would sound so gleeful over catching him in a moment of weakness. "Now will you admit that I was right and send away the one causing this?" Her voice was strident and loud, playing to her audience as always.

"No." Laban was adamant. No child of this village was going into the dark just to feed her paranoia. "But we do need to send help to Maskwatin. Do you have any suggestions, Iamaat?" he asked, knowing what she would say to the village if she was excluded. "What about you, D'vhan?" he asked, noticing the slim form of the warrior leader sliding into the lodge behind Iamaat's bulk. "What is your recommendation for dealing with this attack?"

"The warriors go." The answer was instinctive, the guardian was growling. "Me, Dahi, Y'keta. Sawiea came back a few days ago. Maybe young Coen as well."

Iamaat was nodding. "Take a shaman with you," she said. "Those filth will have desecrated the dead."

"Wise," Laban said. "I'll pack to go with you."

"Then I'm coming too." Ren waddled into the council room uninvited. "If this old crow can make the trip, I can." No one doubted that she was sincere—nothing, especially not her own concerns, ever slowed Ren down when there was a job to be done.

"Not this time." Surprisingly, it was Iamaat who objected first. "You have been given a new life to carry for the People. That must be your priority, not chasing Utlaak up in the mountains."

Ren's face started to cloud over, thunder rumbling in her eyes.

"Iamaat is right, little hawk," Laban said, hating to admit it. "You cannot go, therefore neither can I." He knew Ren's need to be involved, to feel valued. "I will not leave you behind."

He could see Iamaat preparing to lecture him on his duty to lead the rescue party to Maskwatin.

"D'vhan will lead the rescue," he stated, cutting Iamaat's protests off with a sharp hand motion. "This requires a warrior, not a Shaman. I will send one of the younger ones who can keep up on the trek. Get your lodge ready," he told D'vhan. "I want the party on the trail before sunrise. I will speak to Selah," he said, naming one of the shamans who had come to the village in this cycle's Kit'na ceremony. "Although she is new to our village, she has dealt with Utlaak before and knows the ritual for ensuring our People find their eyes and can Walk onto the Road together."

A few frantic hours later the party of warriors were ready. With a murmured word of blessing from Laban, and accompanied by the scout, who had begged to be allowed to return with them, the small group set out in the pre-dawn light. They called it a rescue mission, but every one of them knew that there would be no chance of finding survivors.

Twenty-Five

"Sun of Riad!" Coen gaped as they followed the scouting party into the ruined village. The hollow eyes of the tribesmen gazed up at them in mute recrimination. Their corpses laid side by side in a sick ceremonial display. "We should have arrived yesterday," D'vhan said. "It's my fault. I slowed you down, it should not have taken two days to get here!

"We couldn't have arrived any sooner," Y'keta said, pausing beside D'vhan to gently rest his hand on the older warrior's shoulder. "Even Verlan, running alone, took almost as long." Although his voice was emotionless and clear, the pain in his orange eyes was not hidden.

"Quiet, old crow." Sawiea's use of the old nickname was calming somehow. "We got here today. Yesterday would not have made a difference. Look at these poor people, D'vhan. They started on their Roads days ago. The hania have already been feasting. We saw a flock of them fly up as we entered the village."

"The Utlaak are taunting us," Coen said coldly. "See how they line the corpses up at the entrance to the village. They are mocking us because we cannot stop them. We cannot find them!" The young warrior shook his head angrily and watched as Selah, the young shaman that Laban had sent with them, went from body to body, restoring the eyes of the dead. Making sure that they could find the Sky Road and Walk into the next life with their village.

Selah stood up from her grisly task and slumped wearily against a tree. *Shards*, D'vhan thought, *I know how she feels*. He would never admit it, but the trek from Esquialt had been a long one and even though Siann had restored his lungs the effort of travelling at top speed for two full days had still made his breathing ragged.

D'vhan looked at Pey't, who was kneeling in the middle of the village square, his large frame shaking. Scrubbing a dusty hand across his eyes, he dashed away the tears that seemed to come so much easier now.

This had been the village of Pey't's childhood, D'vhan remembered. Even though it had been almost forty cycles since he lived here, this was his family. The flat, dead look when his eyes met D'vhan's was more frightening than any of the mutilated bodies or the black-winged hania ever could be.

Pey't was everyone's favourite warrior. They called him Pey't the Fat, Pey't the Foolish. The village wouldn't know this cold, stunned stranger, the pain etched into his face so raw that it went beyond anger into absolute incomprehension.

Dahi approached and knelt down in front of Pey't, one long hand gently brushing the dust from his tear-bloated face. "They have Walked," Dahi said. His light tenor voice carrying a surprising resonance of power and authority. "Not one has been lost. The shaman has blessed them all. Let go of the grief, Pey't. You will see them all on the Road."

Pey't looked up, an agonizing need for hope in his empty eyes. "Are you sure, Dahi?" he said, locking one pudgy hand in a death grip around Dahi's corded forearm. "Their eyes," Pey't's voice was a broken whisper; a child's cry for reassurance in the night.

"The shaman has replaced their sight," Dahi said. He didn't try to break Pey't's painful grip on his arm. He knew that the older warrior was clinging desperately to anything that would drag him out of the thunderstorm of grief and despair in which he was drowning. "They will find your People on the Sky Road. Be at peace, warrior." Slowly Pey't's eyes returned to their normal placid brown and he relaxed his grip on Dahi's arm, cursing mildly when he saw the red welts his desperation had left behind.

"I'm sorry, Dahi, I..." Pey't's voice trailed off. He just couldn't find the words.

Dahi shook his head, the red beads in his long hair tinkling softly. "Go and sit at the edge of the village, my friend. There is nothing here that you need to see. Honour your friends by remembering who they were, not what the Utlaak left of them." Carefully he guided Pey't to a patch of green grass on the edge of the village, sat him down facing the clean, snow-covered mountains in the distance and left him to begin the process of coping.

"Something isn't right." It was Verlan, the scout who had run through the night to bring warning to Esquialt, who spoke. His face was grey with pain and exhaustion and the faint smell confirmed that he, along with many of the others, had been physically ill at the brutality of these murders.

"What do you mean?" D'vhan asked. "Everything isn't right!"

"No, Kalixt," he continued. "There aren't enough..."—his throat worked convulsively—"not enough bodies," he finally forced himself to say.

Coen looked at the rows of corpses at the edge of the village, laid out like firewood, one beside the next. "Are you sure?" he asked Verlan. "There are so many!"

D'vhan took a quick count and his eyes narrowed. "Many, but not enough," he said, looking at the young warrior who was fighting to make sense of his first battle. "I see warriors, a few shamans, a few elders, but Coen, do you see any children?"

"There should be at least a dozen green feathers." Verlan nodded vigorously. "And our Mother isn't here either." He pointed at one of the bodies near the village edge. It had once belonged to a giant of a man, tall and broad, with red beads threaded through his full beard. "That is Cami, our Kalixt. But his second isn't here. She wouldn't have left his side without orders. Kalita was his daughter."

"Cub!" D'vhan bellowed for Y'keta.

"Right behind you," Y'keta grumbled. "You don't need to deafen me!"

"Look around for me, look carefully." D'vhan dropped his voice until it was almost inaudible. "I need you to *really* look."

Y'keta's eyebrows climbed into his coarse blond hair. He knew what D'vhan was asking, but use his Waki'tani abilities here? In front of outsiders? "What am I looking for, D'vhan?" he asked, making sure.

"Verlan says that there are not enough bodies here to account for the whole village." His hand swept the open plain around the village. "I don't see anything moving, but can you? Any sign of where they are or if they have been taken hostage."

"The Utlaak don't take hostages," Y'keta reminded them.

"They took you, cub," D'vhan pointed out. "Don't be so absolute, everything changes."

Y'keta stepped to the edge of the village, standing next to the huddled form of Pey't and, being careful to face away from the new warriors, let the change take him. His pupils narrowed, and the raven's eyes emerged. He couldn't see anything on the plain but when he turned back to the village, he could see several areas giving off enough heat to almost burn his sensitive eyes. Blinking quickly to readjust, he turned to D'vhan, hope bubbling like a stream in his heart.

"People, lots of them, underground." His eyes glowed. "There must be tunnels under the village, somewhere that the People could hide."

Verlan jumped and ran towards the ash heap that had once been the smallest of the lodges. "Help me," he yelled. "They must be in the cellars and the entrances are blocked."

Within seconds the warriors were moving debris, flinging lodge poles and scorched hides out of the way with no thought to the damage to their hands or the risk to anyone behind them. It didn't take long to uncover the piece of slate that was set into the floor. "Here," Verlan said, "lift this!"

It took three warriors to pry the slate from the floor and tip it to the side. At first their hearts sank when they couldn't see or hear anything from the opening the slab had hidden.

D'vhan yelled down the hole, hoping to reassure any survivors that might be hiding down there. "Hail Maskwatin, my name is D'vhan," he said. "I come from Esquialt, I come from the Road."

As though they had been waiting for these words, a surge of bodies emerged from the hole. There must have been a tunnel network under the village because people kept coming and coming. D'vhan stared in awe, only coming out of his stupor when the first child started to emerge from the darkness.

"Keep the children down there," he said. "Give us a moment." D'vhan turned to give orders for a quick cleanup of the village, only to find he was too late. At Dahi's direction several of the adults from the village, along with Pey't and Y'keta had moved all the bodies away from the entrance to the tunnel and covered them with blankets from their bedrolls.

"Okay," D'vhan said. "Send everyone out now. It's clear."

A gaggle of children emerged from the darkness, coughing. They looked around with blank faces covered in soot and ash. Leaving them to the village Mother, D'vhan turned to see Kalita, the warrior who had come to the Kit'na ceremony in the springtime. She didn't look at the village, instead her eyes moved from one carefully covered corpse to the next, searching. Then, finally seeing the giant form of Cali, wrapped in a blanket and laid out beside his warriors, she crumbled.

"He is gone," she said. "I knew it, I felt him step on the Road." Kalita's lips tightened, reigning in the feelings that were just too much for speech. "What shall we do?" she asked. "Winter will come before we can rebuild, and we moved our grain and meat stores out of the tunnels to make room for the children."

"Esquialt waits for you," D'vhan said. He hadn't talked to Laban about survivors, they hadn't expected to find any, but he didn't need to. No one would deny these poor souls a place at the fire. "Come now, red child of Maskwatin, let us lead the children home."

Twenty-Six

Siann woke up with thunderclouds circling her head. Every movement seemed to hurt and the Lifebinder burned like a brand where it hung against her chest.

"What in all the Stars is wrong with me?" she mumbled, trying for the third time to get her feet into the soft kaal-hide leggings she wore around camp.

Nothing seemed out of place as she stumbled out of the lodge and towards the main campfire. The sun was shining, it smelled like Hahnee had put berries in the grain this morning, and that annoying hatchling had left the day before. All of those things should have made it a wonderful day, but something in her spirit just didn't think so. Glancing around she carefully pulled the Lifebinder from its pouch around her neck. The crystal pulsed in her hand, flashing from pink to a dull, old-blood red.

Facets of baleful red light flashed through the cavern.

"Closer," the matriarch cackled.

Feeling exposed, and afraid that Iamaat would catch her using the crystal's "unlawful powers," she shoved the stone quickly into its pouch and ducked back into her lodge. She just didn't understand. The crystal only pulsed as a warning, it never gave details or specifics. But the headache, the dread that crawled up the back of her throat like acid, something was trying to reach her. If not the crystal, what?

"Breathe," Siann told herself, dropping down on the untidy pile of bedfurs. "Remember what Laban says when he teaches the young shamans in Grey Lodge, 'Power speaks, but your mind needs to be quiet enough to hear it.'"

Ignoring the noise of the waking camp, ignoring the rush of pain in her temples, ignoring the growling of her empty stomach, Siann drew her mind back towards that place where the snakes and the Lightning twined. A breath in, a breath out, slower and quieter with each breath, until she could hear the hissing of the Lifebinder and the gravelly echo of the Thunderstones.

There is something coming, she thought. *Neither one can speak alone, but maybe if I earn the warning?* Shivering at the thought of trying to touch a power as ancient as the Thunderstones or as dangerous as the crystal, Siann drew her eating dagger from its sheath at her waist. "There has to be blood," she reminded herself. "Blood for the life of the People."

She swallowed thickly, rolling up the sleeve of her tunic. Siann struck quickly, making a small nick in the skin at her wrist, tears filling her eyes from the sudden pain. Reaching again for the Lifebinder and carefully placing it in the palm of her lightning-scorched hand, she watched as the blood dripped down her arm and pooled around the crystal.

Prisms of light flashed from the crystal, throwing red, orange and violet shadows on the walls of her small home. Siann cried out and then, pitching forward, slumped to the floor unconscious, drowning in a sea of fire and light. The flickering crystal rolled out of her limp hand, a trail of blood marking its path across the floor, until it finally stopped, pulsed quietly a few times, and became silent.

When Siann didn't appear for her lessons in the Grey Lodge, Laban was concerned. It wasn't like the young shaman to miss her day as keeper of the scrolls. She loved copying and reading for the other shamans and the young ones. And when Napaay said she hadn't been at firstmeal, that concern became worry.

Striding quickly around to the wooded area behind Grey Lodge, he coughed, approaching the entrance to Siann's home.

"Siann," he called. "It's Laban, are you all right?"

No answer.

"Siann?" he spoke loudly, thinking that the young shaman may be sleeping. "It's Laban. You missed firstmeal and your service in the lodge. Are you all right?"

Silence.

Shaking his head, Laban pulled the hide flap away from the door and, ducking, walked in. Siann lay sprawled across the floor like a broken doll. There was blood, so much blood. It trickled from her palm in a sluggish river, not pulsing, but not stopping, just dripping her life away.

The left arm of Siann's tunic was caked with blood and sticky. Forcibly pulling it away from her skin, Laban cursed. "Foolish hatchling!" he swore at the unconscious girl in his arms. "By all the Stars, what were you thinking!"

Swinging Siann up into his arms, and ducking again to get out of the doorway, he carried her quickly across the camp towards the healers' lodge. "Get Inkiss," he bellowed as he drew close to the healers. "Find my mother and get her here now!"

The young warrior, Coen, had heard Laban's frantic orders and appeared a moment later with Inkiss in his arms. She was spitting and hissing at him in a way that would frighten older, more seasoned warriors.

"Put me down," Inkiss demanded as they drew near to the healers' lodge. "I am not a sack of winter wheat, neither am I a maiden to be impressed by your manly vigour. Put me down!"

Coen gently lowered the frail elder to her feet at the entrance to the healers' lodge, stepping backward quickly to avoid the cane that she swung at him. "My apologies, elder," he said, his light tenor emphasizing just how young he was. "Laban said it was urgent, there wasn't time to explain."

Well done, Coen, Laban thought. *That's one way of getting yourself out of the thorn bushes. Maybe the silver-tongued youth should have been a shaman.*

"And exactly what is so sharding urgent that I can't walk across the compound on my own two feet?" Inkiss was still raging, but now Laban was the target.

"Mother," he said, trying to calm down the fire that was burning in her eyes.

"Don't you 'Mother' me, hatchling." Inkiss was scorched. Laban knew by painful experience that only one thing would work when his mother was this angry.

"Mother," he said, "it's Siann, I needed you." That was all it took. Laban knew that his mother would deal with him later, and that even Coen wasn't safe from reprisal, but for now there was someone who needed healing.

"Then stop blathering, hatchling, and tell me what happened."

Laban sighed. He was the Salixt, head Shaman of the village of Esquialt, first village of the People, and it still didn't matter. To his mother he was forever a hatchling.

"I think she tried to use blood as part of a ritual, and she cut too deep." Laban's frown deepened, remembering the blood-soaked tunic and the smear across the floor of Siann's lodge. "There was so much blood, Maskim."

Shoving Laban out of the way with the end of her willow cane, Iskine clumped into the lodge, muttering about her stupid hatchling. Siann lay on a healer's bed, her face pale and her arm still covered in blood.

"What's going on?" Iskine asked Taycha, one of the younger healers. Taycha flipped her long braid behind her and gestured at Siann's unconscious form. "We've put a poultice on the wound to close it, Mother Inkiss," she said, her soft voice almost inaudible, even in the quiet of the lodge. "I was just going to clean her arm, but I wasn't sure if it would be safe because of this." With a careful movement, Taycha opened Siann's clenched fist, pointing at the lightning-scorched palm. The image of the Tiamat was darker, almost as though dyed by the blood that had poured down her arm.

"Clean off the arm and hand, just avoid the mark if you can," Inkiss ordered. "Until we know what the silly child was trying to do, we can't tell if it's safe to touch."

§

"Laban!" Siann woke up with a screech, bolting upright and then stopping suddenly when she didn't recognize her own lodge.

"Taycha," she called, spotting the willowy young woman who knelt mixing herbs at the fire behind her. "I need Laban. Please, hurry."

"Now, calm down, Siann," Taycha said softly. "You've slept all day, you need to go slowly."

"No!" Siann almost screamed. "It's almost too late. You have to find Laban. Now!"

The noise must have carried beyond the healers' hut because Laban and a very out-of-breath Ren appeared not a moment later. "Now, Siann," Laban started, his face looking stern.

"No lectures," Siann insisted. "There isn't time. The Utlaak are coming!"

"What?" Ren's hand went instinctively to the bump at her waist, protecting the child she carried. "Siann, how do you know this?"

"So..." Laban rubbed his chin thoughtfully, tugging on the wispy moustache he was trying to grow. "Is this what you were using the ritual to see?"

Siann nodded, her face a bit red. "I know it was foolish to try and force the powers to speak. But something was coming—the Lifebinder was pulsing, but I didn't understand why."

"But to take such a risk, why didn't you come and find me, young one?" Laban's tone put Siann instantly on the defensive.

"Because, this is my power to bear. My burden." Shoulders thrust back, chin jutting forward, Siann was the image of defiance and strength. The fact that her face was as pale as snow, and her hands shook uncontrollably took nothing away from the fire in her eyes. "I am not a child, Laban!"

"No," said Ren, stepping carefully in between the two obstinate combatants. "You are a valuable member of this village, and one Laban feels responsible for." Her hand reached out to touch her mate's arm gently. "Too responsible at times." She smiled at Laban gently to take the sting from her remarks. "But, Siann," her voice dropped a bit, taking on a lecturing tone that Siann resented immediately, "while this is your responsibility, the whole camp is his. He needs to know. What did you discover?"

Hmph. Siann breathed out forcefully, trying to decide if being irate would gain anything further at this point. Deciding that it just made her look childish, she dropped the arguments and started to explain.

"I woke up knowing that something was wrong. The Lifebinder was trying to warn me, but I didn't know why." Siann looked at her blood-drenched arm and shivered. "I thought that blood might make the Lifebinder speak. It worked." She bent her arm, wincing as the movement pulled on the tightly bandaged wound. "Worked too well," she admitted. "When the blood hit the crystal, things went crazy. I thought I was burning. The Lifebinder and the Thunderstones were both shouting." Siann rubbed her hand over her aching brow, succeeding in smearing blood across her face. "All I could hear was Danger, Utlaak, and I saw the new moon." Her voice dropped to a whisper. "The attack on Maskwatin was a trick," she said, her voice frightening Laban with its echoes of the ancient powers within her. "They pulled the warriors out and they mean to attack us before they can return."

§

The entire village stood around the campfire that night. Every man, woman, and child stared at Laban, eyes wide with fear as he spoke the words they'd dreaded for moons. "They have found us, my children." His grey eyes searched the silent crowd, trying to hear the thoughts racing behind the People's silence. The children seemed the least concerned, most were fidgeting and bored at all the grown-up talk roiling around them. They were just happy for the excuse to be up late, to sit with their parents and stay out of Green Lodge for a few more hours.

Their parents were not nearly so calm, their silence was filled with worried glances and lowered voices which spoke of their fear.

Ren lumbered to stand beside her mate at the campfire and addressed the crowd. "I am not a shaman." She glanced at Laban teasingly. "I don't know how to speak like one in flying words and flashes of lightning. I am a warrior and I speak with my daggers and my heart." Placing a hand protectively over the gentle swell of her abdomen, pressing her lips into a determined line, she continued, "We are the warriors, we are the shamans, we are the People. Every single one of us knew this was coming. We knew the Utlaak were looking for Esquialt."

Pacing around the fire, Ren's gaze rested on those whom she knew supported Iamaat.

"Some would say"—she pinned the discontented adults with glances as sharp as an emerald spear—"that we have encouraged this attack by breaking with tradition." Her eyes snapped in the firelight, shoulders straight, everything about her shouting defiance. "That is air-headed. The people have lived with the Utlaak attacks since our earliest memories. They always come. They always have." Finally, she allowed her gaze to focus on Iamaat, who stood outside the firelight, obviously separating herself from the other Elders. "It does not matter." She spoke directly to the Green Mother, her sharp features narrowed and accusatory. "Why they come matters no more than why it snows in winter or why the Elder Stars shine at night. They come. We must prepare."

"But we cannot fight," Miah one of the younger mothers spoke up from her place with the children. She was the daughter of Hahnee, and had inherited not only his girth but his soft heart and gentle nature. "D'vhan is gone, and so are most of the warriors—we cannot fight."

"You are right," Laban said, nodding in Miah's direction. "Until D'vhan returns we are not only outnumbered, but in a position where most of our fighters are either too young"—he gestured towards the young hawks that had come during the Kit'na ceremony in the spring—"or for other reasons unable." With a rueful glance he waved at Ren, knowing that his mate would not ever consider herself unable. "Our best option is to retreat," he concluded, "to move to safer ground until D'vhan returns and then make a plan for dealing with this threat once and for all."

Iamaat coughed loudly, making it obvious that she had other ideas of the best way to safeguard the people.

"I know you disagree, Iamaat," Laban said, "but there is no time for discussion now. We will move. Your only choice is to move with us, or to stay here and hope the Utlaak walk past you."

Laban raised his staff and slammed it into the dry earth before the campfire. Lightning shot from the tip of the staff, crackling through the night and reflecting from the beads woven into his hair and ceremonial cape.

"Prepare," he said in a voice that held echoes of power. "The attack on Maskwatin was a diversion to pull the warriors out of camp. We believe that the attack may come with the next new moon, three days from now." Walking around the campfire, looking each person in the eyes as he passed them, Laban ordered, "Take only what you cannot leave behind. Each person must carry their own belongings and enough food supplies for three days. We will go to the highlands and camp on the plains for a hand of days, then send a runner back to inspect Esquialt for damage."

A wave of relief seemed to surge through the gathered adults, going over the heads of the young ones, many of whom were leaning sleepily against their parents. They had a thing to do, actions to fight back the fear. Even though leaving Esqualt unprepared would be hard, it was harder to sit like a target waiting for the arrow to strike.

"I object!" Iamaat, of course. Laban huffed. *Would that woman please just fall into the Watcher's Void and be done!* "We simply draw the Utlaak behind us," she said, pushing her way through the watching villagers and ending up face-to-face with Laban. Her dark complexion was ruddy with anger, eyes hard and black. "You will kill the village because you refuse to sacrifice one person."

Laban straightened up, the Staff of Lightning shooting red sparks into the air as though it echoed the man himself. "We are past that decision, Iamaat," he said in a voice so cold that many of the villagers took an involuntary step backward. "Do you think that the Utlaak will turn aside because Siann leaves? Do you think that they will go back to their tunnels because they cannot find her?" He glanced towards the healers' lodge where Siann watched the proceedings from an open side-flap. She was still too weak to stand unassisted but had demanded that she be a part of this meeting.

"Leaves?" Her voice was weak and her face as pale as the moonlight. Siann swung her legs to the side of the healer's bed and tried to sit up. "Why would I leave?" Her gaze shifted from one Elder to another until it finally settled on Iamaat's angry face. "Mother Iamaat, why would you want me to go?"

Iamaat's dark eyes didn't flinch as they swept over the young shaman, flicked around the assembled villagers, gauging her audience, and straightened her shoulders. "You are dangerous, Siann," she said in a voice that held no warmth or compassion. "This threat to the village comes because of you, and only you can remove it."

"Child," Laban moved towards the hut, hand outstretched. "Don't listen to this. Mother Iamaat doesn't..."

"Don't condescend to the girl, Laban," Iamaat interrupted, taking slow steps until she stood looming over Siann's seated form. "She brought this *thing* to the village, now the Utlaak are coming to find it."

"Iamaat," she said, struggling to get to her feet, to meet Iamaat on level ground. Her legs were still too weak. If Taycha had not been at her side when her knees buckled, she would have been on the floor instead of being eased back onto the bed. "What in the Void are you talking about? There is no reason the Utlaak would be looking for me!"

"Scorch you," Iamaat's voice was venomous, her black eyes holding nothing of the warm, caring Mother of Siann's childhood. "You deny bringing that *thing*"—her pudgy hand reached towards the pouch where the Lifebinder hung around Siann's neck—"to our village?"

"Siann's crystal has saved us," Laban interjected. "It warned Siann of the attack five cycles ago. Without that warning we would have been lost."

"Without that crystal the attack would never have happened," Iamaat insisted, her eyes never leaving Siann's face. "You know that, Laban, all the Elders know."

"Know?" Siann said. "Exactly what do you know about me that I do not, Salixt?"

"Siann..." Laban's voice was calm, reasonable and exactly what Siann didn't want to hear.

"No," she yelled, surprising the nearest villagers with the strength of her voice. "I'm not some kind of freakish thing that you can use when it suits you and treat like a child the rest of the time!" Fire leaped behind Siann's eyes. "I am a shaman. I will not be treated like a child while you interfere in my life."

From just outside the campfire's light a snort of ironic laughter shattered the silence caused by Siann's outburst. "You are caught, my mate. As I warned you would be." Ren's eyes twinkled as she entered the firelight. "Siann is not one to be told to go here or go there like a green feather. She is the child of a Salixt. In her hands she holds the powers of the Thunderstones and the Lifebinder Crystal. Do you think the Elder Stars would pick a weak and biddable vessel for such a task?"

"This has nothing to do with the Elder Stars," Iamaat raved, "Siann has proven herself to be a she-wolf hungry for power. That is why she could not just leave the crystal behind."

If Siann's face could lose any more colour, it did at that accusation. She stared up at Iamaat in disbelief, her wounded eyes flashing from their normal soft brown to the white and red of her power.

"Silence, viper." Ren's cold voice was as cold and lethal as the dagger she held in her hand. "You know Siann, have known her all her life. Nothing speaks here but your own twisted fears and thwarted ambition." A rustle ran through the crowd at her words. People turned to their neighbours with muted whispers, while several of those who stood closest to where Siann and Iamaat faced each other tried to back away. Neither woman looked safe at the moment.

"Enough," Laban said, desperately trying to bring calm to the situation. He turned back to the frozen tableau at the entrance to the healers' tent. Siann and Iamaat hadn't moved. One glared up, the other down. Hatred filled Iamaat's eyes, while Siann's gaze spoke of betrayal and anger.

"Listen," Laban tried again. "There is evidence that the Utlaak are looking for the Lifebinder. This is true." Iamaat humphed. "But," he continued, moving to stand beside the healer's bed where Siann was sitting. "Hear me, Siann. The Utlaak have been attacking the villages for generations beyond count. The Stars alone know why they come. It is not your fault!"

"If you say I must go..." Siann offered, looking at Laban and pointedly not at Iamaat. "I will," she said, trying to stand up and managing it for a wobbly second until she fell back onto the furs with a whuff, knocking the wind out of herself in the process. "But I can tell you this," she said breathily, "I have seen them, they are coming." One hand convulsively grasped the pouch holding the Lifebinder. "Yes," she said, her voice firming up a little as the power of the crystal pulsed through her. "You tell me that they seek the crystal. But think, all of you. Esquialt is the oldest village of the People. Three times we have thrown back an Utlaak attack either by ourselves or with the assistance of the Waki'tani." The bright colour in her face faded as she released her convulsive grip on the crystal and once again became just Siann—pale, weak, mortal. "Do you honestly believe they will just walk past you if I am not here?"

Heads nodded all through the crowd. They had grown up hearing the stories and songs about the battles with the Utlaak. No one honestly believed that, given a chance to destroy their village, the horde would turn back.

"We are done," Laban said, lowering his staff and retreating into his calm, gentle persona. "Esquialt, we are leaving. Spend this night getting your families prepared, tomorrow we will go.. Prepare to go, or to stay. There are no other options." Wrapping his arm around Ren, who was busy throwing daggers at Iamaat from her eyes, Laban left the fire circle and they passed into Grey Lodge. There was a lot to do.

Twenty-Seven

<<<Siann>>>

Be ready to move, Laban had said, it was not as simple as it sounded. But by the middle of the next day we were ready to move the camp, hoping to keep one step ahead of the Utlaak force that was dogging our steps. It hurt my heart to see the green feathers come out of their lodge, faces much too stoic for their age. They didn't play anymore or chase the Elders around begging for stories. They woke up, gathered their little packs and started tearing down the lodge. They were our children, our future, and it didn't look good.

Laban came out of his lodge, Ren waddling beside him. He glanced at me as they started walking over to the cooking fire and I nodded sadly. They were still coming. The Lifebinder crystal hung in its leather pouch around my neck. It vibrated every time the Utlaak came close. For the past two days it had vibrated constantly.

When half our fighters left to aid Pey't's home village of Maskwatin, three days ago, we had thought it nothing unusual. There had been a runner in the night. They were under attack. D'vhan put together a scouting team and left within hours. With D'vhan, Pey't, Sawiea and yes, even the annoying hatchling out of camp we had been an easy target.

Maybe today D'vhan and the rest of the warriors would return, I thought. *They had to come back soon.*

Laban's plan was to move the village towards the high plains. Every day we would walk from dawn through the morning hours, set up camp, and try to hunt or gather berries.

I know that he's delaying just hoping to get the warriors back into camp, hoping that with D'vhan and the warriors we could find a way to turn back the horde and return to our home. *Home. That word means something different to me now.* As a child, home had been Maskim, the Grey Lodge, my father's voice singing around the campfire. Those things were gone now and in its place was a darker, colder world where I didn't seem to belong.

Several of the camp dogs were running around wearing small harnesses. When we were ready to move, they would be fastened to frames of birch and pine and would help to pull loads of dried food as well as the heavier sacred items from Grey and Green Lodge. Titch, the three-legged mongrel, was barking and bossing the other dogs around, obviously convinced that he was in charge of this part of the move and sure we were doing it wrong.

Shaking my head to get rid of the dreary thoughts, I picked up my pack and walked carefully over to Grey Lodge. The shamans had been there all morning, packing the sacred scrolls and rolling the breakable eagle statues in thick bull hides.

"No, Siann." Taycha grabbed my arm, trying to pull me back to the healers' lodge. "You can't carry yet, you're still too weak."

My stomach tightened up at her words. Iamaat was already working her way around the camp, and my mind was weaving horrors about the stories she was spreading. I didn't cry, it would help if I could, but tears would be too easy. Instead the serpents in my heart hissed over and over, telling me all the things I could do to silence her. The crystal pulsed with my pain, picking up my mood and amplifying it until my mind was filled with images of blood and I felt my eyes burning.

Feigning weakness, I put my sleeve over my face and hobbled back to the healers' lodge. "Taycha, I need to talk with Laban," I said. "Can you find him or Ren for me, please?" Once she was gone and the lodge was quiet, it was safe to drop my arm. My eyes burned, and I knew that anyone who looked at me would see blood red in their depths.

Throwing myself on the only pile of furs still not packed, I raged. Anger burned through me until even my hair felt charged with it. Iamaat, the Green Mother, the Mother of my village, the one who had taught me as a child, was telling anyone who would listen that I was the cause of this disaster and that I should be sacrificed, turned out alone in front of the Utlaak horde to die at their hands.

The rage seemed to last forever, but eventually I felt my eyes settle back to their normal colour and my breathing steadied. Then the shaking started. The crystal had drained every scrap of energy that I had and left me feeling cold, so very cold.

There was nothing to say when Laban and Ren walked in a few moments later. Laban took one look at my eyes, red-rimmed with tears, and pulled me against his chest, wrapping me in gentle arms of steel.

"You belong here, Siann," he said. "You are not evil. You are not a changeling or a spirit from the Walker's world, no matter what that old viper says." I thought that I had cried all the tears my heart could hold. I was wrong. His words broke the ice that had settled around my heart. "I know, little one," he said, his hand running over my messy hair comfortingly as I sobbed convulsively into his shoulder. "It hurts, and you must allow the hurt to pass through so that you can heal."

Reaching out to put a long finger under my chin, Ren tilted my head out of her mate's shoulder until I was looking into her sad green eyes. "Hear me, Siann," she said solemnly. "I feel the pain, I know what it's like to have those who were sworn to guard and teach you turn away. After my parents walked on the Road, I was raised by several different Mothers, none of them were happy to have responsibility for a green feather that they couldn't send home at day's end." Her eyes grew distant and her grip on my chin was almost painful. "Ren, they called me, and Ren I became. But my name was Loren as a child. In the language of my village Ren means nothing. I was nothing, no one, not worthy of praise or mention."

Laban's hand touched his mate's gently, his eyes shimmering with tears that Ren could never cry. She smiled softly at him, then switched her spear-eyed focus back to me.

"You are Siann dal Matra, Grey Daughter of Esquialt. You hold the Lifebinder, you have been marked by the Thunderstones and have spoken with the voice of the Elder Stars." The pitch of Ren's voice dropped lower and lower as she spoke, her words holding an intensity that held me motionless. "None of those things matter. None of them! What matters is who you are inside. You are a strong person, one who is finding a way to Walk between all these responsibilities with grace. You are someone who cares for the People, loves your family, and finds joy in the mysteries of the world." The words shook my spirit, soaking in until the tearing pain of Iamaat's betrayal started to fade, at least a little. "This is the person the village needs. Leave behind the rage, let it rest on the heads of those who deserve it. This is who you are."

She didn't hug me, just turned and, grabbing Laban's hand, walked out of the lodge. Leaving me washed clean.

§

We walked out of Esquialt in mid-afternoon, a slow spread-out caravan winding towards the pass into the plains. At the last rise before we entered the forest I turned back. Something told me that if we ever returned to Esquialt, it would be to a very different village than the one I was leaving behind.

Walking beside Napaay, I listened to Vargas and Selah encourage the green feathers, singing songs and setting little contests to keep them moving along the trail. This was the Green Lodge I remembered, full of laughter and gentle lessons.

My heart warmed as I noticed Selah stopping at each rest break to spend a moment with one of the villagers that Iamaat had spoken to. Carefully undoing the poisonous lies that she had been spreading about me. It seemed to be working, the cold stabbing glances I had felt in my back since Esquialt seemed to lessen with every rest stop.

"When are we stopping, Siann?" Napaay said. "My feet are starting to hurt."

"Soon, Gooshoo," I reassured him, making him laugh at the old nickname. "We don't want to get too tired today. Tomorrow will be just as long."

His face fell. "We move again tomorrow?" he said. "Then how will D'vhan ever find us?"

A good question, I thought, and one I couldn't give a good answer for. Scanning up the trail for Laban and

Ren, I pushed forward and caught up with them at the head of the group.

"A question, Laban," I asked. "Napaay was just asking me how D'vhan and the warriors will find us, and I realized that I didn't know how I should answer him."

Laban's eyes crinkled in amusement and he gestured to either side of the trail. Only I didn't know what I was supposed to see there. A few of the younger men were scouting the edges of the forest, cutting wood with their daggers and hauling it along for kindling.

"Watch young K'tan," he said, pointing at the newest recruit to Red Lodge, who was randomly darting in and out of the bushes.

"So?" I was confused. He seemed to be doing nothing but running a few steps off the trail and running back. "Even though he's the youngest in Red Lodge, isn't there something more helpful he could do?"

"Ahh..." Laban's mouth twitched mischievously. "But K'tan is doing the most important job there is. Every time he runs into the brush, he fastens a raven's feather on one of the trees along the trail. You think that D'vhan would miss that? Or even if he did, would Y'keta?"

"You'd do better to use a turkey feather if you want Y'keta to see it," I snarked. It felt good to have something normal to complain about and complaining about that shellhead was about as normal as my life got.

A wave of quiet laughter seemed to spread through the caravan as I heard my comment being passed from person to person towards the back of the line. I hadn't thought that anyone was listening when I said it, but I suppose it was worth the embarrassment to hear the release of tension.

Still, I couldn't help feeling that there would be trouble if the warriors didn't come soon. The vibrations of the Lifebinder in its pouch against my chest didn't lessen or stop. We were still not safe.

Twenty-Eight

D'vhan led the tired group into Esquialt at moonrise. It had been a long two-day march for the tired warriors and longer for the children and the traumatized survivors of Maskwatin.

D'vhan and Y'keta shared a glance as they approached the cold campfire. There had been no watcher on the path to the village. There was no fire in the central camp, the fire stones and charred logs were cold. Something was dramatically wrong.

"Sun of Riad," Dahi cursed when they got close enough to see the trampled remains of the village. "Look at the mess, D'vhan." Piles of ruined belongings were scattered around the main campsite. The smaller lodges had been torn down completely. Only the three permanent Lodges remained standing, although their hide walls had been slashed open.

"Utlaak." D'vhan said, his dark eyes bleak as he looked around the village that had been his home for so long. "Hail Esquialt," he called out the ceremonial greeting, wondering if people were hiding as they had been in Maskwatin. "We come from the Road."

Silence answered.

D'vhan's frown deepened. The call of a hunting bird broke the heavy silence as a single, black shape swooped out of the darkness, flew across the camp and disappeared between the shadows of the trees. "What in the Void happened here?" D'vhan cursed under his breath. "I can't see any sign of bodies or anything that would show a fight, but the Void-cursed grubs have obviously been here!" He kicked angrily at the rubble that the Utlaak had thrown into the middle of the clearing.

"Check all the lodges," he barked, cursing under his breath. "I'll check Red Lodge. They were looking for something. We need to know what they found."

Sawiea ran to the Green Lodge and ducked inside. The emptiness seemed almost physical—nothing moved, nothing whispered. The scrolls that normally hung against the walls were gone as were the berry-picking sacks and the small traps that the Greens used when they learned to hunt. But some things remained. The floor of the lodge was littered with the broken remains of little handmade dolls and drums that the children used in play, someone's rock collection, a pile of raven feathers, all the precious childhood treasures that would never willingly be left behind.

Ducking out of the lodge, she rejoined the tired group around the fire. "Ammarie," she said, addressing the silver-haired woman who had been one of the surviving Mothers from Maskwatin, "take your little ones to Green Lodge, it's has been ransacked, but at least it will be warm once a fire is made for them."

Nodding, Ammarie urged her exhausted charges across the camp and into Green Lodge. A quick glance flashed from Sawiea to Kalita. Sawiea nodded. Two of Maskwatin's warriors grabbed tinder and ducked into the Green Lodge to start a fire for the little ones. The others arranged themselves around the lodge and the trails into the camp. There was no sign of the Utlaak still being in the area, but they did not need any more surprises.

When D'vhan stepped out of Red Lodge, the expression on his face made Sawiea laugh. It wasn't often that the older warrior was confused, but if his face was telling the truth, D'vhan didn't know what to think.

"D'vhan?" Y'keta said carefully, "Is all well in the lodge?"

Looking at Y'keta's square face, and hearing the note of worry in his voice, D'vhan's heart finally settled on an emotion and it was joy. Eyes running with tears, breath coming in gasps, he collapsed onto the hard-packed dirt around the campfire and shook with silent laughter.

"Sawiea," he said when he could speak again. "What did you find in the Green Lodge?"

"A mess," she answered. "Toys, clothes, and—"

"A pile of feathers?" he interrupted. "Raven feathers?"

Sawiea nodded, puzzled.

"In Grey as well, D'vhan," Pey't interrupted, ducking out from under the flap of Grey Lodge. "Not much in there that wasn't ruined, but feathers in the middle of the lodge, on a ceremonial hide."

"So, cub," D'vhan said, turning to look at Y'keta. "How do we solve this mystery? What reason would there be to have feathers piled in all the lodges? It's too odd to be accidental."

"How the Stars should I know?" Y'keta complained. D'vhan was using that voice again, the lecturing one that made his crest rise and took his temper with it.

"Learn, cub!" D'vhan said. "Think! The Utlaak have been here but would they have paid attention to feathers?" he continued thoughtfully. "Hmm, did anyone check Siann's lodge?"

"Why?" Y'keta's voice was more nasal than usual, fighting the impulse to run to Siann's small lodge and make sure she was gone too.

"Because, hatchling," D'vhan said as he shook his head, his growly voice irritated, "she has the Lifebinder Crystal and that is what the Void-cursed Utlaak are looking for."

Y'keta's face went from pale to bright red with embarrassment. How could he have forgotten. Running towards Siann's small home behind Grey

Lodge, he jumped over the remains of the flap and let his eyes change. Sweeping the small family area with his augmented eyes, he immediately saw the pile of raven feathers under the rubble piled in the middle of the floor. Something grey and rigid peeked out from under the black fluff. Carefully moving the feathers aside, he gasped when he saw the parchment that D'vhan had found at the Utlaak camp that winter.

Picking the parchment up from where it had been buried, Y'keta carried it out to where D'vhan was standing trying to start a fire.

"Let me, old crow," Y'keta said, handing the parchment to D'vhan and pushing him away from the fire. "You're useless at this." A few carefully placed sticks and a muttered *"Tlegu"* soon had the fire started. Kneeling beside the crackling fire, feeding it with the small twigs and dried moss that were stacked around the pit, Y'keta glanced over his shoulder towards D'vhan.

"So, oh great and wise one," he teased. "What am I—a lowly cub—missing?"

Red flowers blossomed in D'vhan's tanned cheeks when Dahi hissed in amusement. Y'keta glanced from the older warrior to the handsome new one. *Isn't that interesting,* he thought. *Could D'vhan be blushing?*

Whatever the reason, D'vhan was back to his laughing self as he reached over to take a playful swat at Y'keta's head. "Such respect for your Elders," he said, shaking his head in disappointment. "I fear for our People when this generation is gone."

"Have done, old man," Sawiea said, threatening him with the top end of her bow. "Either get on with it, or I will tell everyone here all the stories of just how silly an old crow can be."

Holding his hands up, pleading for peace, D'vhan turned to the gathered warriors from both villages. "I'm really disappointed that one of you didn't figure it out," he said. "It's so obvious. The People were obviously warned about the attack. If they had been here, we would have found bodies." His face turned an odd shade of green at the thought of what they almost walked into. "Where were the raven feathers?" His voice had slipped into that teaching tone again, leading them on until they figured it out themselves.

"D'vhan!" Sawiea tapped his head sternly with Tonki's sharp end. "We aren't green feathers, just say it."

Eyes rolling, D'vhan shrugged and grabbed a stick to draw on the hard-packed earth beside the camp. "We found feathers in Red, Green, Grey, and Siann's lodge. Connect those places and what do you see?" The drawing that he had scratched on the floor formed the rough shape of a triangle, with Siann's lodge being the only one left outside of its shape. When he connected her lodge to the outline, suddenly it was clear, there in front of them was an arrow pointing north, towards the high plains.

"So, they've moved to the plains?" One of the warriors from Maskwatin asked, "But why? It's not time for the hunt."

"The parchment Y'keta found explains that. We know that the Utlaak are hunting for Siann's crystal." The warriors from Maskwatin looked confused, but the others nodded solemnly. "Laban had that parchment, he would never leave it behind without a reason. So, what is he trying to tell us?"

Y'keta closed his eyes, breathed in, thought about snowstorms, feather-rot, anything to push away the need to scream at D'vhan's constant lecturing. When he felt certain that his eyes would be normal when he opened them, he looked up and caught D'vhan looking at him.

The old demon had nothing but mischief dancing in his eyes. He was doing this deliberately. *You sharding, shellheaded...* Y'keta's thoughts finally slowed down enough for him to hear the echo of Siann's spirit in his mind. Forget Laban, why would she leave the parchment? Suddenly he caught up with D'vhan and veered into his own language, cursing vehemently. "Scorch her!" he finally said. "Why does it always have to be her!"

"Are you all right, hatchling?" Sawiea asked, looking at the red flush colouring Y'keta's face. "Curse who? For what?"

"Siann," he said angrily. "They came looking for her, the crystal warned her, and the village moved."

Slow applause came from where D'vhan sat on the floor near the campfire, smiling sarcastically. "Started to actually listen, did you?"

"Quiet, old crow," Y'keta grumbled. "So, they headed towards the High Plains because Siann's crystal said the Utlaak were coming. It would make sense, the camps there are kept supplied and easily defended. Could that be why so many survived at Maskwatin? It was a diversion?"

"I think so, hatchling," D'vhan said. "Settle the children down for the night tonight. They can't keep going with no sleep and no plan. I want everyone except Y'keta, Dahi, Coen and myself on guard. The four of us will sleep for a few hours and then try to catch up to Laban and bring the village back here." D'vhan pointed at Sawiea and Kalita, his eyes grim in the firelight. "I don't think that the Utlaak will return," he said, "but take no chances! I leave the children in your care." His hand came away muddy from unconsciously tugging on the dirty red braids. "I'm going to the lake," he said. "I need a few hours rest before we find our lost village, and I will feel better doing it if I'm at least clean!"

D'vhan headed off into the dusk, not noticing the tall, tattooed shadow that followed, unobserved, until D'vhan, his bath completed, returned safely to camp.

Twenty-Nine

The people had been travelling for three long slow days. *We're vulnerable*, Ren thought. *Spread out across the high pass like a confused herd of kaal just waiting to be picked off by the kuniak.* She watched from the rear of the column as the green feathers, with Iamaat, who had changed her mind about staying when she saw that no one else was staying behind.

"Not so brave when she's left alone in the village, is she?" Ren muttered under her breath.

"What, Ren?" young Coen, who had been assigned to walk with her today, asked politely.

It was irritating, really, she thought, giving the youngster an undeserved glare, *the way Laban thought a warrior needed to walk with her all the time. I'm neither ill nor incapable!*

They had just reached the first camp on the high plains. Away from the treeline, the sky opened in all directions and the wind in the high grass whispered to her of a million places an enemy could hide.

Dropping back from his position with the other shamans to join her where she stood surveying the camp, Laban asked, "Are you well, little hawk?" and rested a gentle hand on her stomach. Ren swatted his hand away reflexively, then touched his cheek in apology.

"I am well, my mate," she said, "just tired from the travelling and from being treated like a delicate piece of pottery."

Laban shrugged, well past the point where his volatile mate could intimidate him. "You are delicate," he said, watching her eyes darken to forest green. "Fragile, in fact." The forest green took on an icy sheen. "I have to take care of you, my flower."

Laban took a half step backwards as he spoke, anticipating the jab to his ribs that Ren threw a heartbeat later.

"Ren," he continued, his eyes more solemn than Ren expected from such a playful moment. "I took an oath before the Elder Stars to value you, to carry your heart within me as you carry our child within you. Whether you need me or not, I will always protect you."

Ren stopped so abruptly that Laban collided with her, hands automatically coming up to make sure she didn't fall. *What can I say to that?* she thought. *Stars, how will I ever deserve this man?*

Wrapping her in a fleeting embrace, Laban stepped away and rubbed gently at the frown lines between her eyes with his thumb. "You look like me," he said, giving her a gentle push down the trail. "Stop thinking and walk."

By the time Ren caught up with the front of the column, they had already started to set up camp. As always, the dog sleds were unpacked first, releasing the tired hounds to run wild with Titch, getting underfoot and amusing the smallest children.

The warriors threw hides around the makeshift lodgepoles and before Hahnee had a fire going for the mid-day meal they had hauled water from the nearby river and built the temporary lodge that would house the village for the night.

Laban sat with Hahnee in the late summer sunshine, exchanging greetings with every member of the village as they came up to get their food. It was only grain and dried meat, but it tasted good when eaten under the open sky and with friends.

One of the green feathers came up with a bowl and asked for Iamaat's meal. Laban ruffled the youngster's hair and made jokes while Hahnee filled the bowl. "Take this to Mother Iamaat," Laban said, handing the porridge to the young boy. "But tell her that she needs to come and get her own dish at lastmeal." With a backward glance the green feather scuttled off. No one really thought that he'd give the temperamental Iamaat Laban's message.

Thirty

The first thing Siann heard was screaming. From where she slept in the makeshift lodge, she could see the little ones hiding behind the sacks of food, their large eyes panicked. The scaly grey shapes that filled the campsite made her skin crawl and the vibrations from the Lifebinder, in its pouch around her neck, were strong enough to make her teeth ache. So many of them. The last time there had been so many, her mother had died.

From where she lay, she could see the adults making a desperate stand at the entrance to the lodges. Laban was swinging a bone spear, his silver hair dripping with black blood in the moonlight. Ren, standing beside him, was one of the only calm faces in that sea of fear. Calling instructions to the others, and wielding her twin daggers without conscious thought, she danced between the oncoming Utlaak the way Dahi had danced between the fires at the Spring Festival. Lethal and unafraid.

Until she slipped. A pool of black blood and the unaccustomed weight of the child she carried was all it took to send her crashing into Taycha where she stood guarding the little ones. They went down in a tangle of arms, legs, and daggers. Jumping up quickly, Taycha reached down to help Ren to her feet, and when the fallen warrior didn't move, she started yelling for Laban.

With a sweep of his spear, Laban knocked the legs out from under the three Utlaak in front of him and dove awkwardly towards where Ren lay on the floor, unmoving. "My hawk," he cried, scrambling to Ren's side, spear forgotten in his fright. "Wake up, my love!"

Taycha, the normally quiet, soft-spoken healer stood guard over Ren's unconscious form, dagger dripping with black blood. Her face frozen in a terrifying mask of fierce, protective love and bloodlust. Siann pushed away from the pile of grain sacks that she had been hiding behind and tried to crawl towards Ren.

"She didn't land on a knife," Taycha choked out, slashing at the stomach of the nearest Utlaak, forcing it to back away and allowing Siann to crawl close enough to roll Ren onto her back. "I just can't wake her up," she said, glancing worriedly at Ren's limp form.

Siann's hand hovered inches from Ren's lips, the soft puff of breath convincing her that the warrior still lived. There were others who may not be so lucky. "Stay with Ren and the children," she said to Taycha. "The People must not lose them." Taycha took an involuntary step back, then firming her shoulders, nodded at Siann, who had unknowingly used that "other" voice.

Picking up Ren's dagger, wielding it awkwardly in her left hand, Siann crawled over until she could stand up next to Laban. "Laban," she said, grabbing his shoulder and shaking him violently, her voice filled with thunderous echoes. "Ren lives. Your People are dying. Lead!"

Laban shook his head, looking for the first time in several minutes away from his fallen mate to the carnage happening outside the lodge. Several of the people of Esquialt were lying, hurt or dead, on the ground beside the wooden frames for the sleds. Titch, the faithful camp mongrel, was leading the dogs. They ran from one enemy to the next, biting and barking out their defiance. "You're doing better than I am, old man," Laban said ruefully to the hound, who looked up, his grey muzzle covered in black blood, and went on to his next target. "Fire," Laban yelled to those nearest the campfire. "Light the grasses. Flush them out of hiding!"

Varas and Selah grabbed branches from the fire and threw them into the long grass around the camp. Their faces contorting with the pain of touching the burning wood, they reached into the edge of the fire again and again until firelight surrounded the makeshift lodge.

"Don't throw towards the east. Don't block us in, we can still make for the river if we are overrun," Ren called weakly from inside the lodge.

Laban closed his eyes for a moment, giving thanks for the sound of her voice, then ran towards the campfire, waving Varas and Selah back into the lodge where the other healers were setting up a makeshift barricade as a last defence for the little ones.

Titch let out a desperate howl and dove through the smouldering long grass to the west of camp, the other dogs in the village pack charging after him. Yips and growls faded as the dogs disappeared into the smoke. Laban's heart gave up then. The dogs had been harassing the Utlaak, keeping them distracted and disorganized. Without that, the grubs could coordinate their attacks and it would be much harder to stop them.

Setting his lips in a grim line, determined if not hopeful, he glanced quickly at the lodge. Ren sat near the door, propped up against one of the barricades, dagger in one hand, other hand cradling her abdomen protectively. Laban fleetingly wondered where her other dagger was, then saw it. Selah was using it to cut bandage strips from one of the large hides they had used for the lodge walls.

One of the grubs made it to the door of the lodge, eyes fixed on where Siann sat putting salve on Varas' burned hand. Screaming unintelligibly in its own language, he started a wild rush of grey bodies, all determined to get to the young shaman. Chaos erupted.

Varas and Selah stood side by side in front of the children. Iamaat cowered amid her flock like a plump hen with her panicked chickens. No bravery or tradition now. She had thrown her green cloak over her head, hiding her eyes from the reality of the fight and the approach of grey-scaled death.

Varas glanced back at the cowering Elder, his eyes narrowed and assessing. Iamaat was the Mother of Esquialt, leader of the young people, guardian of their future. Yet there she sat, waiting for death, not caring if her charges were slaughtered.

Selah smiled reassuringly at the children. "Quiet little ones," she whispered. "Remember if you are heard, you get to scrub pots at the next meal!"

That produced an instant silence. Scrubbing pots or scraping hides was a job no one would take willingly.

"Not worth it," she said, shrugging off Iamaat's cowardice dismissively. "She may be a coward, but we know our oaths. We keep them."

They jumped as a quiet shuffle came from beyond where Varas stood at the side of the barricade. Young Ihkopi had leaped the barrier and stepped hesitantly between them. His wide expressive eyes were full of fear, but his shoulders squared, and his hand clutched a weapon that looked suspiciously like Iamaat's eating dagger.

"I have not Walked yet," he said firmly in a light tenor voice that didn't quite hide the trembling. "But my intent is to declare for Red Lodge in Esquialt." Shrugging self-deprecatingly, he added, "That is if D'vhan will have me." He spoke with a kind of certainty that only the very young, or the very wise, can express. The young because they don't know how much life can change, the wise because they know that the heart doesn't change, no matter how much circumstances do.

"You have the fire of a warrior, and he would be a shellhead not to see it." Varas clapped the scrawny boy on his shoulder, frowning when he felt the bones under his hand. *There had been no food shortage this cycle,* he thought. *Why then did the boy feel so scrawny?*

There was no time for further reassurances—the Utlaak were pressing again. The adults outside were doing everything they could to keep the front of the lodge clear, but there just weren't enough of them to guard the sides. Soon, the grey-bodied grubs were squirming their way under the temporary walls, trying to get in to where Siann moved among the injured, stitching cuts, bandaging wounds, splinting breaks, doing anything that she could to ease the suffering.

The Lifebinder burned against her chest, trying to escape its leather pouch—magnifying the fear and despair around her into an unbearable wail that pounded into Siann's mind, demanding to be released. Her hand went up to the pouch, touching it unconsciously, stroking, trying to calm the raging power that made her eyes burn and her heart afraid.

"Siann!" Selah grabbed her hand and pulled it away from the Lifebinder. "Stop, your eyes are frightening the little ones." Siann dropped to the floor, eyes closed, head slumped on her chest. She'd almost done it again, almost let that ancient power rage through her, and in front of the children. *What kind of person was she?*

Outside, Laban and the uninjured adults were fighting a losing battle to keep the Utlaak away from the main entrance. Fewer and fewer of the villagers were unhurt, many with crystal cuts and slashes that would need careful attention if they wanted to prevent the crystal rot that had almost taken Pey't's leg. Hahnee, sweat rolling down his fat face wielded the only weapon his hands could find. It was amazing how much damage the cooking cauldron did when swung with the full force of a giant man. *Clang.* The pot hit the side of an Utlaak's head, brains spattered across the clearing, making Laban gag when the gooey grey matter splashed onto his face.

Clang! A grub's foot turned to pulp as the huge pot was slammed into the floor. Squealing in anguish the mutilated invader rolled away from the fight. The other grubs made no attempt to help him, just charged forward, fixated on their orders to retrieve the crystal, with or without the shaman who wore it.

Too many, Laban thought tiredly, his shoulders slumping as hopelessness crept in where defiance should be. *There were still too many.*

Enemy and villager alike stopped and stared as with a triumphant howl the pack raced back into camp, led by Titch, who bounced back and forth on his three good legs yipping like a pup. Laban blinked, stared, and blinked again as D'vhan, Coen, Dahi and

Y'keta strode out of the treeline and into the battle, screaming defiance.

Pulling a long-handled whip from behind him, Dahi struck back and forth among the Utlaak with precision and ferocity. The tendrils at the end of his whip were braided with pieces of sharpened bone and bits of crystal that left the battlefield covered in flecks of blood and lumps of grey flesh.

D'vhan danced among the remaining grubs, knives flying, never noticing the snapping whip that seemed to appear just above the head of any Utlaak that came too close.

Crack, the whip snapped, flashes of light reflecting from the crystal shards. *Thunk*, D'vhan's knife hamstrung a grub who had taken too long to move aside. Y'keta kept pace with D'vhan grub for grub, releasing all the anxiety that he'd carried since they reached Esquialt, and noticed that Siann was missing in huge violent swings of the crystal-edged mace. Spotting one of their adults' weapons turned against them, and the other warriors shooting and slicing their way through the horde, it didn't take long for the last of the enemies to melt into the long grass and disappear.

It was a reprieve, not a victory, and one that they all knew wouldn't last. Siann was too large a prize for them to hope that the Utlaak would just give up. But hopefully it would give them time to pick up their injured and deal with their dead.

§

The last of the Utlaak bodies were piled at the north side of camp, making room for the healers to emerge and assess the wounded. There were so many crystal wounds that Selah had one of the younger mothers, Miah, helping with cleaning the shards from the wounds and handing out strips of leather to use as bandages. *They would be lucky,* she thought, trying to steady Bolin's leg as she picked the almost invisible shards from it, *not to end up with several cases of crystal rot.*

The warriors stood talking with Laban near the edge of camp. They spoke in hushed tones, Laban throwing frequent, almost furtive, glances towards the lodge where Inkiss sat with a pale and shaken Ren.

"How long do you think we have, Salixt?" Dahi's voice sounded thin and weary. They had travelled at top speed for a full day to get to the battle.

"The Eye will still be hidden tomorrow night," Laban replied. "They will come again." Laban looked around worriedly at the tired villagers. Even old Titch was bleeding from tonight's battle, it looked like the edge of a crystal mace had torn part of his ear away. "If we can hold out for one more night, the moon should be rising. They attacked Maskwatin under a waning moon, though. So, shards, I don't know."

D'vhan looked up at the night sky, visible now that the smoke from the grass fires had drifted away. He advised, "For now, we need to get rid of the filth." He gestured to the heap of Utlaak corpses just outside the main camp. "And decide how to get the people back to Esquialt."

"You're right." Laban sighed. "The People are wounded and tired, too weak to stay in the open. At least in Esquialt we have the other warriors, and the people from Maskwatin."

D'vhan nodded. "They have warriors with them, as well as Mothers for the children, and healers for the wounded." Black eyes looked into silver. "They will not stop," D'vhan said. "They cannot."

Rubbing between his eyes, where Ren said that frown lines were settling, Laban nodded. "As we discussed in council," he said, then simply added, "when?"

D'vhan took a deep breath, assessing the night, the enemy, and the argument to come. "I'll wait until sunrise he said. "We need one good sleep, then we can prepare the People for the journey back. Then I'll do battle with Siann if I must."

Thirty-One

<<<Siann>>>

"I will not!" My voice sounded childish and petulant, even to myself. "There are injured warriors here—we need all our healers. I won't run away and be safe when the People are being slaughtered!" I glared at D'vhan. The old crow glared back, his eyes calm, clear, unflinching. My shoulders jerked back, and my lips twitched in anger. They wanted me to slink out of the battle like a coward. This was all my fault and they wanted me to run like a child!

"They are looking for the Lifebinder," he said. "That means they are looking for you. They know the stone you carry, and the power it holds. I believe it could make the difference in this war." D'vhan's hand swept around the makeshift campsite. The smoke from the burning grass hung like fog in the air, opening randomly to reveal the warriors locked in combat with the grey forms of the Utlaak. They had attacked every night since D'vhan and the warriors from Esquialt had caught up with us. Each day we had moved, trying to follow the river so that we would at least have water. We had set up new camps and hunted what food we could find on the run. The children were hungry, the adults were tired, so many were injured, and now D'vhan wanted me to leave?

I sensed movement on my left and whuffed violently as a solid shoulder crashed into my stomach. "Her pride won't let her listen," Y'keta said as he dropped me unceremoniously into the waiting boat. "She feels responsible for the injuries and thinks she's failing by staying safe." The earthy smell of birchbark and pitch made my nose twitch. The boat rocked wildly. A pair of trail shoes appeared in front of me and someone behind me shoved my shoulder ungently, pushing me back down when I tried to sit up. We started moving. I could feel the roll and sway of the water around me and the bottom of the boat, where my face had been so rudely shoved, was getting colder.

After what seemed like an age of rocking and bumping a hand finally reached down and helped me sit cross-legged on the bottom of the boat. I tried to lift myself up onto the raised seat only to run into that shoving hand again.

"Stay down," the person behind me hissed. I turned around and found myself staring at Dahi, his amethyst eyes disapproving. "Now that you are safe the warriors will take small parties of villagers in separate directions and fade into the night. Stop acting like a child who plays at being a grown-up. Start being one!"

Jerking my shoulder out from under his grip I settled back, feeling the cold coming from where my damp legs stretched along the bottom of the boat, and looked around. It was a new moon night, and when the Eye of the Watcher was closed the gods didn't see or care what we did. We floated silently down the river, not even paddling, just allowing the water to pull us along. The silver water seemed deceptively placid in the darkness. The banks rose on either side of us, dark and looming.

Suddenly Y'keta hissed from his position at the front of the boat. The gentle stream of water that we had been floating down so lazily was transforming itself. Where the river narrowed, it was quickly becoming foaming rapids. Steep banks of rock tossed the water back in and upon itself, causing eddies and currents that swept our boat hopelessly out of the calm midstream passage and into a cauldron of silver magma.

"Everyone get down and hold on," D'vhan yelled, his words swallowed up by the roar of the rapids. Dahi pushed me down into the boat and spread his body over mine. His eyes wide in the noisy dark. We slammed from rock to rock as we careened towards a bend in the river. From where I lay in the bottom of the boat I could see caves in the cliff face above me, and now and then even flickers of what might have been fires. It had been hundreds of cycles since anyone lived in those caves and I wondered who might be in there now.

Finally, we slowed down as the boats drifted in to calmer waters past the canyon.

Feeling Dahi climb back onto his seat and hearing the splash of paddles I slowly shuffled back into a sitting position. "Are we out of there?"

"Out of the canyon," D'vhan said, "but not out of danger. Dahi, look for a landing spot on the west bank. We're too exposed here."

Pulling hard against the current, Dahi and Y'keta managed to turn the small boat into the bank opposite the overhanging caves. Sawiea climbed out and disappeared into the gloom. The stillness of the night forest was broken a few moments later when her sharp whistle gave them the all-clear to climb onto the muddy riverbank and start hauling the supplies onto the shore.

D'vhan and Dahi stepped into the water and pushed the small craft back into the current. I watched unbelieving as they just let it drift away.

With a disgusted thud, I flopped down in the dirt. I didn't care if they expected me to help, there was just no way I was going to. The slimy river mud seeped between my legs, making my mood as sour as my face.

"Brilliant plan, D'vhan," I groused. "Three days further from home, and now we have no boat to travel in? Were you trying to make it easy for the Utlaak to catch up?"

D'vhan shook his head mutely. "I'm not going to get into this argument with you, hatchling." Grabbing dry leggings from his pack he unselfconsciously started to strip off his soggy clothes. "We are out of danger for the moment and so are the people of Esquialt," he explained to Y'keta, swatting his hands away when the young cub tried to pick up both his own and D'vhan's pack. "We'll carry on this way for a few days and then double back." Stretching to loosen the muscles cramped up from so long in the boat, he turned to Dahi. "We'll be near Konahi on the walk back. Close enough to speak to their Elders, find out what happened."

"I don't need to know," Dahi snapped, his voice harsher than Siann had ever heard it. "Maskwatin would have called for their aid before a runner would ever have been sent to us. They did not send help. There is no reason that would be good enough."

D'vhan's hand ghosted over his tattooed back as Dahi walked past him. The tall warrior shrugged off the gentle touch and, hunching his shoulders, turned into the forest. "Let's get a camp set up," he said, "but out of sight of the river."

Thirty-Two

The last embers of the fire cast a fading glow over the campsite. The sky was clear and the Dancers sparkled overhead. Dahi and D'vhan had slipped away to patrol. Siann humphed, her thoughts wicked in the darkness. *Sure, patrol, that's what they were calling it.* They patrolled a lot lately. Across the campsite, Y'keta slept, oblivious.

The shellhead had been annoying, more annoying than usual, lately. Ever since he had physically thrown her into the boat, allowing the warriors to carry her away from the temporary camp. She had protested loudly, demanding to stay, incensed that Y'keta had treated her like a stubborn bit of baggage. But, after a few long nights plodding through the forest, she finally had to admit that they had been right. Removing the Lifebinder Crystal had been the only way to lure the Utlaak away from the villagers and that meant moving her. Scorch it!

But lightning strike that hatchling! He never missed an opportunity to remind her that it was her fault that they were trudging aimlessly across the wilds. The

Lifebinder was drawing the Utlaak just as rotting meat would draw the carrion birds.

§

"He's not really sleeping, Siann." D'vhan's gravelly voice echoed from the darkness, making Siann jump. "As much as you don't believe it, he watches over you, we all do."

"But I don't want to be watched over!" Siann complained. "I know I sound childish. You've told me, so many times." Sitting up, Siann grabbed her knees and pulled them to her chest, protecting the huddled ball of misery that was her heart. "I am tired, D'vhan. Tired of being treated like some legendary wise woman, tired of seeing the people that I grew up with falling silent or talking behind my back." Siann's shoulders shuddered and it took a few heaving breaths before she could continue. "I'm just me," she said. "The same me that grew up playing firestarter with the Greens. I'm just Siann from the village!"

Reaching out, D'vhan pulled Siann's hand from its white-knuckled grip on her knees and turned it towards the fire. His rough callused finger traced over the image of the Tiamat burned into her palm. "You are different, child, and it's not a blessing," he said. "The Tiamat marked you, claimed you for something beyond just being a village shaman."

Siann's dark hair flopped limply across her face as her head dropped despondently forward onto her knees. "But I don't want it."

"Don't you?" D'vhan asked gently, tipping her face up and forcing her to meet his eyes. "Aren't you the hatchling who wanted more than to be tied to the village? Who longed for travel and adventure beyond the normal life of a shaman?" he questioned. "If that's not you, then you aren't the same Siann I watched grow up, always underfoot and questioning everything."

"Maybe I did want something," Siann answered, staring into the dying fire, "but not this. Running, hiding, never feeling safe. I didn't want this."

"I don't think anyone asked you." Even now D'vhan's eyes sparkled merrily. "None of us asks for the Road we Walk. We just Walk it." D'vhan's teeth flashed in the dark as a loud humph came from behind him.

"You were talking about something, old crow?" Dahi stepped into the firelight, his tall frame dwarfing the smaller warrior. "You fought against the Road your entire life. Don't tell the hatchling to do what you were always afraid of."

Y'keta cackled, his orange eyes not in the least sleepy. "You three are making enough noise to wake the entire camp. Every Utlaak between here and the high plains will be trailing us by morning."

"The shellhead has a point," Siann conceded reluctantly. "We are trying to escape."

"Not really." Dahi squatted near the fire, the dark tattoos on his arms taking on a life of their own in the flickering light. "We are trying to draw them away from the villagers so that they can return to Esquialt safely," he said. "Why do you think we have been moving so slowly? Making sure they can keep up."

Siann's temper almost snapped at that. Her feet didn't think that they were moving slowly. They ached from hours on the trail and her legs had found every wild thorn and bramble on their path.

"You'll toughen up," Y'keta said, grimacing in remembered pain. "I did." At that rueful admission, Siann had to laugh. She would never forget the first few moons that Y'keta had been in Esquialt. He had minced around camp as though the floor was made of sharp rocks. Every time she had the misfortune to be downwind of him, he had smelled like one of D'vhan's homemade liniments.

Snickering, D'vhan gestured at the Dancers flittering above their heads. "There is enough light for us to move tonight. Less talk. More walk."

A ragged cough interrupted D'vhan's orders, reminding everyone that no matter how much Siann's crystal had healed him, the old warrior was still not well. Dahi's amethyst eyes stared at him worriedly until D'vhan's breathing eased and he tutted. "Stop it, *nimiteh*. I'm old, not dead."

"If you're not dead, old crow," Dahi jibed, concern still darkening his eyes. "Stop talking and let's move."

§

I never knew there were so many shades of grey in the night, Siann thought as they extinguished the campfire and quietly slipped into the forest. Grey trunks whispered, and grey leaves shook in the night breeze. Grey shadows appeared and disappeared ahead of her where D'vhan and Dahi moved effortlessly through the underbrush. Even the mist that had stubbornly held on underfoot looked grey to her night-blinded eyes. The night walk seemed endless. They travelled in a silence broken only by the occasional mutter of *"Shards"* as Y'keta or Siann stubbed a toe or tripped over a root. Dahi never tripped though, and D'vhan, he moved like smoke through the forest as much at home in the dark as he would have been in the daytime.

"Eyes down," D'vhan scolded. "You too, Y'keta. Even the light of the Dancers on a bright night like this is enough to affect your vision. Don't try to see by the light, melt into the dark and use the shadows to travel by."

By the time D'vhan finally signalled for a break they had walked the night down and a rosy glow was building over the mountains.

"We'll sleep until high sun," he said. Then he laughed merrily. Y'keta and Siann had collapsed on the trail and were snoring. Raising an eyebrow at Dahi, he picked up Siann, who just humphed and buried her face into his vest. Moving off the trail, he set her down on some dry moss and watched as Dahi appeared, carrying Y'keta. The two youngsters snored contentedly.

"I'll take first watch," Dahi said, smiling gently at D'vhan. "Sleep, I'll wake you before the sun is high."

D'vhan squinted at the tall figure towering over him. "You'd better," he said, yawning. "I am still the Kalixt, and officially in charge."

"I know who is in charge between us," Dahi's smile became predatory. "And it's not you. Go to sleep."

With an amused humph D'vhan stretched out and slept.

Thirty-Three

The rising sun showed a bleak landscape stretching out beyond the treeline, a vast plain filled with sharp black rocks and deep snowdrifts. "Where are we?" Siann asked, stretching to ease the early-morning stiffness and shivering in the wind that whistled through the small copse of trees where they had camped.

"We are headed to my home village," Dahi answered. "To Konahi. It is time for them to take their part in the fight against the Utlaak. And since it seems they won't help willingly, it is time for us to drag the war to them." Dahi's voice was cold, accusatory, and very unlike his normal mild tenor. Brushing past Siann, D'vhan reached out and put a comforting hand on Dahi's shoulder.

"Peace," he said. "The Road is what it is. Their shame does not stain your soul, their Road is not your Road, their actions do not belong to you."

Dahi didn't answer. He just turned and walked away, his normally straight, proud form hunched and tight as though the weight of a mountain rested on his shoulders.

The sun was fully over the horizon when the tired group walked into the village.

"Hail, Konahi," D'vhan called out the traditional greeting. "We come from the Road."

An Elder emerged from one of the lodges, his stooped shoulders covered in a version of Dahi's white fur vest. "Welcome, strangers," he greeted them, his voice wispy and faint. "And welcome, Dahi. Welcome home. It is a bright star that returns you to us."

"Hail Konahi," D'vhan answered, watching as the villagers came out of the small huts to greet Dahi. Their cries of welcome seemed oddly out of place, given Dahi's tight shoulders and thin-lipped smile and his deep anger at the village for refusing to come when Maskwatin called for help.

"Could we speak to your council of Elders?" D'vhan asked. "We come not with peace but blown by the very winds of war."

A few moments later, Siann and the warriors were seated in Konahi's Grey Lodge, facing the Elders of Dahi's home village. The scent of silversage and ceremonial herbs had seeped through every hide and fur in the lodge and D'vhan breathed deeply, hoping the calming herbs would work on Dahi before he said something unforgiveable. The rangy warrior was wound whipcord tight and D'vhan's hand itched with the need to soothe him. This was not the time, he reminded himself. He was representing Esquialt and all the People, not just himself and one betrayed firebrand.

"Greetings, Konahi," he said, sticking to the ceremonial phrases. "We come from the Road."

"Greetings, Kalixt of Esquialt," the head Shaman replied in a voice that sounded younger than her face looked. "I am Delys, Salixt of Konahi." Her blue eyes took in the small group, fixing on Dahi last. "Welcome, Dahi. You have been missed in our village."

Dahi murmured a response, his voice so quiet that even D'vhan could not hear him.

"Speak up, child," Delys berated the stubborn warrior as though he were the youngest green feather, craning her head back so that her lined face with its ancient blue eyes could fix on Dahi's. "You have never been good at hiding your heart. What is twisting your tail feathers, Dahi, red child of Konahi?"

"I am no son of this village," Dahi blurted out, staring down at Delys with an ice-cold passion. "This village is forsworn. I want nothing to do with you!"

"Dahi..." D'vhan tried to step between the two combatants only to be surprised when Delys, not too gently, pushed him aside.

"This is between me and my grandson," Delys said quietly.

"You are his grandmother?" D'vhan asked.

Delys nodded absentmindedly, her entire focus on the looming warrior who stood, arms wrapped around his chest, glaring down at her. "So, child of my child, what makes you believe that Konahi—" She stopped, took a breath, and continued even more forcefully. "That I, of all the souls in our village, would break my oath?"

"Maskwatin was attacked." The bald statement sent a ripple through the assembled council. Dahi stood with his hands on his hips, every fibre of his body shouting challenge. Daring them to make excuses for refusing to help.

"When?" Delys answered. "We heard nothing of this, why did they not come to us? Our village is closest. Aram," she called out to her eldest warrior, "take two or three Reds and go to Maskwatin, find out what they need."

Aram nodded and was turning to leave, when Dahi's large hand spun him around to stand staring up at the tall warrior. "You dare?" Dahi said. His amethyst eyes glared over Aram's head, pinning Delys like a spear. "You dare say that you did not know?"

"Dahi," D'vhan warned, trying to rein in the boiling anger that was pouring out of his warrior.

"Silence, old crow," Dahi snapped. For once the respect and courtesy that he always showed publicly towards D'vhan was missing. Unconsciously fingering the handle of his dagger, D'vhan waited for Dahi to continue. "This is a matter of honour. I will have an answer from Konahi." The ice in Dahi's eyes could have frozen an ocean and his voice was as cold as wind from the Ice-Lands.

D'vhan looked with pity at the flummoxed warrior standing in front of Dahi. Aram's eyes were flitting from Delys to Dahi and back again, not knowing what to do or whom to speak to. Coughing to get his attention, D'vhan made a quick motion towards the exit and with a thankful glance, Aram bolted.

Turning to follow the retreating warrior, Dahi was shocked to find D'vhan standing in his path, dagger held a hair's breadth from his chest. "Warrior," D'vhan said, his deep voice throwing dark echoes through the lodge. "Where is your oath?"

"D'vhan, I—" Dahi's voice carried so much pain. Not responding burned D'vhan to the core, but he could not.

"Warrior," he repeated. "Where is your oath?"

"My oath is to Esquialt, to the People, and to you, as leader of Red Lodge." Dahi's voice dropped with each word he spoke, until it was barely audible. His head hung down and his shoulders slumped, leaving him looking like a hatchling in trouble with his Elders. "I ask forgiveness, Kalixt," he said to D'vhan, his voice penitent, his normally painstaking courtesy back in place. "I spoke out of turn. I ask forgiveness," he repeated. His eyes carried a plea that his words, at least in public, could never say. He had lost everything, he could not lose D'vhan.

"We will deal with your impertinence in the lodge when we reach home." D'vhan didn't give him an inch of reassurance. This was a matter for warriors, not lovers. "For now, you will wait outside while I speak to Delys," he continued. "You may also wish to speak to Aram, whom you accosted in his own village."

With a curt nod, Dahi stepped outside, allowing the hide flap to close behind him.

"My apologies, Salixt," D'vhan said. "Dahi is a proud man and at times speaks before he thinks."

Delys' faded blue eyes twinkled merrily. "No apologies necessary," she said. "He was always impetuous, and always shall be. I ask that you not be too harsh on him—he means well."

D'vhan's mouth twitched in amusement. "A few days catching and peeling pricklefish for the camp cooks will teach him some patience."

Delys laughed, a tinkling sound that lifted the gloom in the dusty lodge. "Oh, thank the Elder Stars," she said. "He's found someone who isn't intimidated by his 'I am Dahi' routine! But," she continued, the light fading from her eyes. "If Maskwatin called for help, and we did not respond, then it is no wonder he calls us forsworn." Delys looked up to the statue of a perfectly carved crystal bear that hung overhead in the centre of the lodge. The bear seemed to be watching them, holding silent witness as Delys lifted her staff. "Before the Elder Stars, I swear." Her voice took on the echoes of a Shaman's power and the end of her staff sparkled with lightning. "No message from Maskwatin arrived in our village, and if it had, we would have answered."

D'vhan nodded solemnly. "I believe you, but I know the young hothead outside will not," he said, "and for the sake of both our villages we need to know what happened." Thinking quickly, he continued, "I suggest that Dahi and Aram go together to Maskwatin. It would give them time to resolve any hard feelings that lie between them and give us the answer to our questions."

"Agreed," Delys answered quickly. "It is only one day's walk to Maskwatin. Young legs will do it in less than that. So, in two days we will have your answers. Until then you are welcome to stay with our village."

D'vhan pulled on his muddy red braids and glanced at Siann. Putting her hand to her chest she closed her eyes for a second, listening to the Lifebinder Crystal. There was no pulse of warning. Two days should be safe. She nodded.

"We come with danger on our track," D'vhan warned. "Utlaak raiders have followed us for the last moon but I think we are far enough ahead of them that we can stay for two days without putting your people in danger."

D'vhan and Delys walked out of the lodge and into the cold sunshine of the northlands to find Dahi and Aram were talking near the Red Lodge.

"Dahi," D'vhan called, his heart heavy when he saw the clouds of pain that dulled Dahi's amethyst eyes.

"Aram," Delys called her warrior over and outlined the plan for a quick trip to Maskwatin.

"May I speak with you, Kalixt?" Dahi asked once his grandmother had finished. "I would settle this matter between us before you send me away."

"I will speak with you when you return, warrior," D'vhan said. "Our matters will wait until then."

Dahi turned to walk away, shoulders slumped, steps slow. Passing between two of the smaller huts in Konahi he almost ran into Y'keta, who stopped him with a quick touch of his hand.

"Remember, Dahi," he said, his odd-coloured eyes glittering. "This is the D'vhan we told you of. The one who sacrificed himself, or tried to, rather than risk the village." Y'keta's voice dropped to a whisper, not wanting anyone to overhear. "He's doing it again. Sending away what is most important to him because the People need to know what really happened. Because you need to know. That is why he's splitting us up. Stupid old crow."

Touching Y'keta's shoulder in thanks, Dahi picked up his travelling pack and walked behind Aram, out of the village.

Thirty-Four

"Where is Dahi?" D'vhan's deep voice was calm and emotionless. Y'keta's eyes narrowed in concern. To a stranger it may have seemed like just a question. To one who knew the two warriors, the very stillness of D'vhan's voice was a warning. "Aram?" D'vhan asked the warrior who had just entered camp at a run. His voice dropped even lower. "Where is my warrior?" D'vhan's eyes fixed on Aram with an intensity that could have cut through a mountain.

Aram's sides heaved with effort, sweat streaming down his face as he started to explain. "Elder D'vhan," he stuttered.

"Peace, Aram," Delys interjected, throwing a sharp glance towards the visiting Kalixt. "Just take a breath and tell us what happened."

Bent almost double, hands on his knees, Aram took two or three heaving breaths, then straightened up and looked D'vhan in the eye. "Kalixt," he said, speaking slowly to calm the quaver in his voice, "Dahi is a few hours behind me. We found something odd and he is bringing it with him."

Y'keta and Siann exchanged a quick glance as the thundercloud over D'vhan's head evaporated. One of Y'keta's blond eyebrows asked a question, and Siann's nod answered it. *Interesting,* he thought, remembering the sorrow that had hovered over D'vhan for the last few cycles, *maybe the old crow has found some hope at last.*

Dahi walked slowly into the camp as the sun set, a makeshift sled dragging behind him. "Hail Konahi," he said tiredly. Shrugging out of the leather traces he had used to pull the sled, his eyes scanned the gathering crowd restlessly, nodding at familiar faces and giving a small smile when his grandmother, Delys, came out of Grey Lodge.

From behind, a weathered hand gripped his shoulder, spinning him into D'vhan's tight embrace. Only Dahi would ever know that the strong arms that held him were shaking.

"Welcome, Dahi," D'vhan said. "Be welcome, back from the Road." The traditional words meant little, the fire in the black eyes looking up at him meant everything.

"Aram tells us that you found something unusual on your trek," Delys said. "So, son of my son, what did you bring us?"

Dahi looked around carefully, hearing the piping voices of the children who stood in the gawking crowd. "Forgive me, Grandmother, for my behaviour earlier," he said. "But I think this may be a matter for council, and not one for the eyes of the Green Lodge."

Scowling, D'vhan turned to look at the odd-shaped bundle on the sled, faint traces of blood could be seen on the blanket that strapped it down, and a whiff of decay came from what he now presumed to be a corpse. "May we use the Red Lodge, Aram?" D'vhan asked of the slight warrior from Konahi. "This might not be a matter suitable for the sanctity of Grey." Aram was already moving, pulling the sled by its tethers into the shelter of the Red Lodge and chasing away the gaggle of curious children who just wanted to be around Dahi or meet the newcomers.

"Please, Kalixt," he said, respectfully nodding towards D'vhan. "Delys, will you enter and be welcome in Red Lodge."

With a shuffle of feet, a few bumps, and excuse-me's the council of Konahi and the warriors from Esquialt crowded into the small hut.

Siann looked around curiously. She'd been in her own village's Red Lodge several times, but it wasn't like this. The hut was made of woven reeds and the walls plastered with what seemed to be mud and grass. She sniffed, the mud and clay made a dusty, nose-itching smell that wasn't unpleasant, but was making her want to sneeze. Her lips twitched as she noticed that Dahi and D'vhan were carefully on opposite sides of the room, trying to ignore each other. She looked over at Y'keta, who was chortling to himself. *They are so obvious,* she mouthed to him. He nodded vigorously, his lips pressed together to hold back a laugh.

Sometimes he's not so bad, she thought. *Sometimes.*

"So, what did you find, Dahi?" Delys asked, looking at the shrouded figure laid out on the floor near the entrance of Red Lodge.

"The answer to our mystery, Madda..." he said, using the shortened form of grandmother, like he had when he was child. Peeling back the blood-tinged blanket, Dahi let everyone look at the partially decomposed corpse on the sled. There was no doubt that she had been a runner. Slight frame, light clothing, everything pointed to someone travelling fast on a matter of urgency.

"I don't know who this is," he said, "but Aram spotted her about half the day's travel from Maskwatin."

"Her body was pushed into a small pond beside the trail," Aram added slowly, his voice calmer now, the stutter not so evident. "I'm lucky that I saw her. Someone had covered her body with reeds and weighed it down with stones. Poor woman."

"Her eyes?" Delys shuddered as she gave voice to one of the greatest fears of the People. "Were her eyes taken?"

"No, Salixt," Dahi answered. "It seemed strange to us that they were not. Since the Utlaak always take the eyes."

D'vhan paced back and forth across the small hut, thinking wildly. "So, we know a messenger tried to reach Konahi, but didn't get here," he said, ticking off points on his fingers as he spoke.

"And we found out after it happened that the attack on Maskwatin was a feint, a diversion to draw us away from Esquialt." D'vhan chewed on his bottom lip, pulled his hair, and finally stood in front of Delys, his forehead scrunched up in a puzzled frown. "But why not the eyes?" he asked no one in particular. "The Utlaak always take the eyes, it is their way of mocking us."

"Could it have been someone other than an Utlaak?" Y'keta's voice was harsh in the quiet hut. "Could someone else have done this?"

"It would have to be someone from Maskwatin," Delys said, thinking quickly. "No one else would know who had been sent or when."

"But why?" Siann sounded so young in the dusty silence of the hut. "Why would someone murder the messenger? Their village was under attack, by killing the messenger they killed everyone in their village."

Y'keta remembered the blank incomprehension in Pey't's eyes when they reached the razed village, bodies everywhere, eyeless faces gazing up at them in accusation. They had thought they were too late.

Y'keta jumped up from where he crouched with the other warriors. "D'vhan," he said. "It's Iamaat!"

"Shellhead," Siann mocked. "Think, or at least try to! Iamaat was with us in the village all the time."

"Hush for once, will you." Y'keta sighed. "Stars, but it's hard to think with all your chirping." Turning his back on Siann, Y'keta focused on D'vhan, his hands chopping the air to emphasize his points. "Not Iamaat herself, but someone like her—a fanatic, twisted and hateful." Every eye followed him as he tried to draw out the picture that had formed in his mind. "This viper lived in Maskwatin, knew that most of the people would be safe in the tunnels." A gasp went up at this. D'vhan hadn't mentioned that most of the village had survived. "So, they didn't have to kill everyone, just to kill this particular one."

"Not bad, cub," D'vhan said with an approving nod towards Y'keta. "Not proven, but not bad." Looking at Delys, he added, "Is there anyone in Konahi who came from Maskwatin and would recognize this woman?"

"Possibly," Delys said thoughtfully. "Aram, go and find Kade. He may recognize this poor woman."

A few minutes later, a plain, middle-aged man shuffled in, coughed, and looked at Delys for direction. "I'm here, Salixt," he said in a gentle voice. "How may I serve?"

"Kade is one of our Green Lodge Elders," Delys explained. "He has been with us since he Walked, but he was originally from Maskwatin and has visited family there several times."

Kade's bland face scrunched up, his eyes jumping from D'vhan to Delys trying to understand why he had been pulled into the middle of a council meeting.

"Maskwatin was attacked, Kade," Delys explained. Kade's brown eyes grew large. "We did not hear," he said. "Were there any survivors? My family?"

"I don't know, Kade. Perhaps D'vhan can tell you. Esquialt went to their aid." The Konahi Shaman placed a gentle hand on Kade's shoulder. "I need you to do something difficult," she said. "Maskwatin sent a messenger to us, asking for help, but the messenger didn't arrive." Delys sighed and, wrapping an arm around Kade's shoulder, walked him over to where the shrouded body lay. Carefully pulling a corner of the cloth away from the grey and mottled face of the messenger, Delys shuddered and said, "I'm sorry to ask this of you, Kade. But do you know this person? Can you tell us who it is?"

Kade gulped. "Stars, it's Hallie. It's Hallie," he said, turning away, one hand clasped tightly over his mouth and nose.

With a gesture to Aram, Delys led Kade out of the hut, away from the stinking presence of death. As soon as they reached the clean air, Kade placed one hand on the reed wall and doubled over, vomiting noisily.

"I'm sorry," he said, wiping his mouth with his sleeve and reaching eagerly for the waterskin that Aram held out to him. "We were in Green Lodge together. To see her like this..." Kade's eyes filled with an angry pain. "Why would the Utlaak do this, what causes this unending anger?"

Aram opened his mouth to speak, but D'vhan made a shushing motion. "We grieve for your friend," he said quietly, "and before we leave the village, we will see her properly on the Road. For now, be at peace. Your Salixt" —he nodded at Delys— "and I will make sure that her death isn't meaningless." D'vhan looked at Delys for permission to continue, then said, "Take a moment to think, Kade, and then tell us all you can about Hallie. Who was she? What do you remember of her Road?"

Kade looked intently at the older warrior, taking in his whip-thin frame, the short red braids, the butter-soft black leggings that were his trademark. "You are of Esquialt?" he stated. "No tale I have heard of you says that you bore evil towards any, or that you failed to act honourably for the People." Kade's eyes studied the dry ground beneath his feet, then coming to a decision, he continued, "I knew Hallie as a child. She was always different, quiet, alone. The cycle before I came to Konahi she petitioned to join Green Lodge in Maskwatin. Our Mother accepted her, but some were concerned."

"Concerned?" D'vhan's voice was dangerously quiet, listening to the echoes in Kade's voice. "Why would there be a concern?"

"Hallie was different," Kade said, gesturing aimlessly. "She walked the path honourably, but her heart very often put her in conflict with those who held to a strict idea of our traditions."

Y'keta looked sharply at Siann. *"Iamaat?"* he mouthed. Siann nodded. The poison had spread.

"Someone in the village disliked her because she was outspoken?" Delys asked, thinking that if speaking out of turn was an offense worthy of murder, half her village would be dead by now.

"Not just that, Delys," Kade continued. "She mated young, and to a female warrior in Red Lodge. Oh Stars," he said, crumbling to the floor. "Who will tell Kalita?"

"Kalita of Maskwatin was her mate?" Y'keta asked, his shoulders tightening as he remembered how the young warrior had gone from body to body, looking for her father's corpse. "She is in Esquialt and safe. We will bear word to her."

"Thank you for your assistance, Kade," D'vhan said, gesturing to Aram to help the stricken villager back to his lodge. "Delys, I think we need to talk about this. May we use your lodge while the others deal with this poor woman's journey and put her on the Road?"

D'vhan and Delys stood staring at each other across the width of Grey Lodge. The old Shaman stood a hand shorter than D'vhan and looked so frail that she could be broken by a winter wind. But you would not have known it from the ice in her voice.

"What happened in there?" Delys demanded. "What Kade said wasn't scandalous but you acted like a serpent bit you."

"Forgive me, Delys," D'vhan answered, his voice quiet and unusually unsure.

"We've always had people who didn't fit the traditional patterns," Delys said. "The People have respected their choice, it's nothing to be shocked over."

"You are lucky, Salixt," D'vhan said, dropping to the floor of the lodge and gesturing for Delys to sit on a pile of furs beside him. "I grew up believing as you did. But in the last few cycles Esquialt has experienced hatred over such matters, even to the point where people were hurt or injured." *I can see where Dahi gets his beautiful eyes,* D'vhan thought distractedly as Delys' violet eyes widened in the dim light of the hut.

"Surely not, D'vhan." The hand Delys held out to him shook. "I misunderstood you. I must have. Please tell me that such hatred has not grown in the hearts of the People."

"I wish I could, Salixt," D'vhan answered seriously. "One of our own Elders was poisoned so badly that the council had to address her over her cruel treatment of a young one who was two-souled."

"But who would have followed such a bent Road in Maskwatin?" Delys' eyes were clouded, her voice a deep well of sorrow. "And why? When it can only cause pain?"

"I don't know," D'vhan said. "Believe me, I wish I did. Not just for my own sake." Delys smiled at that, remembering the tension she had seen between her grandson and the older warrior. "But," he continued, his deep voice solemn, "if it can happen in Esquialt, it can happen anywhere. And if such a poison grew in Maskwatin, what better time to get rid of the 'aberration' than in the panic of an Utlaak attack."

Delys pulled a small bundle of herbs from the band around her waist and crushed them in her hands, releasing the cleansing scents of silversage and thorngrass. Whispering a prayer for the release of sadness. "But Hallie was killed by the Utlaak, D'vhan, wasn't she?"

"No. I'm sure that this was done by one of the villagers," he answered. "The Utlaak would have taken her eyes. They always do."

"We need to know who did this." For the first time D'vhan could see where Dahi got his temper as a cold wind blew through Delys' eyes.

D'vhan touched the older Shaman's hand comfortingly. "Peace, Delys," he grated. "Most of the people of Maskwatin survived. We will find out who did this and they will face the council of all tribes, as is our law. But for now, I must get my scouts home and make sure that Esquialt is safe."

Delys nodded brusquely. "The Watcher will rise in a few days," she said, calculating quickly. "Together we will perform the ritual for Hallie and see her on the Road with the dead from Maskwatin, then it should be safe for you to leave. The Utlaak should not track you with the Watcher in the sky."

D'vhan snorted. "Should not," he agreed. "But they attacked Maskwatin during a full moon, so there is no guarantee. Still, we will stay to see Hallie on the Road and to give Dahi time to rest and visit with his People."

AUTUMN

Thirty-Five

Late summer had given way to a dusty autumn by the time D'vhan led his small group out of Konahi and slowly across the high plains. D'vhan's eyes felt like all the grit from the dried grasses they walked through had maliciously swirled up and into his face. The air was still. Not even the hania that normally followed the buffalo herds could be seen soaring over the plain. Crumpled leaves and grass flew up into the air with every step. D'vhan wasn't the only one who was coughing, but the cold dry air seemed to be making his lungs ache more with each step.

Dahi was stalking along at the front of the group, his back tense and offended. *I should have spoken to him before we left Konahi,* D'vhan thought. *But there was no private time, and I will not have our business aired out in front of strangers. Besides,* he chortled to himself quietly, despite his tired feet and aching lungs, *it's good to remind Dahi every now and then that I am the head of Red Lodge and, even if only in public, his commander.*

"What are you laughing at, old crow?" Y'keta said, catching up from where he had been walking along beside Siann.

"Nothing important, cub," D'vhan answered. "I see that you and Siann are managing to behave yourselves on this trip. You haven't insulted her all day."

Y'keta's squat form tensed. Siann was a sore point, and something he'd wanted to discuss with D'vhan after they got to Konahi, it just never seemed the right time.

He glanced over his shoulder, making sure that Siann was out of earshot, and spoke under his breath. "I'm worried about her, D'vhan. Something is pecking at her mind, and she's worrying."

"She's been quiet the last few days," D'vhan admitted, but I don't know that it's worrying—she might just be tired."

"Do you remember when you talked to me after the hunt? Taught me about honouring the voices in my heart?" Y'keta's odd eyes were flashing from their normal orange to the black that meant his raven was emerging. "Since Pey't..." He shuffled uncomfortably, straightening his tunic and pulling on the leather breeches he wore. "Well, since I helped her heal Pey't, Siann has been one of those voices." He touched one stubby finger to the middle of his forehead. "In here, I feel her. And she's not all right. She's scared of something, something that happened before we caught up with the village."

D'vhan shot a quick glance back at where Siann plodded along behind them. Her head was down, shoulders hunched. She gave every indication of someone deep in thought. The sky was a beautiful clear blue, the plain was golden and full of the smells of autumn, but she walked through it all head down, oblivious.

That night they camped on the plain. It was too open to start a fire, so they huddled together under their furs and talked of home.

"I can't wait to eat Hahnee's warm rabbithorn stew," Y'keta said, chewing on the dried berries and waybread that they had picked up in Konahi. "Hot and fresh with steam coming from the bowl."

"I think firstmeals are better. I want grain with berries," D'vhan said, deliberately naming one of Siann's favourite meals.

Siann's smile was quiet, tentative. "That's my favourite as well," she said. "Although Napaay usually gets most of the berries before I get to the pot."

Siann's eyes, when she looked up to answer D'vhan, were dark and unfocused, missing the sparkle of teasing he was used to when she spoke of her impish little brother. *"Hmmm,"* D'vhan said under his breath, *"the cub is right. She never calls her brother by his name. She calls him Gooshoo."*

"Settle down close to each other," he said to no one in particular. "It's going to be a cold night and I'm taking first watch." As the small band got ready for sleep, he noticed again how isolated Siann seemed to be. The warriors all spread their blankets together, one undistinguishable lump of snoring flesh in the darkness. Siann slept with her blankets rolled around her, back turned to the warmth of the small group, face turned to the darkness.

With good weather we'll get home tomorrow, he thought, knees tucked under his chin for warmth. *I need to talk to Laban about this before I talk to her. She's a powerful shaman now, not just the green feather I helped raise.*

§

We're almost home, Y'keta thought, *only this day's march and it will be over.* He shivered, pulling his tunic tighter around his shoulders and looking at Dahi's fur vest jealously.

"How can you be warm wearing just that?" he asked. "It's cold enough to see your breath this morning and the Frost Moon has started."

Dahi smiled, running a hand down the white marmot-fur vest that he wore. "Do you want to wear this?" he asked, pulling the warm vest off and handing it to the younger man, leaving him standing bare-chested in the wind. "It's not cold enough to really need it."

A spluttering cough made Y'keta spin around, only to laugh at the sight of Siann staring in amazement at the half-naked warrior. "Don't go giving the hatchling your clothes," she said, "it's freezing!"

Coming out of the bush, D'vhan looked at Dahi, looked away, then shrugging looked back at Y'keta.

"Either wear it or give it back. But for the Watcher's sake, let's keep moving! I'm ready for my own bed."

Thirty-Six

The tired group walked into camp under the light of a waxing moon. It hung red and swollen over the trail, almost full and so low that Y'keta thought he could fly up and touch it.

"When is the full moon?" he asked Pey't, who had been on watch along the trail and now trundled along beside him, chewing at the edges of his greying moustache.

Pey't looked at the sky using his left hand to measure the moon's fullness. "Tomorrow night, I think, or maybe the next one."

Mentally counting off days since they'd left Konahi, Dahi shouted back over his shoulder, "D'vhan, is this the Hunter's Moon? Or is that next moon?"

D'vhan's reddish eyebrows jumped into his hairline. "It can't be this moon," he said. "We haven't been gone that long. Have we?"

As the party came around the last bend leading into the village, they saw flags painted with orange and red moon symbols flying from every lodge. The littlest children raced between the lodges and the communal fire, waving toy bows and spears, and the smell of freshly made stew set their mouths watering.

"D'vhan's here, D'vhan's here," childish voices piped as the little ones spotted them coming into camp. Reaching out to ruffle the hair of one of the little ones hopping around him, D'vhan smiled and slowly started to relax. They were home. They were safe now.

Napaay rushed up to Siann. "I'm so happy you're home," he said, hugging his sister tightly. "I've been eating with the Greens and they don't let me eat berries for breakfast like you do."

"Gooshoo, you never change." Siann laughed, watching her brother race away with the herd of green feathers who were rampaging around camp pretending to be mighty hunters with their tiny bows and spears.

Decreeing that the welcomes, speeches, and reports would wait until morning, an anxious-looking Laban sent the tired travellers off to their lodges for the night.

The Eye of the Watcher shone softly over the forest as the sounds of the camp quieted until only the wind in the treetops and the quiet hoot of a hunting owl broke the silence.

Standing outside Red Lodge, D'vhan watched as the Dancers flew overhead, their green and white lights twisting and swirling in the northern sky. *Shells!* he thought, shaking his head at his own foolishness. *We're all home, everyone is safe, the village is guarded. Yet, still I can't sleep. What under the Stars is wrong with me!*

D'vhan followed the path to the lake edge and sat on the shore, idly throwing stones into the deep water. As much as he loved his warriors, at times they were like overgrown children, and he just didn't have room in his heart for their nonsense tonight.

"What are you waiting for?"

D'vhan spun around, pulling his daggers before he recognized that the voice speaking from the darkness was Siann.

"Don't do that, hatchling," he said, sliding his daggers back into their scabbards and wishing that it was as easy to stuff his pounding heart back into his chest. "I didn't hear you approach. Thank the Watcher that I didn't hurt you! I almost threw my daggers before I recognized your voice."

"What are you waiting for?" the voice that was Siann—but not Siann—repeated. Her eyes shone white in the moonlight, a sign that the Thunderstones were speaking through her to rebuke their warrior. "We gave your life back to the People when you had given it up." The cryptic voice was emotionless, but not cold. "Why do you not step onto the Road we have set before you?"

"Elder Stars..." D'vhan wasn't sure if he was addressing the Stars themselves or cursing at this impossible situation. "I am Kalixt of Esquialt, my life is given to the village, that is the only Road open to me."

"Shells!" D'vhan blinked. The mild curse was the last thing he expected from what he assumed were the ancient beings in the Thunderstones. "And I thought Y'keta was a shellhead." Siann's eyes were her own again, soft brown and dancing with amusement.

"Siann?" D'vhan's voice rose. "Did you hear…"

"Sometimes the powers work through me, without my knowledge." Siann fiddled with a loose piece of beading on her tunic. *I really need to fix some of my older clothes,* she thought, *and I hate to think what Napaay's clothes look like since I've been gone.* "But sometimes," she continued, "what the powers decree and what I want align and I become more than just a vessel for the will of the Thunderstones or the Lifebinder's power." Siann dropped to her knees beside the older warrior and timidly touched his arm with her hand. "You have been a father to me, to this whole village," she said. "It is not a betrayal of Iskine that your heart lives on after she has Walked. It is not a betrayal of your place in the village that you find a reason to live rather than just exist." Her eyes started to flash again and the not-voice spoke. "We are all in agreement, D'vhan of Esquialt. It is permitted to find joy."

Siann touched his arm again and, without speaking, walked into the darkness, leaving D'vhan standing looking towards the lights of the camp. He was caught between the bright light of Red Lodge drawing him towards the duty he had sworn to uphold and the oaths he held sacred, and the flickering firefly light of Dahi's lodge, where a new

Road for him might start, if he had the courage to Walk it.

§

"None," D'vhan said. "I'm as sober now as I was when we walked into camp this evening." D'vhan stood in the entrance to Dahi's small lodge, scrubbing his sweaty palms on the soft leather of his pants.

"Why are you here, Kalixt?" Dahi said, and while his words displayed the normal elegant courtesy that Dahi was known for, the tone was anything but polite. His attention was fixed on a spot just above D'vhan's head, refusing to meet his eyes, his arms wound tightly across his chest. The small fire at the centre of the lodge threw flickering shadows on the walls, creating an illusion of warmth that Dahi's frozen glance didn't share. This was the warrior D'vhan had seen glimpses of in Konahi—proud, unyielding, almost petulant in his anger.

"I am here because this is where I choose to be," D'vhan answered finally. "Where you wanted me to be. Or so I thought."

"I am not a child, D'vhan," Dahi answered, lips folded into a tight line on his normally expressive face. "One whom you can tease and torment when you feel playful and ignore when you do not."

"Sulking doesn't look good on you, warrior." D'vhan stepped further into the lodge, arms relaxed at his side, hands resting loosely on his black leathers. His lips twitched, and he caught himself just before a real smile could show. Dahi's grandmother had warned her about his temper. *He's like a winter-woke bear*, she had said, laughing gently at her over-wrought grandchild. *Don't back down to him*, she had warned. *Stand up to him and he'll calm down.*

Not waiting for permission, D'vhan squatted down on his haunches beside the fire and started throwing kindling onto the sputtering flame.

"You're wasting my wood, old crow," Dahi mumbled from somewhere behind him, his voice still cold and unwelcoming.

"We'll get more," D'vhan said, shrugging his objection aside like the fur cloak he shook off and dropped casually on the floor. He didn't look up, waiting for the next round in this particular battle to begin.

Strong hands gripped his thin shoulders, trying to pull him upright and turn him towards the doorway. D'vhan glanced up, laughed, and dropped to his backside on the reed floor. "Now what are you going to do?" he asked. "Burn the lodge down around me?"

"Don't tempt me," Dahi mumbled under his voice, causing D'vhan to laugh until his sides ached and the ever-present cough threatened to take over. Instantly Dahi's icy façade melted, until nothing but worry showed in the amethyst eyes. "Are you well, D'vhan?" he said quietly. "Do you need water? A healer? Should I get Siann?"

"I am well," D'vhan said. "Did you still wish me to leave?"

"Shards, no!" Dahi's face paled at the thought. "I thought that you had changed your mind. No longer felt..."

"What we are to each other is ours, *nimiteh*," D'vhan said, not looking up at Dahi. "That is not something I was—or ever will be—discussing in front of strangers. Much less your grandmother!"

Strong hands gripped his shoulders again, but warmly this time as he felt Dahi move to sit behind him, long legs stretching out on either side of his smaller frame. "You have called me your heart," Dahi said and D'vhan closed his eyes, feeling the resonance of Dahi's words echoing where his chest was pressed against Dahi's back. "Do you not know that you are, and have been, mine since the night I danced at the fires. The first time I saw your eyes I knew that you were my Road."

"Then let us make a beginning," D'vhan said, resting his head against Dahi's broad chest with a sense of coming home. "As ourselves. Living honestly and Walk the Road that the Elder Stars give us."

"*Nimiteh*," Dahi said, his light voice tight with long repressed emotion. "I could ask no more than to Walk with you for as long as the Road lies before us."

Thirty-Seven

"Siann!" Napaay, Siann's younger brother, came crashing into Grey Lodge, his black hair wet with snow that dripped down the back of his too-small tunic. Skidding to a stop he looked at the gathering of shamans who sat around the edges of the lodge smiling at him. "I'm sorry, Laban," he said, as though just realizing where he was and that he might be interrupting. Dipping his head just a little he continued, "I need to find Siann and this was…well."

Laban smiled kindly. Of course the boy would have come into here without thinking, for the first eight cycles of his life this lodge had been his home. "You are always welcome here, Napaay, this lodge was your home before it was mine." Putting a hand on the young boy's shoulder, he gently urged him to take a vacant spot among the circle and then, squatting in front of him, asked, "You seem upset, little hawk. Can I help you?"

"I wanted Siann," Napaay stuttered, his voice thickening with tears. "I didn't want to bother anyone else, especially you. I know that Ren is ill. Inkiss was telling Iamaat at lastmeal."

"I am here, and it is my place to be bothered." Laban smiled gently. "Isn't that what your mother used to say?"

The tears seemed to hold off for a moment as Napaay remembered his mother, now five cycles gone. "She was always being bothered by someone."

"And now being bothered is my job, even if Ren is unwell." Laban encouraged the young boy with another gentle squeeze to his shoulder. "So," he said, putting on a falsely serious face, "what can I do for you, young warrior?"

Napaay's eyes filled again and he glanced around, but Siann hadn't walked in. "It's Ihkopi," he finally admitted. "He's been gone for days, and Iamaat told us not to look for him."

All joking or pretense disappeared from Laban's face instantly. There had been an early snow storm just two days ago. The wind had howled like a lost soul and the heavy snow had beat several of the smaller lodges into the ground.

"Get the warriors," Laban said, calling out orders as the assembled shamans scurried out of the lodge. "Everyone hunts until he is found, and bring me Iamaat!"

A few minutes of pure chaos ensued as the village organized itself into hunting parties. The shamans and villagers searched nearby, around the lake and down to the seashore. The warriors headed north and south and swept further afield. *They wouldn't find him instantly but, by the Stars,* Laban swore to himself, *they would find him, and there would be a reckoning if any harm came to the boy because of Iamaat's poison.*

§

The warriors found Ihkopi's hideout two days later. The timid teen had found a small cave near the eastern shore of the lake. There were signs of a crude campfire, a flint-chipped spear, and some broken shards of what might once have been a cooking pot. But no Ihkopi.

Fanning out from the cave they searched carefully through the tangled underbrush and woven branches that edged onto the lake shore.

"Y'keta," D'vhan called, "get as high as you can and tell me if you see anything." D'vhan had become more and more comfortable with using the abilities Y'keta had been born with. It was a great "unsecret" in Red Lodge that his eyes were far better than a normal warrior's and that, even though the newer warriors didn't know why, something about him was different.

Y'keta didn't take time to answer, rather, he started climbing swiftly up the closest large tree, hoping to get a view over the area. The tree swayed and bent under his weight and he thought longingly of the talons he didn't have now. But it didn't take long until he could see most of the lakeshore and the surrounding forest. Taking a deep breath and closing his eyes, he allowed the change to come over him, feeling his eyes widen to their true form.

When he opened his eyes, the forest was no longer a mass of trees, rather, he could see every tiny detail. Each creature cast a visible heat signature and movement left an iridescent trail across the scenery.

Starting at the cave he carefully scanned the underbrush. Tiny purple dots were mice or other small animals, larger ones could be foxes or even a stray kaal, but what he sought was larger prey. Five large blotches huddled near the cave. *The scouting party*, he thought. There should be one more. Looking further afield, he started sweeping the forest, eyes looking for any sign of movement. He was almost ready to give up when a flash of purple caught his attention. It was on the opposite side of the lake, he had to squint to make sure it was real. But yes, something large enough to be Ihkopi was over there, not moving, but alive.

Climbing down from the tree in two great drops, Y'keta didn't bother looking for D'vhan and the others, he just started running and yelled, "West side of the lake, in the underbrush."

For once D'vhan wished the lake had frozen early, slogging along the rocky shore added hours to what could have been a short distance. *Not that the ice on this lake was trustworthy*, he thought. It was only five cycles ago that D'vhan had come to the lake, thinking to sacrifice himself to give the people a greater chance of surviving the winter's famine. The hatchling's amazing eyesight had found and saved him then. Hopefully he had found Ihkopi now.

The sun was going down and the winter chill had their breath sending puffs of steam into the air by the time they reached the point on the shore that Y'keta had described. "Not far inland," Y'keta said, "low down, and under brush or something. I only saw pieces."

Coen was the one who found the boy, unconscious at the bottom of a shallow ravine. Ihkopi's fine, sharp-featured face was grey with cold and he didn't wake when D'vhan picked him up.

Within seconds Y'keta had stripped the wet tunic from the boy's body. He threw a worried glance towards D'vhan. It was troubling that Ihkopi didn't shiver. "His temperature is too low," D'vhan said. "His body is hoarding energy—refusing to spend energy, even on shivering. Wrap him in the furs we brought and rub his arms and legs, we have to get the blood moving."

They took turns carrying Ihkopi the short distance back to the village, stopping every now and then to rub his leaden arms and legs and force a sip of Sawiea's vair wine down his throat. The boy's breathing was harsh and, despite the cold, he was sweating, his cheeks flushed and feverish.

Shouting for Laban as they entered the village, the scouting party carried him straight to the healers' lodge, hoping they had arrived in time.

§

"You are a disease." D'vhan's voice was barely audible as he gazed across the unconscious body of the young green feather, his normally merry eyes filled with disgust. "You have served this village and these children for more than a generation. What now brings this poison into your soul? Look at where the hatred in your spirit has led you. See what the venom in your fangs has done to this child!"

The fine-boned young man lay unmoving in the healers' lodge, sweat pouring down his clammy white face. The sharp scent of herbs and the smoke from the fire swirled around him, eddying in slight puffs and billows as he strained to breathe.

"How could you send him into the storm? He is one of your children!"

Iamaat's dark eyes were brittle and hard. D'vhan couldn't find even a glimpse of the loving Mother that the tribe had known for so many years. He tried to imagine her playing firestarter with his son, Dovkine, tried to remember her sitting with his wife, Iskine, through the long, sad hours before her death. These things had happened, but it was as if a spirit from the darkness had stolen all that made Iamaat a Mother and left this woman with her cold eyes and her poisoned heart in her place.

Iamaat stood and shook out her voluminous robes. "The man Walked from the village on his own. He is not one of my children and I will not be responsible for his unbalanced mind." Stepping over the legs of the shivering boy she pushed her way out of the healers' lodge and into the darkness.

Laban and D'vhan gazed at each other in amazement. "What do we do?" Laban said. "She is not my Mother, although I'm going to have to deal with her madness. I cannot let her hateful words drive our young ones into the night." Laban stared at the fire as though the oily smoke could bring some answers. "Would you stay in the lodge with him tonight, D'vhan? I honestly don't know if I can trust her not to come back and try to harm the boy."

Running an agitated hand through his short greying hair, Laban stood up and stretched tiredly. Pulling the boy back from the edge of cold-sickness had taken all that the healers could do, and even now his life balanced on a dagger's edge. He'd asked Siann to use the Lifebinder to try and revive the young one. She was preparing. He just hoped in wasn't too late. "I'll be back in a while," he said. "I need to think and to study the sky."

And to talk to Ren, D'vhan thought, eyes softening as he watched the stooped form of the Shaman walking slowly across the compound. Since their mating five cycles before, the Shaman and the cold green-eyed warrior had become a well-trained team, no decisions happened in the village that both of them did not have voice in. Even now, although the healers had confined her to the lodge and forbidden her to do anything stressful, Ren's presence and opinions were evident in everything that Laban said. *Stars protect her and her little one,* D'vhan prayed. Ren had been injured when the Utlaak had attacked their camp. Since then she had wandered the camp like a ghost from the

Void, pale and shaking. Laban and Inkiss had pampered and fussed over her until she was almost mad from their concern.

§

Siann entered the healers' hut, hands shaking with fear. The snakes in her heart had been whispering that this moment would come ever since D'vhan had brought Ihkopi back to the village. The healers had done everything they could to treat the boy, but nothing was working. He had travelled too far on the Road. Laban had offered his life to call the boy back, so had D'vhan and almost every warrior in Red Lodge. How did she pick someone? Who was she to say whose life was to be risked? This could kill them.

Squatting down beside D'vhan she laid a gentle hand on Ihkopi's brow. He was burning with fever, the skin dry and brittle to her touch. "How can I make this decision?" she whispered softly to D'vhan. "I have no idea how much it will take to pull Ihkopi back and once I begin, I may not be able to stop!"

"It is our oath, Siann," D'vhan said. His voice was solemn, deep and still as a mountain lake. "There is not one of us that will not risk the Road for this hatchling. It is our oath."

He shuffled a bit closer as Miah, one of the younger green leaders stopped at Ihkopi's bedside. Her quiet voice and gentle manner soothing the young boy for a few moments.

"You cannot decide," he said. "It is not fair of us to ask you." D'vhan closed his eyes, took one deep breath to steady himself against the decision and said, "I will do this."

"Nimiteh, no!" Dahi strode across the healers' hut from where he had just entered. "I forbid it. You will not risk yourself this way."

The fire that flashed in D'vhan's eyes would have frightened a lesser man. "You do not allow, Dahi of Esquialt?" D'vhan asked quietly, pressing one weathered hand into Dahi's chest, pushing him away. "I will not"—each word was accompanied by a strong shove that edged Dahi back towards the entrance of the lodge—"see a child of this village die because my life is too precious to risk. What would your grandmother say to you? What would she think?"

Dahi's red face turned pale and, ignoring his stubborn mate, he turned to face Siann with a bow. "I apologize, shaman," he said. "My heart outraces my mind at times and my tongue becomes unruly."

D'vhan humphed. "Unruly?" he muttered.

"My mate is correct." Dahi glanced at D'vhan quickly, hoping that speaking of their mating publicly would soften his temper. "I offer myself, my blood, for healing Ihkopi. I am younger, stronger, and less essential to the village." D'vhan's eyes had turned into black spears.

"Dahi—"

"No," Siann interrupted them both, her voice slipping into that cold, alien tone that meant her power was speaking. "You are all so busy being honourable and self-sacrificing. There is no more time. Ihkopi is a child and his life is slipping away while you decide which of you will be the hero to save him." One too-thin arm swept both warriors aside, forcing them to look back towards Ihkopi's bed where Miah knelt patiently sponging the young boy's brow, talking gently. "That life is being given for his-now-while you argue about oaths. Miah, Green child of Esquialt."

Miah jumped, her whole focus had been on the young boy that their Green Mother had driven away.

"Siann?" she asked, shrinking back a little when she saw the white and red flashes in the normally placid eyes.

"Will you give your life to the Lifebinder to draw Ihkopi back from the Road?" Siann said. "Knowing it may take much or even all of your life?"

Miah swallowed thickly, her pale skin suddenly covered in nervous sweat. "I saw what the Lifebinder did to heal Pey't. Is that what you mean?"

Siann nodded, waiting.

Closing her eyes, taking one deep breath, Hahnee's daughter said, "I am willing, shaman."

"Then come, child," the not-Siann voice said almost gently. Taking her dagger and drawing a thin line of blood from Miah's hand she pressed the Lifebinder Crystal into the pool of life that dripped down onto Ihkopi's unresponsive form. "Blood for the life of the People."

Miah straightened up sharply as though lightning had streaked through her, blinked several times, and then crumpled to the floor. Siann stood unmoving, her whole body surrounded by an eerie red light flickering from where the bloody crystal sat in her hand.

Spring. The cracked voice of the matriarch whispered.

We have found her. It will be ours in the spring.

§

Siann opened her eyes to an ocean of colour. Lights of blue, green and purple seemed to flicker about her. Shapes without form or substance followed the lights like fireflies drawn one way and another. Above her head, or where she assumed was her head, a path of stars stretched from horizon to horizon. *I'm on the Road,* she thought. *The crystal drew too much and I have passed onto the Road.* Ahead of her a small figure seemed to be standing within the dancing lights, waiting for her.

"Maskim?" she said in a voice that sounded much younger than her twenty-one years. Focusing on the figure seemed to pull her close enough to see that it wasn't her mother but Ihkopi who stood ahead of her watching the flickering lights that danced between the earth and the Road.

Swallowing a sob of disappointment, Siann tried to reach out to the young boy. "Come back, Ihkopi, all is well. The People do not wish to lose your light."

The smile that Ihkopi gave her was peaceful. "Can you see the Dancers?" he said in his light, soft tone. "Look how they move between the earth and the Elder Stars, Siann, it's so beautiful."

"Come home," she tried again. "Napaay misses you. Go into Red Lodge as you had planned. You have much to give our world, Ihkopi, do not Walk away."

"My Walk is done, Siann, I am happy so." Ihkopi's form slowly shimmered, turning from the image of a boy into a firefly flicker made of blue and green lights. "Say farewell for me."

§

Siann collapsed across the boy's unconscious form. Tears rolling down her face, sobs racking her trembling frame. "He does not want to return," she choked out. "He has chosen to Walk." Power drained, heart broken, Siann's slender body could not bear the burden, and she fainted.

Dahi picked Siann up in strong arms and placed her on a pile of furs beside where a sleeping Miah was resting. "What do we tell everyone?" he said.

"That Siann tried," D'vhan answered, his eyes full of tears for both young lives so brutally damaged. "Let the healers do their job, they will anyway. Maybe they can hold Ihkopi's body here long enough for his Spirit to turn around."

D'vhan slept on the floor between Siann and Ihkopi's pallet, waking every time the healer came to add more wood to the fire or pour sweet wine seasoned with honey and medicinal herbs down the boy's unresponsive throat.

Sweat poured from Ihkopi's body no matter how much liquid the healers made him drink. Just before dawn he started to moan, his body shaking with convulsions. D'vhan and Miah stretched themselves out across the boy's unconscious form, trying to hold Ihkopi in the bed, to stop him from harming himself.

A heartbreaking stream of muttered phrases, words of apology, pleas for forgiveness poured from the boy's tortured soul. They heard of his wish to become a warrior, his desire to be like D'vhan who could choose his own Road, his love for his parents and his pain when they had listened to Iamaat's poison and disowned him.

Tears ran down D'vhan's face, he had never felt so helpless. How had he not seen this happening? How could he have ignored the depth of Ihkopi's pain? Siann had tried to warn them, the Lifebinder had said that Iamaat meant to harm the boy but they had trusted their Green Mother, believed that she would not harm one of her children. Now look where that blind faith had led them.

Thirty-Eight

"No one saw you, Gooshoo," Siann said, wrapping her arms around Napaay's shaking form and turning his tear-stained face into her shoulder. "And if they did, they would only cry with you."

The village watched helplessly as the shamans of Grey Lodge wrapped ceremonial skins around the body of Ihkopi. Laban would cleanse his remains, leaving his spirit free to walk the Sky Road with those who had gone ahead.

"Ihkopi walks the Road," Laban said, his voice sombre, quiet against the whisper of the stars. "He was young, one of the bright lights of our future, his Star has flickered and gone out." Laban held the Staff of Lightning and Thunder over the wrapped body and allowed the power to reach through him. The staff glowed red, then white, and finally incandescent blue. Power blasted from the staff surrounding the corpse in a purifying blue aura, then it was done. No lightning, no power, no sing-song voice of Ihkopi around the campfire.

Laban turned in a slow circle until his solemn face had surveyed everyone in the gathering. The whole tribe was standing in a silent circle around the fire—well, the whole tribe minus two. Iamaat, who was noticeably not there, and Ihkopi, who would never be there again.

"It is darker tonight," Laban said, staring at the bier, now simply a stand made of sticks and hide. "Our light is lessened by Ihkopi's passing, but the light of the Stars will be ever brighter for his presence on the Road. We can rejoice in this, even though our hearts are torn." Laban paused, his very silence demanding attention. "We have a greater darkness among us than the loss of one life, no matter how precious, can create." A cold wind blew through the camp as he spoke, his voice harsh and unyielding. "Iamaat, with her intolerance and hatred for anything that she did not understand, allowed prejudice to be born among the People. This ugly vine grew, watered by childish pranks and by indifference from Elders, who should have known better, now has brought a bitter harvest. We all bear the responsibility for Ihkopi's death."

The stars over Laban's bowed head twinkled quietly, not dancing the way they normally did, just a sombre sparkle that gave no warmth.

"When did we learn to fear?" Laban's quiet voice, mesmerizing by its very lack of heat or anger, held the attention of everyone in that solemn circle. "We are the People. We Walk together on the Sky Road. All of us. Ihkopi Walked the path of two souls, with his early passing we have lost both sides of the gift he was meant to be."

Thirty-Nine

Iamaat was gone. D'vhan stared around the family area of Green Lodge, watching as snow drifted across the hard-packed floor. The wind howled through the back of the lodge where the hides had been slashed open and her belongings removed. All signs of the demanding green leader's presence had been swept away.

Laban gestured aimlessly from the empty lodge to the pieces of clothing thrown around recklessly. His eyes just didn't believe what they saw. "I can't believe she'd be such a coward," he muttered. "She was so sure of herself and her twisted beliefs, I thought she would stand in Council to argue that she was on the only right Road."

D'vhan looked sheepishly at the floor, his bloodshot eyes squinting in the light from the open door-flap. "Well, I may have had an argument with her last night," he said, idly scuffing his boots through the packed dirt.

Laban peered at D'vhan. Between the smoke, the frustration, and the mixture of grief and guilt he felt over Ihkopi's death, his eyes looked like shrivelled berries this morning. "What did you say?" Laban asked. His grey eyes weren't condemning. D'vhan was doing a good enough job of condemning himself.

"I called her out for her part in Ihkopi's death and generally for her venomous behaviour." Gnarled hands twisted in the material of his dark tunic, D'vhan sighed deeply then, squaring his shoulders, continued, "She said I was 'unnatural' for the way Dahi and I live. I could have handled that, but after what happened to Ihkopi I just couldn't listen to her poison."

Laban scanned the floor outside the lodge. Footprints marked where Iamaat had come and gone several times, moving things out the slashed tent wall. "She loaded up a hand sled, I can see the drag marks headed west towards the mountains." The last sunlight glinted through the trees as Laban spoke. "We should probably try to track her down, but to be honest I really don't want to. She chose not to face the Council, she left."

§

The campfire that night was a solemn and quiet one. News of Iamaat's flight had shaken the village, most of whom had grown up under the care of the blustering green leader, it was like finding out that your mother was a stranger. Everyone was hurt and not quite meeting each other's eyes, as though they were wondering who would be next, who could really be trusted.

"But who becomes Green Mother?" Hahnee asked. Hastily summoned, the Elders stood around the campfire trying to deal with Iamaat's final betrayal. "The hatchlings will be frightened if we seem to be rudderless."

"I don't know, Siann," Laban said. "Who is available for Green?" Laban thought out loud, tugging on the leathers of his tunic. "Varas is too young, too new here. Selah has been here her whole life, but she has a family of her own and may favour them over the village's children. Is there anyone else? I can't think!" Shoving his hand through his dishevelled hair, Laban's shoulders slumped tiredly. "This is beyond me, I don't know how to decide."

"Let the Tiamat decide," Siann spoke up from the darkness just outside the council fire. As always, the young one had been listening. "The stone decided that you should be Salixt, it decided that Savohn should go to Atiskaat when their Mother died, both of those decisions were for the good of the People. Trust it now."

It was what Laban called her "power voice." The normally soft voice of the shaman echoed with the sound of rumbling thunder and the sharp bright echoes of crystal. Pacing over to the edge of the firelight he invited her in.

"Welcome to our council, Siann, Matra's daughter, even though you were not invited, your council is welcome."

Power fading from her eyes, Siann stepped hesitantly into the firelight. "I'm sorry, Laban. I watched the council when my mother was Shaman and I have never been able to hold my tongue."

D'vhan laughed merrily. "I remember many councils where your words brought wisdom, as well as laughter," he said. "If it wasn't for you, we wouldn't have our young bear cub Y'keta with us and the Utlaak would have destroyed the village five cycles ago."

"Not one of my better decisions," Siann muttered to herself, not noticing how many of the adults heard her, smiled, and then flicked amused gazes to the Red Lodge where Y'keta, totally oblivious to their discussion, lounged talking to Pey't.

"Still," Laban said calmly, his normally stolid manner back in place, "I think that given the wisdom you have shown and the power you have been given over the last five cycles, that it's past time for you to step into this circle and take your place at council."

Siann shivered, feeling the responsibilities that she had fought so hard to earn locking around her like iron shackles. "I'm not sure," she said hesitantly.

"I'm not asking you to join the council, you are too young for such a burden, merely to hear and give advice."

If ghosts could go pale, that was the colour Siann's face went as what Laban was saying penetrated her panic. They were not locking her in to the council, they were not making her responsible for the village.

"Breathe, young one." Laban laughed. "The village needs your input, but we aren't expecting you to know everything, at least not yet." Taking a quick look around the gathered Elders, judging their moods, their reactions to what Siann had suggested, Laban decided. "Gather the People, I will bring out the Tiamat, we will see who holds the Green Heart of Esquialt."

It didn't take long for the drums to call everyone out of their lodges and into the firelit centre of the camp. A tired, subdued mutter was running through the villagers. It was really unusual for a full camp meeting to be called at such a late hour.

"My apologies for disturbing you, children of Esquialt," Laban said, stepping into the firelight. "We have a decision to make tonight, and the People are needed."

His cloak was covered in feathers—red, green, and grey for the Lodges and in his hand the Tiamat cast shards of emerald fire into the crisp night air.

"Iamaat, our green leader, left us. Betrayed the children who were her charges and followed a twisted path into the dark. We must choose a new Mother." Pacing around the open area in front of the fire, Laban lifted his hand above his head, allowing everyone to see the flashing crystal in his hand. "We cannot risk a bad choice. The People are in danger, and our children are our future. We ask for the wisdom of the Elder Stars to show us who is the heart of Green Lodge."

Drawing his dagger from the loop in his belt, Laban carefully sliced the palm of his hand and placed the green crystal into the flowing path of his heart's blood.

Turning slowly, making sure that his gaze swept every face in the now silent crowd he began the invocation, "Green for our forest, stone for the mountains we came from, red for the blood connecting the hearts of the People." Holding the stone high in the air, light pouring from its heart, blood pouring from his hand, he continued, "Hear us Elder Stars, your children are lost and bewildered without your guidance. We have been betrayed but we are not broken, our children have been damaged, but we will heal them. Show us the one to bring health and wholeness to our young ones."

Light flared within the crystal and a beam of pure green light shone straight out in front of Laban, striking the Lifebinder where it hung on Siann's chest, making her flinch at the strength of the contact.

"Behold," she said in the thunder voice that was only hers. "Behold the Green Mother of Esquialt." The green light that struck the Lifebinder speared out, illuminating a small figure kneeling quietly beside the Green Lodge, talking to the crying child in her arms, oblivious to the ceremony going on in the centre of the camp. "See her, even now she kneels with your children, healing and holding while you talk. That is the heart of a mother."

The light died out. Siann crumbled. No one noticed except D'vhan and Y'keta, who scrambled to her side, pulling her up from the cold ground and supporting her protectively. The attention of the camp was on the small grey-haired woman who stood beside Green Lodge, blinking in bewilderment.

"Ammarie," Laban spoke softly, trying not to startle the child clinging to her legs.

"Yes, Shaman?" The older woman spoke quietly, gently chiding the young one back into Green Lodge. She stepped up to where Laban stood in the firelight, the village in a semi-circle around him.

"You were not at the fire circle tonight. Where were you?"

Ammarie looked down at her hands, uncomfortable to be speaking with so many eyes on her. "I was in the Green Lodge," she finally answered. "So many important people making important decisions, but the little ones were left alone. They are scared, Laban. The only leader Green Lodge has known in their lifetime has run away from them, it has torn their worlds apart. They needed to know that they were still important, still cared for."

Laban smiled as bright as a summer morning. The Tiamat had it right—this was a Mother for the village. "You are exactly right, Ammarie. But you need to know what happened in the council meeting tonight. With the assistance of the Tiamat, we chose a new Green Mother."

"Ahh," she said, unselfconsciously tucking her loose tunic back into her baggy pants. "I thought I saw a green light. Who did the stone choose?"

"It chose you. You are the Mother our children need in this time."

Ammarie tilted her head, silver hair falling over her shoulder. "Really?" she said. "I have just arrived in your village, surely there is someone else, someone your children know, who can take Iamaat's place?"

Laban's smile was sad as he looked at the older woman, so gentle, so much more the Mother this village deserved. "The Mother of Maskwatin must surrender you first, of course," he said. "But the Tiamat spoke clearly, you hold the Green Heart of Esqualt, if you choose to take it."

Ammarie dug a toe into the ground, tracing idle patterns in the sand. As though on cue, one of the youngsters from Green Lodge ran up to her. Kneeling to talk to the little one, she dealt with his problem and sent him back into the lodge with a laugh.

Laban sighed in relief. There had been no mistake, this woman was born to be a Mother.

"I walked from my home village to Maskwatin to serve in Green Lodge," Ammarie said. "Maskwatin has three Elder Mothers, Esqualt has none. If my own Elder releases me, I will serve."

Forty

What kind of sharding dream was that! Y'keta had woken up in a panic, lightning shooting from the tips of his wings, talons gripping deep into the wood of his perch. Sitting up, he looked around the dark interior of Red Lodge and shook his head. A tingle like an electric shock pulsed from his shoulders, down his arms, leaving him with shaking pins and needles from his hands.

The lodge was quiet—well, as quiet as it could be with D'vhan and Pey't snorting like piglets in their sleep. *I just need to look at the stars,* he thought. *It's just a dream.* Still, the tingling in his arms was spreading, the back of his neck itched now, and he felt as though his bones would jump out of his skin if anyone startled him.

Something at the bottom of his stomach churned over, a noose tightening around his nerves. Grabbing a fur throw from his bedroll, he quietly pushed his way outside and stood, breathing deeply. His chest heaved as though he'd been fighting and a thin sheen of sweat made his tunic cling to his chest.

Memories attacked him in flashes, D'vhan's blade dancing with the adult Utlaak, Pey't with his leg crushed to pulp under the heavy mace that Y'keta had claimed as his own, the smell of phosphorescent lichen and honey burning through Utlaak hide. And power, memories of power, flaming through his hands and vaporising the hallway full of grubs. His eyes snapped open, orange pupils swallowed by the raven black. Rubbing his hands up and down his arms he shivered as he saw tiny sparks jumping from skin to skin. Something was here.

Reaching into the lodge, trying to move as silently as a shadow, he succeeded in tripping over a stack of spears near the door.

"Scorch it, cub!" D'vhan grumbled, rolling over to look at him. "Could you be clumsier if you tried?"

"Go to sleep, old crow," Y'keta said, grabbing his daggers and heading back towards the door. He had to hurry, the lightning was building on his skin. Soon even a half-conscious D'vhan would see it. "I'm just going for a walk. I need some air." Ducking out of the lodge he turned towards the west and started walking. West, the prickles in his skin told him, and faster.

Every step crackled and snapped in the bed of dried pine needles that lined the forest floor. Consciously relaxing, taking deep breaths, trying to let the itch on the back of his neck tell him which way to walk, Y'keta was surprised—but not really—when he ended up behind Grey Lodge.

"Of course," he muttered under his breath. "If there is trouble tonight it just has to involve her." There was no light coming from Siann's small lodge. Nothing moved, nothing seemed out of place, but the twitch behind Y'keta's neck was almost painful now. Pushing him towards the young shaman's home. "She won't want me interfering," he tried to convince himself. "The last thing she wants to see is my face in the middle of the night."

It didn't work. Shoulders hunched, fighting every step of the way, he moved closer. A rustle in the lodge startled him. He froze. Something was moving in there.

§

Siann slept uneasily, her head resting on a small rabbit-skin pillow, her mother's bag of herbs and potions clutched against her chest. Even now, five cycles after Matra stepped on the Road, the ghostly aroma of silversage and the sharp tang of wild mint clinging to the cured hides of the bag comforted her. It reminded her that there had been a time when things were not so complex, a place where she could hide when the world got too frightening. And it was all too frightening now.

She tossed restlessly, moaning softly, unaware of the figure that slid through the opening to her lodge and stood, unmoving, beside her bed.

A low incoherent mutter came from the brooding shadow. "I have to," the shadow murmured, in a voice not loud enough to wake Siann, and one that even now her mind didn't accept as an enemy. "She's unclean, tainted. Cannot allow her to corrupt the People." The figure swivelled left and right, just two steps in the tiny main room of the lodge. "She's Matra's child, from my village, my lodge, how can I?"

The edges of the figure blurred and swirled as Iamaat pulled her heavy cloak away from her body. The lodge was dark, warm even on a cold autumn night. Flashes in the banked embers of the central fire revealed a feral, almost hypnotic intensity to Iamaat's eyes as they stared at the child-woman sleeping innocently. "For her own good," she murmured. "The demons twined within her will be gone and she will Walk with her mother." Moving deliberately, Iamaat removed the heavy cloak, ceremoniously folded it and then folded it again until she held only a single piece of cloth, wide enough to cover Siann's face and thick enough that no one would be able to breathe through it.

One pudgy hand touched Siann's face, brushing aside the unruly hair that lay plastered to her forehead. Whispering a blessing, a prayer for forgiveness, she struck.

Siann woke, trying to scream, her muffled cries echoing uselessly through her brain. Something was over her mouth and nose, cutting off her air. She kicked and twisted, trying to dislodge the heavy cloth over her face, choking on the cloying smell of wild roses that clung to it. The smell of Iamaat.

"Mother, no!" Siann screamed against the smothering weight, struggling to sit up, to push away the cloth, to breathe. Her mind was running wild. She couldn't fight. Couldn't run. Her eyes bulged out, small veins popping as her body fought for breath.

"You are a she-wolf," Iamaat said, her voice not angry or hateful, just sad and weary. "It was you and the crystal you carry that drew the evil of the Utlaak to the People. That crystal will destroy everyone if I do not stop you." Her massive weight pressed further into the cloth over Siann's neck, cutting off the blood flow to her brain.

This can't happen, Siann thought. *Can I truly be such a monster that the Mother of my own village believes I need to die?* A rushing sound filled her ears, making her think that the wind was coming to save her, until a cold clammy sweat enveloped her body, and all the sounds stopped.

The door flap to Siann's lodge was torn away and Y'keta stormed through the entrance. Blue lighting flashed up and down his arms in ripples of uncontrolled power. "Viper," he said, grabbing Iamaat's hands and throwing her against the far wall of the lodge. "What have you done?"

Flying across the room to where Siann lay, unmoving, he pulled the folded cloak from her face and gently laid a hand on her chest. *Still breathing. But not conscious,* he thought, *or she would have slapped me for touching her.*

Turning from the unconscious shaman, he stalked across the lodge to where Iamaat was sidling towards the exit. "You aren't running this time. Void, curse you!" Y'keta's voice was cold and unforgiving. His broad hand grabbed Iamaat's tunic and effortlessly lifted the large woman straight up into the air. "You've cost enough lives in this village, Iamaat." With each word Y'keta grew larger, his body expanding in the dark interior of the lodge. His eyes were filled with a burning rage that danced across his face.

"You are not of this village," Iamaat squawked. "Alien, not even one of the People! You, like that she-wolf, bring death to everything you touch."

"I did not sneak into a young woman's home and attempt to murder her." Y'keta's voice was calm, but that didn't take any of the cold fire from his eyes or tame the lightning that flashed up and down his arms.

Siann moaned, drawing the attention of both combatants. Sitting up, she put her hand on her throat, feeling the red welts where Iamaat had attempted to suffocate her. "Mother," she croaked, her voice raw and painful. "Why?" Tears tracked down her face as she looked at the woman whom Siann had known all her life as the Mother to Esquialt. Her shoulders jerked convulsively with the pain of every sob torn from her damaged throat.

Y'keta's heart hurt with her betrayal—he wanted so much to go to her, to hold her close and reassure her that there were people who would care for her. He remembered the pain when his father exiled him, sending him alone and hurting into a world he knew nothing of. But he had found a family, a place to belong that no one could threaten. Siann would too, he was sure of it.

His mind distracted, he failed to notice the small bone dagger that Iamaat pulled from her waistband until it dug painfully into his wrist. Cursing, he released her and Iamaat dove past him, towards Siann, the dagger waving wildly. "Siann, she-wolf, you are a poison in the heart of the People," Iamaat hissed wildly. "You have to be stopped before everyone is tainted."

Siann's eyes flashed red and white as the twin powers within her fought to rouse themselves. One hand pressed to her aching throat, the other wielding the small dagger she used to cut her food, she stepped forward to confront the crazed woman.

"No, Siann," Y'keta said, stepping between them. "She is broken, her mind is damaged. There is no honour in this and you are already hurt."

Siann hissed, a painful sound. Even now the Void-scorched hatchling stood in her way.

Iamaat lunged past Y'keta, her substantial weight throwing him off balance for a second. Her dagger swung wildly, slicing through Siann's exposed forearm, blood dripping. Cradling her wounded arm against her chest, Siann backed away, her face pale with shock. Bright light pulsed through the room as blood from her wound soaked through to the crystal around Siann's neck.

"You are bent," she said in that other voice, the one that wasn't only hers. "Your daughter died, and you allowed that grief to bend you away from the Road. Your spirit no longer Walks with the People. You are alone, there is no place for you among the Elder Stars."

An unearthly wail came from Iamaat's mouth and her eyes became wild, uncomprehending as she flailed towards Siann, thrusting with her dagger again and again. "You did this!" Spittle flecked her cheeks and her mouth foamed at the corners. "You made this happen. She-Wolf!"

Siann dodged, trying to avoid the larger woman's fury but there was just no room in the lodge, nowhere to hide.

Y'keta stepped toward them, roaring, trying to distract Iamaat's attention with his sheer volume. He bumped into Siann, hauling her into his arms and swinging her behind him.

They touched. Her blood on the crystal, the lightning on his skin. Iamaat rushed him. Her dagger aimed at his heart. "Stop her," Siann whispered, terrified.

"*Illix*," he said, his voice crackling with the power of his own People, and Iamaat stopped. Her face went slack, her spirit unhoused, she crumbled.

"What did you do?" Siann cried, pushing him aside and dropping beside the fallen woman. She put a hand on Iamaat's chest but could feel no heartbeat, no breath from her pale lips. "Y'keta, what did you do!"

"I said stop." Y'keta blinked, his eyes refusing to focus, refusing to acknowledge what lay at his feet. "I stopped her."

Forty-One

<<<Siann>>>

"The Utlaak won't attack once the snows come," D'vhan predicted, looking up at the leaden sky. The icy winds hadn't come yet. Birds still swam in the open spaces on the partly-frozen lake, but soon the snow would come.

Laban, his silver eyes flat and hollow, had agreed. For now, if not at peace, we were safe.

I knew that they were right. The twisted, burning thing in my mind gave no warning, its hunger sated with Iamaat's death.

They had buried Iamaat's body on the lakeshore outside of camp. There had been no ceremony, no final Walk on the Road. Just sorrow for the woman she was, and relief that the thing she had become was gone from among us.

§

Finally, the snow came. The storms blew across the lake, freezing it solid. And, just as frozen, I moved numbly through the winter days. The sun rose and set, the People slept, ate, and slept again and I walked through it all alone. I hadn't known how many ways there were to be alone. It was my fault.

I stomped a pathway from my lodge to the main campfire, following the tracks I'd made the day before, the storm before, the moon before. No one else's tracks led to my home. Snow dropped from the pine boughs over my head, sending a frozen shower down my back. I cursed loudly. No one laughed. I was alone.

So maybe, I thought, grabbing my meal and running back to the lodge, *I could hide in here and pretend that the very walls aren't coated with Iamaat's poison.*

For the first few days after Iamaat's death I had slept in Grey Lodge with Laban and Ren. But it felt wrong to be intruding, it was too soon after the death of their little one. D'vhan offered to open Red Lodge to me, despite all the traditions, but being under the same roof as Y'keta—after what I'd made him do—I just couldn't.

Staring blankly at the walls of the lodge had become a nightly event. The whole horrid memory unreeled every time I closed my eyes. Iamaat's curse, the dagger burning through my arm, Y'keta whispering the word that stopped her. Because I asked him to. My fault.

The smell of panic and wild roses filled the air and I ran out of the lodge, choking. Pelting blindly across the clearing, not even thinking where my feet were going, I didn't stop until I tripped headlong, rolling face first into the trampled earth. A high-pitched yelp and a cold nose under my hand told me who had stopped my headlong flight. Titch. The poor old dog was standing beside me, his nose pushed against my hand, one of his three good legs padding at the ground tenuously. *Oh Stars,* I thought, *I've even hurt the dog.* Without thinking, my hand clutched the Lifebinder in its pouch on my chest. My eyes flashed bright red, and I reached out. It wasn't like healing a person. Titch's mind couldn't guide me to the injury or stand in my way if I searched too deep. Sending a wave of crimson power racing through his body, I could only hope that I didn't kill him.

A whine and a nudge from his grey muzzle broke my concentration, I could feel the itch behind my eyes fade and looked around guiltily. It was all too easy. The power of the crystal required nothing, it took all I gave, and always left me hungering for more. But it was wrong, some saner part of my mind insisted. Power without limit, without control, is dangerous. *Maybe Iamaat was right. I'm a she-wolf, a predator, always looking for the next opportunity to use my power, hunting for prey.*

I forced myself to stand. My breath coming in frosty puffs as I swatted at my legs trying to remove the mud that clung in frozen clumps to my leggings. I was in front of Red Lodge, I could hear the sound of D'vhan's deep rumble and Dahi's lighter reply.

Heart thumping, I spun around as a hand touched my arm. It was Y'keta. Of course, it was.

"Siann," he said tentatively. I hadn't spoken to him since that night. It's hard to avoid someone in a small village like Esquialt, but shards, I'd tried.

Turning, I moved back towards that lodge full of fear and memories. Eyes fixed on the muddy trail at my feet. *Don't look up,* I thought, *if you don't look at him, you can't hurt him.*

"Siann," his voice was quiet, but insistent. His hand locked around my forearm, over the tender spot where Iamaat's dagger had struck. "You need to talk to me."

"I don't need to do anything, hatchling," I said, no longer bothering about being quiet. The impulse to fight with him was far too ingrained. "The only thing I need is for you to let go!"

"I won't," he said, his hand moving to tip my chin up and force me to meet those orange eyes. "Just talk to me."

"How can I?" My words stumbled over themselves, about as graceful as I'd been when I'd tripped headlong over Titch. "What can I say?"

"Well…" Y'keta's nasal voice was calm, his hand on my chin warm, but strong. Not letting me go. "You could start with saying you forgive me. That's what I need to hear."

"Forgive you?" I blinked, mouth gaping open like a fish gulping air. The cold wind blowing off the lake was biting, reminding me that my leggings were damp and clinging, my feet frozen from running out of the lodge in nothing but slippers.

I jumped as an arm snaked around my shoulders and Y'keta pulled me in to his chest. "You're shivering," he said, rubbing his warm hands up and down my arms. "Let's go back to your lodge." I stiffened, not ready for the memories that lived there. The warm arm tightened, "Shards," Y'keta said, "I can be such a shellhead." His steps guided me down the path behind Red Lodge. "Dahi and D'vhan are both in the main lodge, they won't mind if we borrow their fire. You are too cold to be outside."

Numbly I let Y'keta push me through the entrance to Dahi's small lodge. My lips twitched and I snorted softly.

"What?" Y'keta asked.

"I've never been here before, I don't think anyone has," I answered. "Well, anyone other than D'vhan."

Pushing me down onto a pile of furs and muttering something that set the small fire blazing, he shook his head. "Shells, those two are funny together," he said. "You should have seen the argument before we left for the Ice-Lands in the spring. It was unforgettable."

"Oh," I said, "what happened?" Stretching my hands to the warmth of the fire, feeling the pins and needles fade from my feet and legs, I started, just for a moment, to think of something beyond the battle in my mind.

"I will tell you," Y'keta said, "I promise. It's worth it. But," he sighed, "as much as neither of us want to, don't you think we need to talk about Iamaat?"

Talk? I dove back into my thoughts, the darkness there sucking every trace of warmth from the room. "No," was all that came out. There was no way to explain—I didn't even understand how I felt about Iamaat's death. Talk about it? Maybe in whatever moon came after I stepped on the Road.

Y'keta's hand touched my arm again, and again it was over the spot where Iamaat's knife had struck. "I know what it feels like," he said. "When my father cast me out, I felt betrayal, anger, and so much guilt because I believed that my own actions had caused it all." Y'keta ran a hand through his coarse blond hair, making me notice that it wasn't sticking up in spikes now. His hair was getting longer, almost to the point of resting on his shoulders.

Quelling a traitorous urge to smooth down the wild blond tangles, it struck me that I'd never looked at Y'keta before, not really. He was just that annoying hatchling. The one who managed to irritate me just by walking through a room, who talked too much, knew too much, and saw far too much that I wanted to keep hidden.

"Y'keta," I said, reaching out but not quite touching his hand. "I don't blame you for what happened. Really, I don't. Well, most of the time." My brain was stuttering again, twisting the words around and totally failing to make sense. "Please," I asked, "talking won't help, just let me forget."

His busy eyebrows shot up incredulously. "You won't forget. You can't. Shards, I can't. I carry the memories like stones in my mind." His nasal voice penetrated the fog that wrapped around me. "Try to talk to someone, Siann," he pleaded gently. "If you don't, you'll break under the burden."

I stared at the fire as it crackled and popped, wet wood hissing in the flames. There was no answer that I could give, not to him, not to myself. The ordinary smells of the lodge, D'vhan's herbs and Dahi's leather soothed my senses, keeping my mind focused on where I was and away from all that had been.

"You're staying here for the next few moons," Y'keta informed me, not asking, just saying it and then getting up to leave. "There is no reason for you to stay in that place full of hateful memories. I'll let D'vhan and Dahi know. He shrugged casually. "It was their idea anyway."

"You jumped-up, half-witted hatchling," I started to curse at Y'keta for leading me through this elaborate charade just to offer me something that he knew I wouldn't be able to refuse. But I couldn't, it was so typical of the way we reacted to each other that I laughed until tears rolled down my face. Then, the dam broken, finally I cried, cradled in the arms of the only man who understood, my nemesis, my friend, Y'keta.

Y'keta gestured offhandedly to a bundle of furs along the side of the lodge. "Those came from your lodge," he said. "D'vhan thought you'd want your own things."

With a final shrug, Y'keta stepped out of the small lodge and I was alone. It lasted for two heartbeats before his head, orange eyes squinting against the light, popped back through the entrance.

"We'll bring the rest of your things in the morning," he said. "Don't argue with me. Just rest." I shook my head in amazement. Only he, the Void-cursed know-it-all, could make a sincere act of kindness into something that set my every nerve on edge.

"Thank D'vhan and Dahi for me," I said, waving him out of the lodge. "And make sure to tell them I appreciate *their* kindness." A snort was the only reply I heard as I looked around the tiny sanctuary that Red Lodge had provided for me, a place away from the memories and the roses. Opening the bundle of furs brought the tears back again. Not only were there thick warm bed furs and clothes from my own lodge, but a small cooking pot, a cup and a package of herbs that smelled like the calming tea the healers made.

I spread the furs near the fire and was just settling down when something flew past my head, making me jump nervously. The laugh from outside was unmistakable, even before a blond head popped back in and said, "Sleep well, hatchling." Grabbing the brown package he'd thrown through the entrance, I went to pitch it back at him when a familiar smell stopped me. It was my mother's healing bag. The shellheaded, arrogant hatchling had gone back through the snow to my lodge and brought the one thing that he knew I needed. A reminder that I had been loved, and safe, once. My face buried in the soft worn leather, breathing in the scent of silversage and home, I finally slept.

<<< *The End* >>>

The Characters

Waki'tani, The Sky Lords

Surta (Sir-tah)	Chief of the Sky Lords
Y'keta (yuh-**Kee**-ta)	Exiled son of Surta

The People

In Esquialt (Es kwee-alt)

Coen	Young warrior, Red Lodge
D'vhan (D-**vaan**)	Kalixt, Warrior Leader, Red Lodge
Hahnee (**Hah**-nee)	Shaman, Grey Lodge
Iamaat (Ee-a-mat)	Head Mother,
Ihkopi (Ih-**Copi**)	Young boy, Green Lodge
Inkiss (Ihn-Kiss)	Elder, Laban's mother
Laban (Layban)	Salixt - Head Shaman, Grey Lodge
Miah (Me-ah)	Young mother, Green Lodge
Napaay (Nah-pay)	Siann's younger brother
Pey't (Payt)	Warrior, Red Lodge
Ren (Ren)	Warrior, Mated to Laban
Sawiea (Suh-**wee**-ah)	Warrior, Red Lodge
Selah (**Seh**-lah)	Young mother, Green Lodge
Siann (See-**ahn**)	Youngest of the Shamans
Taycha (**Tay**-zha)	Young healer

Y'keta (yuh-**Kee**-ta)   Warrior, Red Lodge

*In Konahi (Koh **nah** hee)*

Aram	Kalixt - Leader of Red Lodge
Dahi (**Dah**-hee)	Warrior, Red Lodge
Delys	Salixt - Head Shaman, Grey Lodge
Kade	Elder, Green Lodge
Xliat (**Klee**-at)	Shaman, Grey Lodge

In Maskwatin (Mas squat in)

Ammarie (Ah-marie)	Mother, Green Lodge
Cali (Kali)	Warrior Leader, Red Lodge
Hallie	Young Mother, Green Lodge
Kalita (Kaleeta)	Warrior, Red Lodge
Verlan	Scout

*In Atiskaat (a-tis-**Caht**)*

Savohn (Suv-**ohn**)	Shaman- Grey Lodge

How do I say that?

The language of the People borrows liberally from several modern languages which I have 'aged' in different directions to suit the Road. Pronunciation can therefore be as varied and quirky as the People themselves.

Gooshoo	Piglet- Nickname for Siann's little brother
Hania	(han-ear)Carrion birds
Illix..	(Waki'tani) Literally - stop.
Kaal (kahl)	Deer-like creatures used for food and hides.
Kalixt (kay-lix)	Warrior leader of the village Leader of Red Lodge
Kit'na	(Kit-nuh)Literally, traveller – a young man/woman who leaves their own village to join another

Kuniak(koo-nee-ak)	Small dog-like pack hunters
Nimiteh (nih-ME-tay)	Endearment - my heart
Salixt	(say-lix) Head Shaman of a Village- Leader of Grey Lodge
Utlaak	(uht-lak) Vicious tunnel dwellers. They have attacked the villages many times through their history.
Tlegu	(Waki'tani) Calling for a lightning strike
Vair Wine	A potent drink made from the Vair berry.
Waki'tani (Wah-ki-tah-nee)	The legendary Sky Lords The ones who fly between the Walkers' world and the Elder Stars.

About the Author

As a child in England, stories and legends surrounded me, I learned how important imagination was. When I was eight, we moved to northern Canada and the legends changed. Stories of the Fae and the little people were replaced by legends of the Thunderbird and stories of the woodlands. I never stood a chance. What could I be but a writer?

Growing up in Northern Alberta gave me a great love and respect for the wildlands and indigenous cultures which made its way into the worlds I create. A mythmaker at heart, I started writing poetry in middle school and graduated to epic fantasy.

I now live in Calgary, Alberta with my husband and son, both of whom I love dearly, and have put up for sale on e-bay when their behaviour demanded it. My day to day life is a balance between my outside life as a paralegal counsellor and my inner life as an author/poet. In between, I work on improving my writing, studying history and languages, writing book reviews, and blogging on my website.

Media Links:
Facebook - @SandraHurst.Author
Twitter -   @_SandraHurst
Website: www.delusionsofliteracy.com

Professional Credits

No author creates in a vacuum, there are always a great many talented people who stand behind the scenes and make the wheels go 'round.

I wouldn't be here without these people. They are consummate professionals, team players, and above all great friends.

Managed by *Ink-N-Flow Management Group*
www.InkNFlowManagementGroup.com
email:Hello@InkNFlowManagementGroup.com

Cover Design: *Amy Queau – Qdesign*
https://www.qcoverdesign.com/

Editing: T. Morgan Editing Services
http://tmorganediting.weebly.com
email:tmorganediting@gmail.com

The Sky Road Trilogy

Two strangers, one running from responsibility, one dying to be given it, together they can save the People, but only if they can stop arguing.

A young exile, Y'keta, finds a place to belong, only to find his new home threatened by secrets from his past. If he reveals what he knows to the villagers, it will tear their history and traditions apart but sharing his secrets may be their only hope for survival.

Siann has always dreamt of being a shaman. She longs for the day when she will be one of the Elders of the People. Her power whispers that this newest warrior is hiding something, and she has sworn to uncover his secrets.

Exile is an epic fantasy set in an ancient world, where legends Walk and the Sky Road offers a way to the stars.

Coming in 2019!

Look for the exciting end to
Siann's story and the climax
of the war with the Utlaak.

LifeBinder